BAD GAMES

BAD GAMES

JEFF MENAPACE

MIND  MESS
PRESS

2019

1

Patrick was fairly certain the white Pontiac was following them. Nothing to be too alarmed about on a country road with few detours, but still, he had that feeling.

When the Pontiac passed his silver Highlander at the first sign of a dotted lane, Patrick looked left. The driver looked back—longer than necessary.

Asshole.

And yet, a few miles later, it was the same white Pontiac that made Patrick stop for gas. Had the car not been parked next to one of the pumps at the battered station, Patrick would have driven past without even tapping the brakes. The place looked barren.

Will there be a confrontation with this guy if I stop?

Nah. There were no horns honked. No middle fingers given. Not even a tough-guy scowl during the long glance. The man simply passed him on a country road—and Patrick *had* been driving slowly. Alone, his right foot was usually a lead boot on the accelerator, but with his family in the car, Patrick was an old man behind the wheel. Besides, they needed gas. Who knew when they'd come upon another station out here?

He turned in and took the only other pump in front of the Pontiac. The metal tank was a beaten rectangle. It offered two grades:

REGUL R and PR MIUM—vowels, Patrick mused, apparently being the preferred meal of the elements around here. He chose PR MIUM and began filling the Highlander.

And that was when he first met the man with the white Pontiac.

"A Penn State man huh?"

Patrick looked over his shoulder. The man sat smiling on the hood of his car, the pump's black hose winding out of the Pontiac's tank like a stubborn snake latched to a meal beyond its means. The man had apparently flipped the metal latch beneath the handle to keep the pump running hands-free. Patrick fingered the latch on his own handle, wondering why he hadn't thought to do the same himself. He carried on squeezing anyway.

"Excuse me?" Patrick said.

"Your license plate," the man pointed.

The Pennsylvania plates on the Highlander read that the owner was an alumnus of Penn State. Patrick often forgot he had them. "Oh," he finally said with an even smile. "Yeah—class of '92. You go there?"

The man pushed off his hood and stood upright. Patrick guessed him at just under six feet with a slender but sturdy build. His pallid complexion was in contrast to the charcoal eyes that were fixed beneath a full head of black, messy hair—the result of little sleep and no comb, or perhaps the latest fashion trend. Likely, a mussed, unkempt look was the latest style; Patrick wouldn't have had a clue. At thirty-eight and with a family, he was admittedly as up to date on fashion trends as he was on who Paris Hilton was currently dating.

"Sure did—class of '98," the man said. "I guess that would put about six years between us, yeah? No chance of ever crossing paths."

Patrick gave a nod and added, "Well with the size of Penn State, we could have graduated the same year and still never met."

The man laughed. "Very true."

Yes—his initial assumption had been correct; there was no confrontation here. Quite the opposite, in fact. Yet it still didn't deter Patrick from willing the inevitable click from either of their pumps to come sooner than later. Small talk was a hemorrhoid to him.

Patrick looked through the rear-side window of his SUV and made eye contact with his wife, Amy. She gave a quick flick of the head towards the stranger, the curious frown on her face asking who and what. Patrick replied with a subtle roll of his eyes. Amy returned a sympathetic roll of her own, blew him a kiss, and then turned her attention back to their two children in the backseat.

"So do you still visit from time to time?" the man asked.

Patrick shook his head. "Not really. I used to try and make a football game every once in a while, but with a family now, it's kind of tough."

The man pecked forward and looked through the rear window of the Highlander. Amy could be seen leaning over the front seat, entertaining the two kids. She looked up and caught the man's eye. He stared back, holding his gaze.

If it were a game of chicken, Amy would have lost. She was first to look away, quickly bringing her head back down towards the children as if caught staring at something taboo.

Seconds later, she glanced up again. The man's eyes hadn't shifted; he was still staring at her, his expression calm and curious, like a man entertaining a riddle. "Huh," he said softly.

The man brought his attention back to Patrick, started smiling again. "Well, I can sympathize with you on that one, my friend." He pointed a finger over his shoulder. "I've got two of my own."

Patrick leaned his torso away from the car and looked through the windshield of the man's Pontiac. He squinted through glass and glare to see two child seats in back, each one occupied by a dark, fuzzy little head sticking out of a blanket.

Patrick smiled. "How old?"

"One and one," the man smirked, his expression one of blatant delight for the riddle to tantalize before hitting home.

Patrick got it immediately, but accommodated him anyway. "*Twins?*"

The man all but giggled. "Yup."

"Whoa."

The man was beaming now. "That's what I said when I found out. Hit the lottery my wife likes to kid. Hasn't been too bad though really; they're good boys. What about you?"

"One boy, one girl," Patrick said. "Four and six."

The man said, "Nice."

Patrick felt it was now his dutiful turn to initiate some sort of generic inquiry before one of the blessed clicks. "So I take it you haven't made any recent visits to our alma matter then either?"

The man shook his head, a saddened dip on the corner of his mouth. "Nope. Could have made a detour and stopped for a quick visit on the way up here, but the wife was having none of it. Broke my heart." He breathed in deep as though reliving a tragic event. And then, switchblade-quick, the smile was back. "Still, my wife's family has a nice little cabin out here in the boonies. She thought it'd be a nice overdue getaway for the four of us. Shake off city life for a little while I guess. She's there now with her folks, waiting for me and the kids."

"You're kidding," Patrick said. "Where are you staying?"

"Middle of Nowhere, PA," he joked. "Why?"

"Weird coincidence, that's all. My family and I are pretty much doing that same exact thing. Made the trek all the way from the 'burbs of Philadelphia. My wife's family even owns a cabin out here as well. Crescent Lake. You ever heard of it?"

The man's handle clicked and the chipped-paint numbers on the old tank rolled to a stop. He turned and headed to the rear of his car, talking over his shoulder as he worked. "No, can't say I have." He lifted the handle from its hole and locked it home on the tank. "We're from Philadelphia too—city, not 'burbs—so I'm pretty darn clueless around here." Screwed the cap back on, and closed the hole's lid. "In fact, to tell you the truth," he headed back to his spot in front of his car, "I get more creeped out around places like this—way out in the country—than I would on a wrong turn in North Philly late at night."

Patrick chuckled. "I know what you mean. Our cabin is in a small community surrounding the lake I mentioned. It's nice and cozy, but it's out there—lets your imagination get the best of you sometimes. Guess I've seen *Deliverance* one too many times, yeah?"

The man smiled. "Good movie."

Patrick nodded. "Good but disturbing."

"Disturbing how?"

Patrick's chin retracted. "You serious?"

The man said nothing, just waited for elaboration.

"That scene," Patrick said. "That one scene? The one with Ned Beatty?"

"Oh right," the man said. "Didn't like it, huh?"

Patrick's chin retracted again. "Did *you*?"

"Thought it was funny."

"You got a sick sense of humor, man."

"You should meet my brother."

Patrick smiled. "I think I'll pass."

The man put a hand over his heart and made a face as if wounded. "Ouch."

Patrick quickly said, "Oh I didn't mean any offense by it, man. It's just that most people—guys especially—found that scene in the film pretty disturbing. Did for camping what *Jaws* did for swimming if you ask me."

The man chuckled and stepped forward with his hand extended. "Well put. And no more of this 'man' stuff—call me Arty."

Patrick's handle clicked. He replaced it on the tank before taking the man's hand. "Patrick."

"That's a heck of a grip you got there, Patrick. Did you *play* football for Penn State?"

In clothes, Patrick looked like a powerful man at six-three and well over two hundred pounds. However, the lines of definition that had sculpted his body in his youth had been systematically erased over the years thanks to children, work, and Krispy Kreme donuts. His once treasured six-pack stomach was now a smooth one-pack, but the bulk on his wide frame was still there, and modestly maintained by the occasional weight session in their furnished basement back home.

"No, no, I played in high school," he said. "I could have never made the roster at Penn State."

"I see," Arty replied. "Well at least you're honest. No *Al Bundy* delusions of grandeur for you, yeah? Wondering what could have been if you weren't *Married with Children*?"

Patrick got the joke (a fan of the show, he actually found it amusing) and fed the man's wit. "Oh no—my wife makes an excellent Peg Bundy. Keeps me nice and humble."

Arty laughed loud then asked, "So...what's your damage?"

Patrick hesitated.

"*Gas*," Arty said, pointing at Patrick's pump. "What's your damage?"

"Oh..." He read the meter. "A hell of a lot. In a million years I never thought I'd own one of these things. But it's pretty convenient when you've got kids, and—"

"Well I'll tell you what, Patrick," Arty interrupted, "any alumnus of Penn State is a friend of mine. This round's on me." He pulled a wad of bills from his front pocket and began heading towards the cashier in the glass booth.

"No," Patrick said, "I can't let you do that. Arty, please."

But the man was already en route. He simply waved a hand behind him as though shooing away a dog.

Arty returned a few minutes later, shaking his head and pointing a thumb over his shoulder. "*That* guy was a winner," he said. "Could smell him through the glass."

Patrick dug for the right words. "Hey, man, that was really generous of you. I don't know what to...thank you very much."

Arty smiled. "Please, don't give it a second thought. I like to think that if we show kindness to others often enough it'll become contagious." He folded his arms. "Some people say environment makes us who we are. So, I guess it's up to us to *change* that environment, make our world a friendlier place to live in."

Patrick raised an eyebrow; he couldn't help it.

Arty broke out laughing. "I sound like a goddamn politician, don't I?"

Patrick shook his head. "No, no, it just took me off guard, that's all. I uh...I was just...yeah, you did kinda sound like a politician."

Arty laughed again.

Patrick smiled. "But it's nice to have someone be generous just for the sake of it."

"Well it was my pleasure." Arty reached out and patted Patrick twice on his upper arm, squeezing its girth hard on the final pat. It was an odd gesture that almost had Patrick yanking his arm free. The move seemed primitive—like he was being sized up.

As if reading Patrick's mind, Arty placed both hands behind his back and started rocking on his heels. His aura had hardly dipped though; it was brighter even. He just grinned and said, "Have fun at Crater Lake."

"*Crescent* Lake," Patrick said, rubbing his arm, claiming it back.

"Right, Crescent Lake," Arty said. "Hope it's relaxing for ya."

"Same to you."

Patrick watched the man get into his Pontiac, then lean over his driver's seat to check his kids. When Arty faced front again he spotted Patrick watching him through his windshield. He waved before backing up.

Patrick waved back, nodded and smiled a goodbye.

Amy spoke the second Patrick was back in the Highlander. "Who was that?"

"Some guy named Arty. He went to Penn State."

"You knew him?"

"No. But he saw our license plate and we just started talking. He was an okay guy. A little odd. Believe it or not he bought our gas."

"*What?*"

"I know, can you believe it?"

"Why did you let him do that?"

Patrick started the engine. "He didn't really give me a chance to argue. He was halfway towards the attendant before I could object."

"That's bizarre. I wonder what he wanted."

"That was my first impression too. I thought he was a salesmen or something— buttering us up before giving us his big pitch." He put on his seatbelt. "But the guy had his kids in the car with him, and they were heading west to meet his wife and family so…"

"Weird."

"Yeah," he paused, trying to figure it all out himself. "I guess he's just one of those guys who's desperate to be liked. You know, started buying people's affection as a last resort?"

"He was *weird*."

Patrick shrugged. "Okay fine, he was weird. But at the end of the day he did save us some money."

Free gas, even for a guzzler like theirs, did not seem to deter Amy's pessimism. "That's *strange*, Patrick. People don't just do that."

He sighed, exasperated. "I know Amy, but it's already done. What do you want me to do about it?"

She said nothing.

"Okay then, maybe the guy's just got a little dick and he's compensating by flashing around wads of cash."

Amy slapped his leg and Patrick jumped. Carrie, their six-year-old, leaned forward after witnessing her mother's reprimand of her father. "What did Daddy say?" she asked.

"Nothing. Daddy's just being a dummy."

Carrie giggled and flopped back into her seat.

"That's nice, honey. Give our children a nice heaping bowl of respect for their father."

"Yes, well if their father would watch his mouth around his children—"

Patrick grabbed his wife's thigh and she screeched. A rapid-fire assault of noisy smooches followed. Amy squirmed away from her husband's probing lips, her laughter rising into playful screams. "Stop! Stop!"

One final obnoxious kiss and Patrick returned upright into his seat, more than a little pleased with himself. Amy laughed, straightened herself up, slapped her husband on the shoulder, then laughed again. Patrick turned to his kids in the backseat and flashed a silly grin. They grinned back, each one seemingly revolted yet delightfully entertained at their parents' public display of affection.

Patrick faced front again. "Okay, we're off."

Arty pulled his white Pontiac to the side of an isolated road not far from the station. He got out and opened one of the back doors.

"Come on, boys," he said, reaching in and snatching the blankets off his twin sons. He grabbed the children each by a leg and dragged them out of their car seats. Walking off the gravel road, Arty headed up a small hill towards a stretch of woods about twenty yards from where he'd parked. The boys dangled by their ankles in his grip.

Arriving at the most condensed border of the wooded area, he held the boy in his right hand up to his mouth, kissed him softly on the bottom, and punted the child deep into the woods.

The second boy got the same treatment, landing further back into the mass of green and brown than his brother. Arty raised both hands in the air like a referee confirming a touchdown.

"Take care, boys," he said to the two plastic dolls he had just booted. And then, softly, smiling, "You served your daddy well."

Arty strolled back to the Pontiac. He opened the driver's door but did not enter right away. He stood there, eyes closed, breathing in one deep breath of autumn air until his chest could hold no more. He exhaled slowly, feeling the tingle radiate throughout his entire body.

"*Fuck yeah*," he breathed.

The start of a new one. The exquisite foreplay. So good.

Arty settled into the driver's seat. Gunning the engine, he cranked the wheel hard to the left, gravel spitting out from beneath the tires as the car fishtailed before righting itself. Before too long he was back on the main road heading west. He smirked and occasionally giggled the entire drive.

2

"Daddy, Caleb said he was hungry. How much further?"

"No I didn't!" Caleb took a swipe at his sister that missed.

Patrick glanced at his wife. "You think we should stop some-where? We've still got about a half hour to go."

Amy looked at the clock on the dashboard then double-checked it with her watch. It was twelve-thirty. They hadn't eaten since seven. "Yeah, maybe we should. Where though?"

"I'm sure we'll come across something soon," he said. "People around here like to eat."

"Probably because it's the only thing there is to *do* around here."

"Well that's the whole point, right?"

"To eat?"

"No—to have absolutely nothing to do. Eat, drink, s-e-x, and eat and drink some more. We're going caveman-style, baby."

"Just as long as you don't start dragging me around by my hair."

"No hair-pulling? I thought you liked that?"

Amy opted for the pinch to the arm instead of the slap to the leg this time. "Would you *stop*?"

Patrick jerked away from the pinch. "Ouch." He rubbed his arm. "They won't know what that one means."

"Our kids? Don't be so sure, *caveman*."

Patrick turned to the back seat, scratched his head like a monkey would, then grunted, "*You kids want food, ya?*"

Both Caleb and Carrie exchanged uncertain smiles. Their father's playful change in manner was not out of character, but this new material—the caveman—had managed to suspend their laughter for a few seconds while they tried to figure out just *who* exactly their nutty dad was trying to portray this time around. It mattered little anyway. Caveman, pirate, monster—it was the frequent shift in character they loved. There was no need for a formal introduction to the day's performance; the sincere attention and child-like zeal their father constantly provided was enough.

"*What food you want?*" Patrick grunted again.

"Pizza," Carrie giggled.

"*What 'bout Caleb? What food Caleb want?*" His left hand on the wheel, Patrick reached behind his seat with his right and began tickling his son's stomach. "*Pizza okay with Caleb?*" A "yes" managed to squeak its way out of the boy between fits of laughter.

"*Pizza! Pizza! Pizza!*" Patrick leaned for a grab at Carrie. The little girl wriggled as far away as her car seat allowed, screeching with delight each time her father's fingertips grazed her.

Amy, who was finding it near impossible not to smile, couldn't resist a dig at her husband. "You're such a dork."

"You love this dork," Patrick replied, now in twenty-first century English.

"You have your moments."

Patrick instantly began crooning Edwin McCain's "These are the Moments."

Amy slapped both hands over her ears and winced. "Please make it stop."

Patrick continued his attempt at singing (a little bit louder now to ensure proper annoyance, of that she was sure) while grinning at his wife like a loon.

She turned away from him, but succumbed to the smile. "Dork."

3

If one was to drop from the sky and land in front of Tony's Pizza, one might think it was the only restaurant in existence. At least that was Amy's opinion. Looking east gave you nothing but mountains and trees, and looking west gave you an infinite stretch of highway that eventually dwindled to a point on the horizon. In addition to that, the restaurant's spacious parking lot held more cars than a movie theater premiering the newest *Harry Potter* film.

"Jeez, popular place," Amy said.

"That's a good sign," Patrick said. "Means they have good food."

Carrie looked out the window, her chestnut eyes shifting from car to car as they cruised for a spot. "Are we going to park?" she asked.

"Daddy's trying, honey."

Carrie pulled her head away from the window and wiped her brown bangs out of her eyes. "Mommy, I need a haircut."

Amy, who was a hawk in her quest to find an empty spot, answered in a slow, dreamy tone—her daughter's comment finding its way in, but only deep enough for a mechanical reply. "Okay, honey…"

"Can I get one today?"

"Hmmm...?"

"Mommy?"

Amy's gaze broke with a snap and her tongue was quick again. "Carrie, can you hold on a minute please? Your father and I are trying to find a parking spot so we can *eat*."

Carrie huffed and scooped up her doll. She moved its legs back and forth like pistons to pacify her frustration.

Caleb watched his sister with amusement. "I need a haircut too," he said to her.

Carrie set the doll down and glared at her younger brother, his attempt at camaraderie only appearing to agitate her further. "No you don't," she said. "You don't even *have* any hair." She finished her sentence with a hard swipe down her brother's head of buzzed brown hair. Caleb shoved her hand away and scowled.

"There's one!" Amy pointed.

"*Nice*. Good catch, honey." Patrick swung the Highlander to its left and worked it gingerly into the empty space. "I hate parking this damn thing."

Amy exited first, followed by Patrick, who seemed focused on the task of not banging his car door into the Chevy next to him. Both kids waited for their mother and father to collect them.

Patrick opened the back door and unfastened the belts on Caleb's child seat. "Let's go, brother-man." Caleb leaned forward into his father's arms. Patrick intentionally grunted as he lifted. "You're gettin' huge, dude." He plopped his son down and kissed him on the top of the head. "You been working out?"

Caleb squinted into the sun as he looked up at his father and smiled. Patrick took his hand, squeezed it twice, and winked at him.

Carrie, who was insistent on making her *own* way out of the car without the help of her mother, nearly had a conniption once she realized Amy was intending to shut the car door before Josie had a chance to exit.

"Okay, okay, relax." Amy reached into the car, grabbed her daughter's doll, and handed it to her.

"Everything okay?" Patrick asked.

"Almost forgot Josie," Amy replied in a tone ripe with sarcasm. Carrie, who could not define sarcasm for all the toys at the North Pole, could sure as hell identify it when slung. She therefore rewarded Amy with a two-handed grip on her doll and refusal to hold her mother's hand. Amy snorted and snatched her daughter's hand up in an instant. "There are too many cars around here for your attitude now my little ain-pay in the utt-bay."

As expected, the restaurant was teeming with patrons. Although it was only September, in western Pennsylvania it may as well have been January. Flannel and blue jeans with the occasional wool coat filled every booth, stool, and table. Large, well-fed people walked in and out of the restaurant, each time igniting a small bell over the glass door, something Caleb found damn near impossible to ignore whenever it chimed.

A short, unmistakably Italian woman approached the family. "Hello, four it is?" she asked in broken English.

"Yes, four," Patrick said.

"A booth, if possible," Amy added.

The woman smiled, nodded, and then led the family towards an open booth, their route passing by a large candy display near the cash register. Carrie instantly zeroed in on it, and did not hesitate to mention her find once they were seated.

"They have candy here," she announced.

Caleb's eyes brightened, only to dim after Amy said, "No candy."

Carrie was not giving up so easily. "Why not?"

"Because it rots your teeth."

Carrie turned to her father. "Daddy, can I—"

"Whoa, whoa, are you trying to get Daddy in trouble with Mommy? Mommy said no candy. Sorry, kiddo."

Carrie let loose her patented huff and turned away from both parents. Patrick glanced to his left and gave Amy a wink. She returned a tired roll of the eyes and ran both hands through her thick auburn hair, pulling tight at the peak of her grip. Patrick rubbed her leg under the table.

"So," Patrick began, leaning towards his kids, "we're getting anchovies on our pizza right?"

The kids gazed back in horror.

Patrick was in the restroom with Caleb while Amy stood by the register, paying. Carrie was tight to her side, eyes stuck on the candy display inches from her face.

"Please, Mommy?" she asked.

Amy handed the cashier two twenties then glanced down at her daughter with a stern face. "I said no. End of discussion."

The cashier, a man whose appearance and thick accent suggested he was no less Italian than the hostess, asked, "Do you have change?"

Amy looked at the total again. If she gave the man thirty-five cents she could get back an even five. Stuffing her wallet into her mouth, she mumbled, "*I think so,*" and began digging into her back pocket with a concerted effort.

After retrieving a runaway dime, Amy eventually handed the cashier thirty-five cents. The cashier smiled at her struggle, then handed her back a wrinkled five. Amy tucked the bill into her wallet just as Patrick and Caleb returned.

"Where's Carrie?" Patrick asked, looking at his wife's knees.

Amy spun. Carrie was gone. "Carrie!" she called out.

"Your daughter?" the cashier asked.

"*Yes,*" Amy nearly yelled. "Where did she go?"

"She is out there." The man pointed towards the entrance where the back of Carrie was visible through the glass door. She appeared to be talking to someone just out of view.

Amy bolted for the door. Patrick quickly scooped up Caleb and followed his wife. With one foot barely out of the restaurant, Amy seized her daughter's arm, pulling her off balance and nearly to the ground. Carrie's eyes bounced wide with shock, her mouth falling open...revealing a blue tongue.

Amy looked down into her daughter's hand, and spotted a large blue lollipop held tight in her fist. Amy's anger for her daughter's negligence was stalled with confusion. "Where did you get that?" she asked.

Carrie said nothing, her head down.

"Carrie Lambert, where did you get that candy? Did you *steal* that from the restaurant?"

Carrie's head shot up; she looked her mother in the eye. "No, Mommy, I didn't steal, I swear. A man gave it to me. We traded."

Now it was Amy's mouth that fell open. Her next question was obvious, but she balked for a moment. Her daughter's words made no sense. "What do you mean *traded*? What man?"

Patrick, still holding Caleb tight to his chest, noticed something. "Where's your doll?" he asked.

Carrie looked up at her father. "That's what I traded."

Patrick frowned, confused.

Amy's expression was an easier read. She was livid.

"You traded *Josie* to a man for a piece of *candy*?" she said. "To who? What man?"

"Whoa," Patrick said. "That's a coincidence." His attention was now off his daughter and further out into the parking lot. Amy's eyes left Carrie's and followed her husband's.

The entire family stood silent, staring at the same white Pontiac they'd seen over an hour ago. Arty was behind the wheel, a big grin on full display as he waved to the four of them.

Carrie pointed her little finger towards the exiting Pontiac and said, "To him."

4

Arty pulled the Pontiac into the big driveway and stopped halfway. Exiting the car with Carrie's doll in hand, he took a good long look at the house in front of him. It was perfect, so isolated and serene. Not a hint of worry for miles.

The last few weeks in such a place had been more than he could have ever hoped for, adding many delightful bonuses to the game. New material had been happily introduced without neighbor concern; any screams managing to echo their way outside would have far too much ground to cover before falling on curious ears.

It would be sad to leave such a house. But Arty was no dummy. He knew that the game had time limits, and that planned time limits were the key to successful transitions.

But all was not lost. Yes, they were leaving, however they would be moving on to something Arty believed held far more potential.

Embracing the tingle he'd bathed in earlier, Arty wasted little time unlocking the front door and hurrying up the carpeted stairs. At the top of the landing, to his immediate right, was a bedroom door. It was closed.

"You better not still be asleep."

Arty turned the knob slowly, paused, then exploded into the room with a bang. His brother Jim jerked upright from a king-sized bed.

"Lazy bastard," Arty smirked.

Upon recognizing his brother, Jim frowned and let out the breath he'd stifled from the sudden intrusion. "The fuck, man?" He flopped back down onto his pillow and started wiping sleep from his eyes.

The second Jim's torso was horizontal again, Arty got a good look at the entire bed. He was not pleased. "What the hell is this?"

Jim went to answer but his voice cracked from sleep. He coughed, snorted, then sat upright again, his bare back resting against the headboard. He ran his hand back and forth over his shaved-bald head and looked at his brother through puffy eyes.

"What?" he finally said.

Arty kept his eyes locked on his brother while he eased into the room, eventually standing firm at the foot of the bed.

On Arty's left was Jim, his torso still upright against the headboard, his lower half covered in blankets.

Next to Jim was a woman, uncovered and stark naked. She was also bound and gagged. The woman was not struggling, whimpering, or even moving, but she was alive. She just lay in a fetal ball away from Jim, her glazed eyes hopeless and defeated like a mental patient doped to the gills, staring out a hospital window.

"What the hell did you bring her up here for?" Arty asked.

Jim looked irritated. "Because every woman in this hick town is a fucking pig." He motioned to the bound woman next to him. "I miss hot city bitches like this. Thank God these two yuppie fucks decided to build a second home out here in Mayberry." Jim reached to his right and grabbed his cigarettes from the nightstand. He lit one and inhaled deep.

"You took a big risk, Jim. What if the husband put up a fight?"

Jim laughed, choking on his recent drag. "Come on Arty, you know he wasn't gonna try anything. We practically broke that pussy from day one." He sighed, flicked a stray ash off his chest. "I miss Philly."

Arty thought of their mother, their sole reason for being in the western part of the state. "Get over it," he said.

Jim grunted.

"Yeah, well, whether your dick likes it or not, this is the way it is."

"I guess," Jim said. "But the way Mom's been lately, we could have probably moved her ten fucking feet from the old house and told her she was here…probably wouldn't have known the difference."

Arty banged the base of the bed with his knee, rocking it. "She's not that bad yet, dickhead. Show some respect."

Jim hung his head and took a short guilty drag from his smoke. "You're right, my bad."

Arty and Jim had moved their mother to western Pennsylvania when her condition was demonstrating more off days than on. Her wish was to live her remaining years near her place of birth, and despite the boys' initial reluctance, they weren't about to deprive their ailing mother of such a wish. No way.

"Anyway," Arty began, "we'd been pushing our luck around Philly lately. We're needles in a haystack out here. It's perfect for now."

Jim exhaled both pessimism and smoke. "Yeah, perfect if we can continue to find people like these two to play with."

Arty's lips nearly split from the grin that spread over his face. "Well I might just have some wonderful news for you then, little brother."

Jim's pessimism dipped, his black eyes flickering hope. "Yeah?"

"Oh yeah." Arty tossed Josie onto the bed. Jim stuck the cigarette between his lips and picked Carrie's doll up with both hands.

"*My, oh, my, oh, my,*" Jim said out of the corner of his mouth, cigarette bouncing with each word.

"I met the husband. He's a sturdy guy; they won't break easy."

"Awesome. The wife?" Jim asked.

"Very nice. Hot."

Jim grinned. He held the doll up and wiggled it at Arty. "How many kids?"

"Two—boy and a girl."

"How old?"

"Four and six."

"Lots of potential."

"Indeed."

The woman in bed sighed deep through her nose then resumed her trance. Both men looked at her.

"Jesus, man," Arty said. "She hasn't bathed in over three fucking weeks."

"I know that," Jim said. "I threw her in the tub first. Scrubbed that ass until it squeaked."

Arty hung his head and shook it, fighting off a smile. "You're a sick man."

Jim took a final drag of his cigarette then crushed it out on the nightstand. "So where are they?"

"In a cabin. Place called Crescent Lake. Don't suppose you've ever heard of it?"

Jim shrugged. "If you've never heard of it, then how the hell would I?"

"Well I asked around. I'm thinking we can venture out there in an hour or so. Sneak around a little and get our bearings."

"Are we gonna take the cabin for a bit when we're done?"

"I don't know, I doubt it," Arty said. "The husband mentioned it was a *community* of cabins, or something like that. It might be too risky. Plus they're only gonna be up for the weekend. Who knows who'll pop in after."

Jim nodded, yawned, and rubbed the remainder of sleep from his right eye. "Alright, so what's the next move?"

"Well first things first. We need to get the hell out of here. If we want to do this next one right, we need to start moving."

Jim rolled over towards the naked woman. He slapped her hard on her bare bottom, a section of the pale flesh instantly glowing red in the shape of Jim's hand. She hardly flinched. "So should I assume we're dealing with her and her hubby *right now*?"

Arty nodded. "Yeah. We're not killing them though."

"What? Why not?"

"Because we only kill if it's necessary...or part of the game. It's neither."

"We've done it before."

"And?"

"I think it's necessary."

"I don't."

Jim frowned. "They'll ID us, Arty. Jesus, they saw our faces every time we fed the fuckers. This bitch could ID my *dick* if she wanted to."

"Yeah, well that last one is your problem. Still, we can fix it so they can't ID us."

"Yeah, I know we can—by killing them."

"No."

Jim snorted. "How then?"

"Stand up," Arty said.

"What?"

"Stand up."

"Why?"

"Just stand up."

Jim kicked off the blankets and stood. He was just under six-feet with a powerful physique that he owed mostly to good genetics as opposed to hours in the gym. He was also very naked.

"Jesus," Arty said, the second he got an eyeful.

Jim made no attempt to cover himself. He just splayed his arms. "What?"

Arty hung his head again, shaking it slowly, biting his tongue. He did not want to encourage his brother's lewd, and often risky, behavior, but found it damn hard not to laugh at his audacity once in awhile.

Jim scratched his naked groin and asked, "So how do we fix it so they can't ID us?"

Arty raised his head, took a step forward, and jabbed his fingers into his brother's eyes.

There was a wet squelching sound, and Jim dropped to his knees, grabbing his face with both hands. "*What the fuck?!*"

Arty instantly held up four fingers and said, "How many fingers am I holding up? Jim! How many fingers am I holding up?"

Jim made several attempts at looking up at his brother, trying to focus, each attempt heightening the pain, his head whipping away from Arty's hand every time as though it flashed a beam of white light. He finally gave up and tucked his chin into his chest, rubbing furiously around his eyes with the palms of his hands.

"You see what I'm getting at?" Arty asked.

"Yeah…I get it," Jim said. He rubbed his eyes some more then launched himself upward, driving his right fist deep into his brother's gut. Arty doubled over instantly, and now it was his turn to drop to his knees.

Jim hopped up and danced over his brother, laughing hysterically, his genitalia flopping left and right. Through his pain Arty still managed to witness the unsightly phallic jig occurring overhead, and although his breath had left him, he could not resist an attempt at a laugh.

"*Sick…fuck…*"

Jim continued his dance around the room, eventually leaping onto the woman, gyrating on top of her still-fetal body while hooting and hollering like a horny chimp.

Arty got to his feet, holding his stomach, wheezing out more chuckles as he watched his brother carry on, his gyrating atop the woman stopping, changing to the missionary position as he began miming wild intercourse, his hooting louder with each imaginary thrust. "Get over here, dickhead," he said.

Jim hopped off the woman and sauntered over to his brother. He walked with an exaggerated strut, like a cowboy entering a saloon. His eyes were rimmed red from Arty's recent attack, but it hardly seemed to bother him now. He was grinning like a kid.

"So you know what I'm getting at then?" Arty asked, still breathing hard, still holding his stomach.

"Yeah, I think so," Jim said.

"We're just taking their eyes, Jim. That's all."

Jim nodded, paused, thought for a moment, and then asked, "What about their tongues?"

"Huh?"

"Well wouldn't it make sense to take their tongues too? See no evil, speak no evil—wait—what's the other one? *Hear* no evil? Yeah…it's hear no evil. So that means the ears too, right? We'll take the tongues and ears too?"

Arty gave the suggestion a few seconds, smirked, then palmed his brother's bald head, running his hand back and forth over it as though rough-housing with the family dog. "Why not? Such a clever brother I've got."

Jim kept grinning. "Hey, maybe we could preserve everything when we're done. You know, dry 'em out like beef jerky, and then make a necklace for them. Something to remember us by."

Still smirking, Arty waved a playful finger at his brother and said, "James, now you're just being mean."

5

With the half-eaten blue lollipop now discarded, and Josie the doll in the hands of a stranger, it would likely take Santa Claus himself to bring a smile to Carrie's face—or perhaps a dog.

As the silver Highlander pulled into the gravel driveway of cabin number eight bordering Crescent Lake, a mangy Border terrier began yipping and yapping at the SUV with an enthusiasm that suggested it might explode at any moment.

"Daddy! Look at the dog!" Carrie yelled, straining against the binds of her car seat to get a better look.

Patrick needed only a second's glance at the dog before saying, "Don't go near that thing, honey. He doesn't look very clean."

Carrie ignored her father's comment and continued to gape, letting out anxious squeaks and smiles that matched the dog's eagerness for contact. Caleb leaned over and took a hard, wary look at the dog the moment Carrie began shrieking.

Patrick caught his son's expression in the rearview mirror, reached back and rubbed his knee. "Don't worry, pal, it's no big deal."

"You think it's a stray?" Amy said.

"Probably. Stay in the car for a couple of minutes though. I'll get out and shoo it away."

The instant Patrick stepped out of the car the terrier leapt towards his thigh, begging for affection, its spastic behavior accompanied by a multitude of whines that could crack glass. Patrick shook him off and nudged it away with the tip of his shoe. He clapped his hands loudly. "No! Bad dog! Get out! Shoo!"

The terrier took a few cautious steps back, regrouped, then dove after Patrick's leg for a second try.

"No! Get out of here! Bad dog! *Bad!*" Patrick yelled louder, nudging harder with his foot. This time the dog took several steps back and eventually sat. It quivered and whimpered from its spot, spring-loaded, anxiously waiting for Patrick to succumb to its canine charm so that it could rocket forward again.

Patrick opened the driver's door and poked his head in. "You know what? Why don't we take the kids inside, and then we'll unload everything. It seems harmless enough, but looks pretty dirty. I don't want the kids touching it."

Carrie whined. Amy reached back and squeezed her daughter's knee to quiet her. "Okay, that's a good idea," she said.

Carrie folded her arms and grumbled, "No it's not."

With both kids now safe in the cabin, Amy and Patrick began unloading the rear of the Highlander.

"So what do you think?" Patrick asked, taking a brief look around before reaching for a bag. "Seems just as peaceful as last time, doesn't it?"

Amy turned her back to the car and looked down the driveway and beyond, out onto Crescent Lake. The lake itself was man-made and about half the size of a football field. The surrounding homes that bordered the green water were in contrast of one another. Some were rustic blocks of wood that looked as if they'd been erected by pioneers hundreds of years ago, and some were more modern establishments that resembled basic, one-story homes you might find in any modest suburb throughout the country.

Crescent Lake was not flashy; that wasn't its purpose. Its purpose was serenity and solitude, and in that, it excelled. Amy turned back to Patrick, smiled, and said, "Just as peaceful."

Patrick smiled back and breathed in deep. The smell of wood, leaves, and mountain air calmed him to no end. The trees that surrounded the rear of their cabin, and nearly every cabin bordering the lake, narrowed upward from a mighty base until their tips were lost among an explosion of red and orange, with not a single leaf daring to fall to the earth just yet.

"It really is, isn't it?" Patrick said, more to himself than Amy. He breathed in the earthy scents again and closed his eyes, the gentle calls of nature singing to him, more acute with his eyes shut. He thought it might actually be possible to fall asleep standing up.

Amy took hold of a small duffel bag and slung it over her shoulder. "What do you want to do about food?" she asked.

Patrick snapped from his daze and brought his attention back to the Highlander. He took a small black suitcase from the car and set it at his feet. "You want to go shopping now?"

Amy grabbed another small duffel bag and balanced it atop the black suitcase. "Might as well get it out of the way before we get comfortable."

Patrick shrugged. "Okay. You want me to go?"

"Nah, I'll go. You can take the kids for a walk around the lake or something."

"Oh, I get it. Dump the kids with the naïve dad and the new mangy mutt while you drive off to reunite with your forbidden mountain man."

Amy raised an eyebrow, and did not smile when she said, "Actually, I was going to go look for your little buddy, Arty."

Patrick dropped another bag at his feet, stood upright and sighed. "Yeah, that was kinda weird, wasn't it?"

"*Kind* of weird? That was flat-out *bizarre* Patrick. What would a grown man want with a little girl's doll?"

"Well, I'd like to think he didn't actually *want* the doll, Amy."

"So explain then."

"I don't know. My guess is that he was just using it as a way to give Carrie a piece of candy. I mean let's face it, the guy did have a bit of an odd way about him, to say the least." He paused for a second, smiled and added, "I guess we must have forgotten to give our daughter the 'don't take candy from strangers' speech."

Amy shot him a disgusted look. "It's not funny, Patrick. She was out of my sight for less than a minute. It couldn't have been a coincidence."

Patrick frowned. "What do you mean?"

"Well for starters, how did this guy know Carrie wanted a piece of candy so badly? Was he watching us in the restaurant? Listening to our conversation at the table somehow?"

Patrick's back stiffened. His wife's question was a damn good one. He had sized Arty up from the moment he met him and did not figure him a physical threat in any way. Weird? Hell, yes. But a threat? No. The man's actions at the gas station and the restaurant were no doubt bizarre, but Patrick still felt comfortable that if push came to shove, he could deal with Arty with little trouble.

Amy continued. "I mean that whole thing at the station with the free gas was strange enough."

Patrick steadied himself, took a deep breath. "I don't know what you want me to say, honey. Maybe in his weird little world, it's his way of being friendly. You know there are some people out there who just don't know where the line is."

"Bullshit. The way he smiled and waved as he was driving away from the restaurant…that was…that was something different than being friendly."

"Like what?"

"Like, I don't know. Just *different*, okay?"

Patrick held up both hands. "Okay."

Amy shook her head and rubbed the back of her neck. "And what the hell was that whole thing with the doll? Carrie barely lets *us* hold that damn thing, yet she gives it to a strange man for a piece of candy in less than a minute?"

Patrick felt his wife's frustration and shared it equally, if not more so, but he desperately wanted to put it behind them in order to focus on the weekend ahead. It was the role he often played in their relationship. Amy was strong, tough, and outspoken, but she was a worrier, and Patrick frequently found himself assuring her all would be well, even if it meant bottling up his own fears and misgivings for the time being.

"Honey, I agree, what the guy did was exceptionally odd, but let's just think about things for a second. He's got a wife, in-laws, and twins to entertain while he's up here. I highly doubt we'll ever run into him again. Chances are, he was probably just passing by the restaurant, spotted our sore-thumb-of-an-SUV in a parking lot full of battered pick-ups, and decided to...I don't know...reach out again.

"If you ask me he's just a very strange guy who never received the handbook on acceptable social etiquette. *Please*, let's not let it ruin our weekend, okay?"

Amy gave a weak smile, leaned forward and rested her head on Patrick's chest. He stroked her long dark hair. "You know I would never let anything happen to you guys."

"I know," she said softly, her head still in his chest. She remained quiet for a moment before lifting her head and looking up at him. "You *do* realize we're going to have to buy Carrie a new doll right?"

Patrick nodded. "Maybe I'll go buy some lollipops and canvas the local pizza shops later. You know, look for a trade?"

Amy slapped his chest hard and pulled away. "You're sick."

Patrick took a step back and rubbed his chest. "Ouch," he laughed. "That hurt."

"Good," she said without a trace of a smile. She picked up one of the small duffel bags and started walking towards the back door of the cabin.

A second later, the censor button on Patrick's sense of humor appeared—late as usual.

6

Amy drove the Highlander along the only gravel road leading out of Crescent Lake. The large wooden sign that welcomed the family to the lake upon arrival now informed her that she was leaving, just in case the obvious had managed to elude her.

She recalled from previous years spent at the cabin that a Giant Food supermarket was a convenient three or four miles past the lake and would provide a decent go-to spot for any necessities that might pop up during the course of their stay.

As for now, Amy's list was as basic as basic gets: some meat, some liquid, and some starch. Caveman-style, Patrick called it.

Remembering her husband's expression brought a small smile to the corner of her mouth. When she recalled Patrick's goofing around with the kids in his caveman voice the other corner of her mouth rose as well. She was suddenly overwhelmed with an immense feeling of love and gratitude for her husband—such a wonderful man who not only loved her unconditionally, but was the ideal father to her two babies.

The smile was now full-blown. Her light-brown eyes rimmed hot with happy tears. Amy laughed a small laugh, wiped the tears with the back of her hand, and pressed down on the accelerator.

She wanted the food shopping over with so she could be back home with her husband and children as soon as possible.

"When *will* you let me pet him?" Carrie asked.

"When we take him to the vet and get him checked for every possible disease known to dog," Patrick replied.

"When are we going to do *that*?" Carrie asked, looking over her shoulder at the four-legged bundle of dirt and fur that was following the three of them around the lake.

"That was a joke, sweetheart. We're not going to be doing that. Besides, he probably belongs to someone else around here."

Father, son, and daughter had walked halfway around the lake—Patrick in the middle with Caleb staying tight to his left, Carrie occasionally straying from his right in order to check the status of the terrier.

Despite the lake's moniker, it was not crescent-shaped. If anything, it was more of a perfect square. However, Patrick believed he was correct in the assumption that "Crescent Lake" carried a bit more flair than the alternative "Square Lake" when it came to attracting potential residents.

Not that there were many vacancies. Crescent Lake was a small community—a secret of sorts. And the locals preferred it that way. If they wanted glamour and tourists they could have gone to any one of the fancy resorts in California, Arizona, Florida. Perhaps one of many island paradises that seemed almost fictional in its extravagance. But here, tucked away in a wooded nook of western Pennsylvania, they remained anonymous, truly to themselves—a prize forever cherished from the moment received.

Patrick and the kids stopped their walk for a brief moment to take in the view. Caleb bent over, picked up a shiny flat rock, and then handed it to his father. Patrick weighed the rock in his hand, then skimmed it across the lake's surface, where it jumped a good four times. Caleb looked on as though it was quite possibly the single greatest thing he had ever seen in his four-year-old life, and began frantically searching the ground for more flat stones to give to his father.

"Who?" Carrie asked her father.

Patrick turned away from the lake and gave his daughter a funny look. "Huh?"

"Who does the dog belong to?"

"I don't know, sweetie, maybe our neighbors. Do you remember the Mitchells?"

Carrie nodded and immediately continued her inquiry. "They didn't have a dog *last* year," she said.

Patrick sighed and answered, while turning back to Caleb who had just pushed a second flat rock into his father's belly. "Well maybe they just got him, honey."

Carrie glanced over her shoulder at the dog for the umpteenth time. The terrier was maintaining a cautious ten feet behind the trio lest he suffer the wrath of Patrick's shoe again. "He doesn't have a collar," she said.

Patrick skimmed the rock harder this time and managed five skips. Caleb nearly fainted with delight.

"Daddy, he doesn't have a collar," Carrie tried again.

Patrick breathed in deep through his nose and let it filter out slow. With the most patient of smiles, he said, "Carrie, what would you like Daddy to do? *It isn't our dog.* Chances are he's a stray."

Carrie made a funny face. "What's *that*?"

"It's a dog that doesn't have an owner and lives on its own."

Carrie's face lit up and Patrick quickly added to his definition before her little mouth could form a word.

"—*But*," he began, "that also means he's probably very dirty and might be carrying some kind of disease. So it's best to stay away from him."

She scrunched her eyebrows. "Disease?"

"Yes, like rabies. Ever heard of *Cujo*?"

"What's that?"

"Never mind. Bottom line is that he's very dirty, and I want you to stay away from him."

"How 'bout we give him a bath then?"

"How 'bout you listen to your father for a change and do as you're told?"

According to Amy, if you've seen one Giant Food supermarket you've seen them all. So for her, this particular one in western Pennsylvania was no horizon-broadening experience. She moved up and down each aisle with a purpose, grabbing only what was needed, affording no second glances towards impulse items. She enjoyed food shopping as much as she did a pothole after an alignment. Plus, she was still pining to be back with her family so they could settle in properly and let their weekend officially begin.

"Excuse me?"

Amy was in aisle seven deciding between two types of instant rice. They were fortunate to have a microwave oven in the cabin, and the convenient Uncle Ben's pouches that plopped steaming rice onto your plate in ninety seconds were a godsend to hurried families and frozen-waffle-bachelors alike.

"Excuse me, miss?"

Amy turned over her shoulder and locked eyes with the man behind her—his black to her light brown. The man was solidly built with a shaved head.

"Are you talking to me?" Amy asked.

The man smiled, forcing a squint in those black eyes. "Yeah."

"What do you want?"

"Some help."

Amy was backed up against the rice display so she took a step to her left to create distance. The man did not appear an immediate threat, but he had a confident, straightforward way about him that made her feel vulnerable.

"Help?" she said.

"Yeah, can you help me?" The man smiled again, a bigger one this time, more confident.

Amy did not answer right away, and for a good five seconds there was a moment when the two just stared at one another. The man never blinked, and did not speak again until Amy responded. His smile was close to becoming a leer.

"I don't know…I…what do you want?" Her words were close to a stutter. She wanted to turn and walk away, but the man with the shaved head had not crossed any physical boundaries. It was his *demeanor* that seemed to be taking liberties—it held her still despite the desire to move.

"Help," the man said once again. "Actually, more like some advice about something."

"I don't know—"

"You see, I'm cooking dinner for my girlfriend tonight, and I'd be lying if I said I knew my way around a kitchen."

Amy heard the word "girlfriend" and expected a sense of relief that she was not his motive. But there was no relief. The way he continued to look at her…

"I was kind of hoping you might be able to suggest something I could whip up real quick that wouldn't take all night, something that wouldn't set my house on fire?" He ended his quip with a satisfied chuckle, all but licking his own eyebrows as the smile officially became a leer.

"I'm sorry, I'm in a hurry." Amy took two more steps to her left. This time the man did move. He took one step towards her.

"Are you sure? I could really use some advice on this. You see, my girlfriend kind of looks like you. And I figured maybe the two of you might share the same kind of tastes."

Amy felt a tight chill down her back. She contemplated leaving her cart and just exiting the store. But then a twinge of anger surfaced alongside her trepidation. She straightened her posture and a surge of confidence spoke for her. "No," she said. "I'm sorry, but I can't help you. Excuse me." She threw both packets of rice back onto the shelf, gripped the handle of the cart with both hands, and went to maneuver it past the man, hoping he would take the hint and step aside. He did, but very slowly, looking her up and down as she worked passed him.

"I understand," the man said. "I didn't mean any harm, you know."

Amy ignored him and never once looked back as she pushed the cart up to the self-serve checkout line. She regretted not taking the rice, but for now starch could—and would—wait. Besides, she could pick some up somewhere else. Or better yet, have Patrick do it.

Amy quickly scanned the meat and juice over the scanner, only pausing long enough to make certain each item emitted the definitive *boop!*

Stuffing the items into the plastic bags next to the scanner proved more cumbersome than it should, and she cursed her nerves. She thought of people in movies who struggled to put keys into locks when they were scared—fine motor skills that went out the window due to the effects of adrenaline. Who knew bagging groceries could be a fine motor skill?

Just get it done and go, girl.

She was on the second to last bottle of juice when Amy knew that the man with the shaved head was behind her. She refused to turn and acknowledge his presence. Only two more beeps and a swipe of her debit card and she was out of there.

"You know, miss…in a way I was giving you a compliment," the voice behind her said.

She ignored him.

"My girlfriend is a beautiful woman."

One beep down.

"I'm not kidding."

She could hear his breathing, low and heavy.

"The two of you could be sisters."

Second beep. Swipe the debit card and you're done.

"I wonder if your tits are the same."

She froze.

"You wanna turn around and give me a little peek?"

Amy spun. "*Fuck you!*" She actually shot spit when the expletive left her mouth.

The man with the shaved head just laughed and held up both hands in playful surrender. By now several curious eyes were on the pair. The man met the stares of each onlooker—an arrogant smile for all of them—before leaving through the hiss of the automatic doors.

Amy breathed in and closed her eyes. Purple blotches swirled inside the black canvas of her eyelids. Her legs shook. She placed both hands on the rim of the conveyer belt to steady herself.

"Are you alright, ma'am?" A pleasant female voice said behind her. Amy nodded but kept her eyes closed, facing the register. She took one final breath, opened her eyes, and swiped her debit card. She punched in her code, waited for approval, ignored the receipt, grabbed the groceries, and headed outside.

Amy was close to the Highlander when she stopped and dropped both bags of groceries to the ground. She doubted her vision. What she was looking at couldn't be what she was looking at. But it was. And the fact that a stranger had left two packets of instant rice on her windshield wasn't nearly as unnerving as the fact that the stranger knew which car was hers.

7

Amy was still shaking when she pulled the Highlander into the cabin's driveway. She switched off the ignition and leaned to her right, collecting both handles of the plastic grocery bags in one grip. With an angry tug that was more forceful than it needed to be, she jerked the groceries onto her lap and slid out of the car. The second her feet hit the driveway she heard the sounds of laughter echoing behind the cabin.

Amy recognized Lorraine Mitchell as soon as she turned the corner. Their neighbor's short white hair and tall lean physique looked exactly as it did a year ago. Lorraine was standing with both hands on her hips, a smile bordering on laughter aimed towards the wooded area behind the cabin. In that wooded area, a very wet Patrick was attempting to wash the Border terrier in a large metal wash basin while Carrie and Caleb looked on with great amusement.

"Hi," Amy said. Her voice was unsteady.

Lorraine turned to Amy, her previous smile bordering on laughter now changing over to one of joy. She walked forward with arms outstretched for the impending hug. "Hello, Amy!"

Amy set the groceries to the ground and hugged her neighbor with as much enthusiasm as her still-rattled mind would allow.

Patrick's head snapped up the second he heard his wife's name called. He raised two soapy hands in the air as though a gun had been pulled on him. "Let me explain."

Amy pulled away from Lorraine. She spoke softly and motioned that Patrick should follow her into the cabin. "Can I talk to you for a second?"

Patrick wiped his hands on his jeans and nodded. "Sure. Lorraine, can you watch the kids for a minute?"

Lorraine nodded back but her smile had faded. She looked concerned as the couple entered the cabin.

The second they were inside, Patrick started rambling like a guilty man. "Honey, let me explain. Lorraine says the dog is *very* safe and *very* friendly, and I figured if we gave him a bath—"

Amy walked towards her husband and wrapped both arms around him in a tight embrace, silencing him. She started to cry.

"*Motherfucker,*" Patrick hissed through clenched teeth. "You're sure it wasn't our friend Arty?"

Amy had stopped crying but her nose still ran. She sniffled and said, "No, his head was shaved." She then held both hands out to the side as if measuring a pair of invisible shoulders. "And he was wider, broader."

Patrick took a steady breath, but his right fist was clenched at his side. "And you're sure he was the one who left the rice packets?"

"Well who else would it have been, Patrick?"

Her intolerance was justified, and he didn't dare question her tone. He spoke his next query in an even manner. "Okay, okay…I'm just wondering how the hell he knew which car was yours."

"I have absolutely no idea. My only guess is that he'd been watching me from the moment I entered the store. Maybe even followed me there, I don't know."

Patrick went rigid the second his wife voiced her speculation. "Followed you? From where? *Here*?"

"I don't know. Maybe."

"Do you remember anyone following you when you left the lake?"

Amy dropped her head and shook it. She didn't remember anyone.

Patrick's right fist clenched tighter, the knuckles glowing white. "Son of a bitch must have clocked you when you pulled into the supermarket then."

"I want to leave," she said, wiping her nose with the back of her hand. "I think we should leave. First we get the weirdo with the gas and the doll, and now this? It's like bad karma or something. I think we should just pack up and leave."

Patrick shook his head emphatically. "*No*. We've been here less than three friggin' hours. I'm not gonna let a couple of assholes ruin our trip."

"Then what do we do, Patrick? Wait for something else to happen?"

"Nothing else *will* happen. I won't let it." He reached out for both of her hands. She took them, but did not go in for the hug.

"He was so creepy, Patrick. So…sure of himself. I mean, I've met some strange men before, but this guy…there was something different about him. Something…*wrong*."

Patrick played his role, swallowing his own rage. "Honey, relax, you're getting a little too worked up. I'm sure he was just an arrogant pervert, that's all. The kind of guy who fancies himself a player—always on the lookout for the next notch on his bedpost. When you weren't taking his bait it probably angered him, and that's when he got crude. I wouldn't read too much into it."

"I'm not so sure. What kind of player states that he has a girlfriend *before* implementing a pick-up line?"

Patrick shrugged. "I don't know. Maybe it was to bring your guard down. Who knows how a guy like that operates?"

A solid minute of silence passed. Amy's eyes were unblinking and staring off into nothing, reliving the experience and weighing her husband's words simultaneously.

"You know what though, honey?" Patrick eventually said. "If you stop and think about it, much of this *is* your fault."

Amy didn't pull away. She didn't yell. She didn't even frown. She just stared at her husband, certain she had heard him wrong.

"What?" was all she finally said.

"Well just think about it for a second. If you weren't such a *stunningly, sexual succubus*, none of this would have happened in the first place." Patrick delivered one his trademark alliterations dripping with cheese and network-anchor eyebrows.

Amy was aware of what her husband was attempting to do, and she instantly began pulling her hands out of his grip. His attempt at levity felt too soon. She managed to pull one hand free but Patrick held on tight to the other.

Patrick continued. "I mean if you're going to go to such a happening spot like the supermarket, you need to ugly yourself up a little bit…"

Amy tried to tug her remaining hand free, a smile was working its way to her face and she would not give him the satisfaction of seeing it.

"Maybe pad your butt and belly with big pillows, make 'em look huge…"

She tugged harder. He was grinning, her elusive smile now on the line and being reeled in.

"Forget to brush your teeth, let the stank-breath blow…"

She tried to pull free with both hands now, her head down, hiding the smile at all costs.

"Oh and forgetting to bathe for a few days might help as well."

Amy stopped pulling and changed tactics; she used Patrick's own leverage against him by going *with* his resistance and launching herself forward into his sternum, knocking him to the kitchen floor with her on top.

Patrick began laughing once his back hit the linoleum and Amy instantly straddled him, pretending to choke him with both hands. "You make me *crazeeeeeeeeeeeey!*" she yelled between fake throttles and psycho eyes.

Still laughing, Patrick reached around and pinched his wife's butt. She squealed and bounced up, only to come crashing back down onto Patrick's stomach, causing him to let out a definitive *OOMPH!*

"What? Are you saying I'm *fat?*"

Patrick's mouth opened, searching for the answer that was never correct under any circumstances, but Amy had already taken the initiative to lean forward and sink her teeth into his ear.

"Ow! Ow! Ow! Okay, okay, you win! *You win!*"

Amy cinched herself further up onto her husband's chest. "Damn right I do." She then brushed the hair out of her face and let out a long sigh. "So you think I'm overreacting by wanting to leave?"

Patrick rubbed his recently chomped ear. "No, not at all. It was a freaky moment that spooked you, and your initial reaction was totally understandable and justified. The guy was a perverted asshole, plain and simple. And like I told you before, I would *never, ever* let anything happen to you and the kids." He kissed his first two fingers and reached up to touch them to his wife's lips. "And from now on, *I'll* be the one who does the food shopping."

"Mmmmm…Spaghettios and cereal," she said.

"And Pop-Tarts."

Amy bent forward and kissed him, her hair falling forward around both their faces. "I love you, baby."

"I love you too, honey," he said. "Does this mean I'm forgiven about the dog?"

8

Arty and Jim sat across from one another at a diner not far from their mother's house.

"So what did you think?" Arty said.

Jim shoveled a scoop of mashed potatoes into his mouth and spoke with it full. "She's fucking nice. I can't believe she squeezed two kids out of that body."

Arty sipped his iced tea and smiled. "Those kids are going to make everything *so* much better. You wait and see."

The two brothers sat silent after that, hardly blinking, each one lost in a world they loved. Controlled, practiced breathing teased the exquisite sensations they shared like a man capable of orgasm without ejaculation so that he may savor the erotic dance again and again. Control was everything.

In their eyes, they were not serial killers, although they had certainly murdered enough to be officially labeled as such, and they were not kidnappers or thieves with simple financial motives. Sex, or more appropriately, rape, sometimes occurred, but that too was no primary motive, at least not for Arty. Jim was often guilty of indulging more often than necessary with their female captives, but Arty understood and forgave him for that, it was just his younger brother's way.

Their primary motive for what they did was summed up best by Arty years back when a previous female captive asked the all-too common question:

"Why are you doing this to me?"

Arty had thought hard for several moments after the question; he was searching for something clever that would define it all with swift decisiveness. And when the perfect response had finally hit him all at once, and his eyes had settled contently with an odd mix of pride and foreboding, he leaned in close to the female captive and did not give an answer, but instead asked a question.

"When you see someone trip and fall, what do you do?"

The female captive had looked at Arty through swollen red eyes that were still capable of projecting confusion.

"I'll ask again. When you watch someone slip, trip, or fall in everyday life, what do you often do?"

When the answer had appeared on the woman's face, it was obvious. Those swollen red eyes had discarded confusion in order to project shame. Arty wondered if she would tell the truth.

"I guess I sometimes laugh," the woman admitted, looking away.

Arty had been pleased with her honesty; it allowed him to continue with his perfect response.

"Thank you for being honest. We laugh too. We just raise the bar a little in order to keep laughing." Arty then stood, smiled, and added, "I hope that helps you understand. And I hope I don't disappoint when I say...it really is as simple as that."

9

Amy still wasn't wild about the newly polished terrier, but Lorraine had assured her the dog was safe, and had actually been coined the unofficial mascot of Crescent Lake this past year.

"So he just showed up one day?" Amy asked Lorraine. "Out of the blue?"

"Yup. I was out tending to some things in the garden when I heard this pathetic little whimper. The poor thing looked as though it hadn't eaten in weeks. I stuffed his belly and we haven't been able to get rid of him since."

"And people here don't mind?" Patrick asked.

"Some do," Norman Mitchell replied. "But he's a clever bugger. He knows who to go pouting to—and it looks as if he's found a winner in your Carrie."

"*Wonderful*," Patrick and Amy said simultaneously.

The four adults sat around a large wooden table on the back porch of the Mitchell's cabin. It was past five and dusk was just starting to gray the light. The grill was fired-up and leaking smoke out of both corners, filling the air with the heavenly aroma of all things char-grilled.

Carrie and Caleb ran and giggled further back in the yard as the terrier yapped and darted at their heels, both siblings completely oblivious to everything else in life except the newfound joy that was fifteen furry pounds of endless entertainment.

"I don't know who's got more energy, that mutt or your kids," Norman said. Norman Mitchell was a short, squat man with a cherub face that said friendly no matter which way you looked at it. His black hair was gone save for the long strip that wrapped around the back of his head from ear to ear. Patrick had told Amy a few years back that he was the spitting image of a slightly taller Danny Devito and she had instantly agreed.

"I'm putting my money on Carrie," Patrick said. "Caleb will poop out soon. He's like his old man—prefers to kick back and relax and watch others do the work. Now Carrie on the other hand, she's my lovely wife's child. She—"

Amy reached over and gripped her husband's ear. "Yes, honey? Please go on."

Patrick gave an exaggerated wince of agony. "You see this?" he said, pointing to the ear still in Amy's clutches. "This happens all the time. Spousal abuse."

Amy let go and pushed his head away. "Oh boo hoo, you big sissy."

Patrick pointed at his wife again. "Psychological abuse too. I'm a broken man inside."

"You're my bitch. Accept it," Amy said.

Both Mitchells laughed. Patrick shook his head in defeat, finished his beer, and raised the empty bottle. "I think I may need a refill here, Norm. Gotta ease the pain on my wounded ear and shattered ego."

Norman smiled at the couple and headed towards the back door leading into the kitchen, grilling spatula still in hand. He stopped in the doorway and turned to the group. "Anyone else? Amy? Sweetheart?"

"Sure I'll have another," Amy said, her head now resting on Patrick's shoulder.

"Sweetheart?" Norman said again.

Lorraine smiled at her husband and shook her head.

"More for us I guess," Norman said, winking at Patrick and Amy.

"Bring it on Norm," Patrick said. "I'll rent your entire supply."

Norman made a face. "Rent?"

Amy rolled her eyes. "Oh God, Norm, I thought you knew better than to feed into my husband's pathetic cheese he calls a sense of humor."

"Ohhh…now I've got it," Norman said. "The old, *you don't buy beer, you only rent it,* joke." He pointed the spatula at Patrick. "The scent of Gouda is strong with you, my son."

Patrick bowed his head. "Thank you, Obi-Wan."

"You're quite welcome. But sadly, I'm afraid I look more like Yoda."

Lorraine said, "I always found Yoda to be quite sexy."

Norman pointed the spatula at his wife while looking at the Lamberts. "Is there any wonder why I love the woman?"

The grill was off and Patrick's waistline was stretched to capacity. Amy, who was usually a light eater, was equally stuffed.

"You missed your calling, Norm," Patrick said. "You could have started your own barbecue pit up here and made millions."

"Why thank you, good sir," Norman said. "You two sure you had enough?"

Amy put a hand to her mouth and pretended to stifle back vomit. Patrick chuckled and said, "I'm afraid I'll have to agree with my charming wife's subtle gesture." He then looked at a drowsy Caleb seated on Lorraine's lap, the toddler struggling to keep his head from rolling off his shoulders. "How 'bout you champ? You had enough?"

"I don't think he's long for this world," Lorraine said as she stroked Caleb's fuzzy head as though petting a cat.

"He *always* falls asleep too early," Carrie announced.

Amy looked at her watch. It was almost eight. "Yeah, well, you won't be up much longer either, missy."

"I want to play with Oscar a little more," Carrie said.

The table of grownups exchanged looks. It was Norman who said, "Oscar?"

"That's what I'm calling him. Because he used to be dirty like Oscar the Grouch."

"Makes sense," Patrick said with a wink to the rest of the table.

"So can I go play with him?" Carrie asked.

Amy looked over her shoulder and out onto the lawn where the now sprawled-out-in-a-blissful-heap terrier resided. "I think Oscar might want to rest for a bit, sweetheart. He ate more than all of us."

It was past ten, and Caleb was now a wad of ooze in Lorraine's arms. Carrie had apparently swallowed her pride and decided that her brother was on to something because she too looked equally sedated in her father's arms.

Dessert never made an appearance and was happily replaced with more beer and wine. The porch lights were on and did a fairly decent job of allowing more than silhouettes to be visible to one another.

"My goodness, that's awful," Lorraine said. "What a terrible way to start your weekend."

"Tell me about it," Amy replied. "I wanted to leave."

Norman shifted in his seat and scratched his bald head. "And you've never met these two men before today?" he asked.

"Nope," Patrick said. "I met the Arty guy for the first time at the gas station, and then we saw him later at the pizza place with the whole doll and candy debacle. But this guy Amy ran into at the supermarket was something completely unrelated. And the bastard *must* have been following her from the moment she arrived at Giant. How else would he have known which car was she was driving so he could play his hilarious little game with the rice on the windshield?"

Amy nodded at Patrick, sipped her beer, and said, "We encoun-tered a doll-loving weirdo and a rice-giving pervert before we even had a chance to get unpacked."

"That's awful," Lorraine said again. "My goodness, how long have we been coming up here, Norm? Twenty years? We've never met any characters like that."

Norman nodded emphatically. "On the contrary, everyone here tends to be too friendly."

"Yeah, well, we always felt the same way," Patrick said. "It's one of the reasons we love it out here so much." He took a swig of beer. "Don't know what happened this time though. Bad luck I suppose."

"It was a freak occurrence," Norman said, raising his beer bot-tle. "The important thing is that you're safe now and you've got a lovely weekend ahead of you."

Only Patrick and Lorraine raised their drink with him. Amy just gave a weak smile then sipped her beer as though it was a pacifier.

"You don't agree?" Norman asked her.

She shrugged. "I guess..." She took another sip. "I think I'm just still rattled about the idea of that pervert at Giant following me without my realizing it. And of course there's this Arty character and his interaction with my daughter." Another sip. "I mean the creep even knows where we're staying for Christ's sake. Patrick told him."

Patrick frowned. "Honey, the guy called this place *Crater* Lake. And that was *after* I'd already told him the correct name. Hell, I'll bet he probably forgot it again the minute he left the station."

"But he was right there at the restaurant with us an hour later, trading a blue lollipop for a fucking doll." She looked away, disgusted.

Norman and Lorraine exchanged an uneasy glance.

"I'm not saying it isn't bizarre, Amy—it is—I'm just saying that with a wife, in-laws, and twins on his plate, I doubt the guy's got any time to pop in for a surprise visit, *if* he happens to remember the name of the lake."

Amy took a deep pull from her beer.

"Come on, honey," Patrick began, "we've already been over this. I hate what happened too, but it's done, right? We need to put it behind us now."

Norman leaned to his right and rubbed Amy's shoulder. "Here, here," he said. "Just dumb luck is all it was." He then smiled and added, "Besides, you've got Oscar to protect you now."

All four adults looked out onto the grass where the still-heavily stuffed and clinically zonked Oscar hadn't moved for the past two hours.

"Great," Amy said. "I feel safer already."

Over an hour had passed before Amy and Patrick were able to crawl under the sheets together.

Inching over, Patrick placed his lips on Amy's neck and mumbled into her warm flesh. "You better not be ready to go to sleep just yet."

"You're not tired?" she asked.

"Does it feel like I'm tired?"

Amy reached under the sheets and touched the front of her husband's boxer shorts. "Oh my," she said. "No, I would say you're, or should I say, *he's* wide awake."

They both chuckled. Amy rolled over on top of her husband and began kissing his chest, periodically darting her tongue in and out, flicking his nipples. "Although I'm not sure I gave a good enough inspection," she said, her tongue sliding down his torso towards his waist. "Perhaps I should take a closer look?"

"I, I mean *he,* would like that very much."

In the twelve years they had been married there was one undeniable truth both Amy and Patrick could never deny: their sex life was amazing. As incredulous as it sounded to other couples in the same chronological boat, their physical attraction and passion for one another had never once dimmed from the first time they'd touched each other's skin. Tonight's marathon of intensity proved to extend that streak even further.

"I think I'm done for now, baby," Amy said. She was on top, Patrick still inside her (the sheets long since discarded in a heap on the floor), and panting heavily, perspiration rimming her hairline. "I'm starting to get a little sore."

"You okay?" he asked between pants of his own.

She leaned down and began kissing him, pausing and breathing hard between each kiss to say, "I came twice." Kiss. "Yes, I'm okay." Kiss. "I'm *very* okay." Kiss. "I think I just need some healing time if we're ever going to do it again on this trip." Kiss.

Patrick laughed and said, "Okay, dismount."

She giggled and slowly pushed herself off. He leaned forward and wrapped his arm around her waist, pulling her onto her side and close to him so they could spoon into one another. He kissed her softly on the nape of her neck. "I love you," he said.

Amy reached back and rubbed his leg. "I love you too." She took a deep breath into her nose, and let it filter out slow and heavy through her mouth—any previous anxieties gratefully expelled with her therapeutic sigh. She felt her eyelids getting heavy. "We better pull the sheets back onto the bed," she said. "If the kids come in…"

"Good idea," Patrick mumbled, his eyes already closed. "You do that."

"Such a gentleman," she replied, gently slapping his leg.

Amy sat up and reached over the side of the bed. She glanced outside through the bedroom window and saw the man with the shaved head staring back at her. She screamed louder than she'd ever done before in her life.

10

Patrick and Amy sat huddled together on the steps of their front porch waiting for the local sheriff to arrive. They each gripped a mug of tea prepared by Lorraine who was now next door keeping an eye on Carrie and Caleb until matters could be resolved. Norman stood next to the seated couple.

"I think this might be him," Norman said, pointing out in the distance towards a pair of headlights entering Crescent Lake. Seconds later the flashing red and blue left zero doubt.

"It only took him half an hour," Amy said. Her bitter sarcasm was anything but subtle.

"Not much ever happens around here, Amy," Norman said. "Heck, it's just the one sheriff and a couple of deputies patrolling the area. Guess they figure they can take their time."

Amy had been chatting up a nervous storm the entire time they waited for the sheriff. She fired out questions, each one flowing immediately into the next, giving neither man a chance to answer. This was oddly appropriate; neither man *had* answers.

Patrick's behavior on the porch was the opposite of his wife's. His rage for what Amy had seen in their bedroom window was consuming him and had taken hold of his tongue. He had stormed outside immediately after the incident, keen on a confrontation.

After several minutes of fruitless searching, he eventually broke down and phoned the police. And now, having no other option but to sit and wait (while the son of a bitch in the window was being given *ample* time to get away), he felt as if a sea of bile was burning holes in his stomach.

The sheriff's car rolled to a stop in front of the cabin. The flashing red and blue continued their show while the sheriff exited the car and began his walk to the cabin.

"You the Lamberts?" he called, still a good ten feet from the couple.

Amy and Patrick set their mugs to one side, stepped down and walked a few feet forward. The porch held two lanterns on either side of the front door, each one powerful enough to cast a decent light onto the sheriff as he came into view. He was in full uniform, right down to the wide-brimmed hat. His pallid skin was heavily wrinkled, eyes dark and narrow. A long, thick gray mustache touched both corners of his chin. His physique was the odd combination of skinny and fat: a sunken chest, pipe cleaner arms, and a belly that bubbled and hung over his belt.

"Yes," Patrick said as he extended his hand. "I'm Patrick. This is my wife, Amy."

The sheriff took Patrick's hand and gave it a half-hearted shake while looking in Norman's direction. "That you, Norm?" he asked.

Norman nodded and gave a small obligatory smile, discouraging drawn-out pleasantries. Patrick was grateful.

"How's Lorraine?"

"She's fine."

The sheriff nodded then turned his full attention to Patrick and Amy. "So who can tell me what happened here tonight?"

Amy and Patrick took turns relaying the bizarre events that took place earlier in the day—Patrick when it came to the incidents with Arty, Amy when it came to the man with the shaved head at the supermarket. When the telling of events ultimately arrived at the episode with the man at the window, Amy took over entirely.

"And I glanced up at the window for a few seconds and he was there…staring at me," she said.

"And you're sure it was the man you saw earlier in the supermarket?" the sheriff asked.

"Positive," Amy said.

The sheriff fixed on Patrick. "And you say you ran outside after the guy?"

"That's right."

"But you didn't find anyone."

"No."

The sheriff went back to Amy. "And you're absolutely *sure* you saw a man in your window?"

Amy looked at the sheriff as though he'd told an offensive joke. "*Yes, I'm sure.*"

The sheriff showed Amy both palms in a placating manner. "Okay, okay, I'm just suggesting that after the ordeal at the market today, maybe this guy's face might have been on your mind some. Maybe caused you to see something that wasn't really there."

"I just got finished making love to my husband. I can assure you that creep's face was *not* on my mind."

Norman blushed at Amy's comment, bit back a smile and looked away.

The sheriff's reaction was similar but different. He too blushed, but there was no smile to fight; he seemed flustered by Amy's bluntness, avoiding eye contact when he said, "Okay, ma'am, I'm just here trying to put your mind at ease, that's all."

"Well you're accusing me of not seeing something that I *know* I saw."

Another placating gesture of the hands. "Okay, okay…"

"So what now?" Patrick asked.

The sheriff answered Patrick by addressing Amy. "You mind showing me which window you spotted him in, miss?"

"It would be my pleasure."

Amy led the sheriff around the side of the cabin with Patrick and Norm close behind.

"Here." She pointed to the only window of the cabin that looked directly into their bedroom. "Right here."

The sheriff looked into the window for a brief moment, then squatted down into a catcher's stance, grunting the whole way. He pulled the flashlight from his belt and waved it along the ground for several seconds before mumbling, "Huh."

"What?" Patrick asked.

The sheriff remained squatting, still shining the flashlight on the ground. "Kinda muddy."

"So?" Amy said.

The sheriff glanced up at Amy, a mild look of annoyance now trumping the uncomfortable berth he'd initially given her. When he brought his attention back down to the ground, he proceeded to wave the flashlight over the muddy grass in slow, deliberate circles. "I can't make out a shoe print. Can you?" he asked.

Patrick squatted down next to the sheriff. "Can I borrow that?" he asked, nodding his head towards the flashlight.

The sheriff seemed reluctant, but eventually clicked his teeth and said, "Sure thing."

Patrick took the flashlight, waved the cylinder of light over the area beneath the window. He saw nothing that resembled the tread of a shoe or a boot, but he did see something. "There's a few indentations here," he said. "It kind of looks like the earth was pressed flat in spots. Maybe he was barefoot?"

The sheriff stood slowly upright, groaning more so than he'd done during his descent. "Perhaps," he said. "But I can't see a man running around out here without a pair of shoes on. Wooded area like this would tear his feet to bits. Hardly worth it for a little peepshow."

Amy made no attempt to hide her disgust over the sheriff's choice of words.

Patrick stood and handed the flashlight back to the sheriff. "So then how do you explain what my wife saw?"

The sheriff clicked off the flashlight, hooked it back onto his belt, and let out a long sigh, the delay in his response seemingly intentional, as though he considered his wisdom a privilege, worth the wait.

"Can't say for sure," he finally said. He faced Amy. "It's obvious you're quite upset, miss. And I don't doubt your word. If you're friends with Lorraine and Norm here then I'm sure you're decent folks who would have no reason to make up such a story." He turned back to Patrick. "You say you went out after the guy."

"Yeah, I told you that."

"How soon?"

"What?"

The sheriff enunciated slowly. "After your wife spotted the man, how soon after did you go out looking for him?"

Patrick struggled for a quick response. The sheriff's patronizing tone made him feel guilty for some reason. "I don't know—a minute maybe? I had to throw on some pants and shoes first."

"And you say you never saw the guy in the window to begin with? Nobody was there when *you* looked?"

"That's right."

"But you still went out anyway."

"Absolutely. I trust my wife."

"How long did you look for him again?" The sheriff didn't look at Patrick when he spoke; his flashlight was out again, waving about their surroundings, more obligatory than necessary.

"I don't know—a few minutes? I kind of ran the perimeter of the cabin a few times, then wandered further out."

"But you never saw anyone."

Patrick gritted his teeth and steadied himself. "No."

The sheriff looked at Norman. "What about you, Norm? You see anything out of the ordinary?"

"Lorraine and I were asleep."

The sheriff nodded once and clicked the flashlight off. A brief moment of silence followed. The cacophony of chirps and clicks from the surrounding nightlife echoed throughout the dark surroundings. Such sounds were usually demoted to white noise after only a few minutes of exposure, but now they seemed intent on rising above their disregarded status in a bid to set an ominous mood for current events.

"Well," the sheriff finally said, holstering the flashlight again, adjusting his wide-brimmed hat, "I've got all your information. I'll alert my deputies to keep an eye out for anyone fitting the description you gave me, and I'll send a cruiser out periodically this weekend to do a brief check around the area. My guess is that if there *was* a guy here then he's long gone by now, especially when he saw a big fella like this coming after him." The sheriff smiled and patted Patrick on his upper arm, finishing with a firm squeeze. Patrick flashed on Arty's similar gesture at the gas station and this time he yanked his arm free. The sheriff dropped his smile and stared. Patrick instantly regretted his action. Not because the sheriff was a good guy (he seemed like an asshole), but because his ego still regretted the physical liberty Arty had taken with him. And of course, the sheriff was law—that was a big one too.

"I'm sorry," Patrick immediately said. "I'm just...I guess I'm just frustrated. I'm very sorry, sheriff. I didn't mean any disrespect."

The sheriff slowly put his smile back on. "That's alright, son. You've had a heck of a night. Can't blame a man for getting frustrated when it comes to protecting his family."

Patrick smiled and nodded a silent thank you.

The sheriff turned to Norman. "Nice seeing you again, Norm." He looked at Amy, tugged the brim of his hat and said, "You take care now, folks." He did not look back at Patrick.

The sheriff sauntered back to his vehicle with all the urgency of a man out for a midnight stroll, painfully obvious to Patrick that the sheriff had felt his time had been wasted, that he was eager to get back to the station so he could put his feet up and continue watching his belly grow.

Giving a final wave over his shoulder before oozing into the driver's seat, the sheriff started his engine and left.

"Asshole," Amy said once the flashing red and blue were colored dots in the distance. "Is he always like that, Norm?"

"Can't say. I've only met him at picnics and community gatherings and such. He seemed okay there. This was the first time I ever saw him on the job. Seemed a bit condescending at times, didn't he?"

"And then some," Amy said. She turned to Patrick. He looked strange. "Patrick? You alright?"

"Yeah," he said a little too quickly, shaking himself from the blender of thoughts in his head. "Yeah, I'm fine."

Amy did not seem convinced. "You believe me, right?" she asked. "You believe I saw someone? The guy with the shaved head from Giant? You *do* believe I saw him outside our window right?"

Patrick did believe her. Initially. Now he was unsure. He knew how upset his wife had been earlier, and he knew that if you coupled that fact with the dark and relatively unfamiliar environment they were in, it was very possible that she *did* see something that wasn't there—a cruel but common trick of the eyes.

And then there was the evidence. There was none. No shoe prints in the mud, no sign of the guy when he ran outside after him. As much as it pained Patrick to even consider it, maybe the asshole sheriff had been spot-on in his assumption that what Amy truly saw *was* an image of a man locked away in the recesses of her mind—unwillingly set free for a fleeting moment when her guard was down.

Still, Patrick was smart enough to know that betraying Amy's trust was about as wise as pissing off Lorena Bobbitt, so he prayed his uncertain response gave authenticity. "Of course I do. I'm just flustered right now, that's all. That sheriff was a dick."

To Patrick's delight, Amy did not appear to second-guess his response. She just walked over and put her arms around him in a tight embrace. He hugged her back and kissed the top of her head.

"Would you like Lorraine and I to keep the kids for tonight?" Norman asked.

"Would you mind?" Amy said, pulling away from her husband and facing Norman. "I'd hate to wake them again. Plus it kind of makes me feel better to know they're not...I don't know...at the cabin *he* was looking in."

"Wait, wait," Patrick said. "I'm not too sure about that. Maybe it's best if the kids are with us."

Amy repeated herself, adamant. "I don't want to wake them again. And I *don't* want them to be in the same cabin that he was—"

Patrick held up a hand. "Fine."

"What will happen tomorrow?" Norman asked.

Amy gave an uncertain shrug. "I guess we'll figure that out to-morrow. But don't be surprised if you find us leaving first thing in the morning. As for right now I'm just thinking about..." She sighed. "I don't know what I'm thinking." She looked at Patrick. "Maybe we *should* wake them." She looked back at Norm and sighed again. "I don't know...I'm not making any sense, am I?"

"No, you are," Norman said. "I'd be confused and uncertain too. It's completely understandable."

"You're sure you don't mind keeping the kids for tonight?" she asked again.

"Absolutely not. You know we love having them. You two go on in and try and get some sleep."

Amy snorted. "Right."

"We'll bring the kids over first thing in the morning when they wake," Norman said.

"Thanks, Norm," Patrick said.

Norman stepped forward and gave them each a hearty hug. "We'll see you in the morning. Goodnight." He flashed a reassuring smile, turned and headed back towards his cabin.

Patrick took Amy's hand and gave her a gentle pull. "Come on, honey, let's go inside."

They were a few feet from the back entrance when Oscar appeared, wagging his tail and whining for affection.

"And where the hell were *you* during all this?" Amy said.

Jim had watched every second of the aftermath unfold. He was only fifty yards away during the sheriff's entire stay—nestled safely behind an enormous oak at the rear of the Lambert's cabin.

His feet did ache, but the two thick pairs of wool socks he wore dulled the sharp edges that jabbed into his soles when he fled from the window.

Watching the couple fuck had proved arousing. But that show was a mere bonus. Anticipation had been the true culprit for the thumping in his heart and the tickling in his groin—waiting for that sweet, sweet moment when Amy (he knew her name now; he heard it spoken from behind the oak) would spot none other than *his* face leering back at her from the bedroom window.

The game was officially gaining momentum.

11

Arty was nursing a beer when Jim entered the bar. It was nearly 2:00 A.M., and in this particular dive that meant the remaining patrons were still around for two reasons: sex or a fight. Or both. Arty was the exception. He was waiting for his brother to arrive so he could find out how his solo venture at Crescent Lake had gone.

"It's about time," Arty said as his brother took a stool next to him. "Any problems?"

"Nah—I wore the socks like you said. No serious prints or anything. My feet hurt though."

"Can't make an omelet."

"Yeah."

Arty slid a bottle of beer over to his brother. "It might be a little warm. I didn't think you'd be this late."

Jim took the beer and sipped it. "It's fine." He took another swig. "I planned on getting here sooner, but I was enjoying myself a bit too much I suppose."

Arty laughed and sipped from his own beer. "Tomorrow's going to be a good day."

Jim looked off into one of his thoughts for a moment, a smile on his face that managed both malice and delight. When he returned he quivered and shook his head hard as if trying to wake himself up. "I think I need a shot. You want one?"

"No, let's get out of here. There's some big inbred fuckers at the end of the bar who were giving me shit earlier."

Jim looked past his brother, down the length of the bar. Three big men stared back with drunken, arrogant smirks. Two slovenly women accompanied them.

"Those big hicks? What'd they do?"

"Just said some shit. Took some cheap shots because I was on my own. Thought I was an easy victim. Trying to impress those pigs with them I guess."

Jim was adamant. He continued to stare at the three men as he spoke to his brother. "Well fuck them—I'm not leaving because those hillbillies are looking to start something. Let them fucking try."

Arty put his hand on his brother's forearm. It was as solid as a baseball bat from the angry grip he had on his beer. "We don't want to draw any attention to ourselves, bro. Two guys from out of town fighting with locals will put a beacon on our backs. It's nearly closing time—let's just let it go and leave."

Jim watched the three men lean in and whisper to one another. The shift in their body language said it all. "They're not gonna let us leave here without a fight, Arty."

Arty glanced down the end of the bar and saw exactly what his brother saw. The three men were fidgeting, psyching themselves up. "Well if it comes to that I've got a back up plan I took care of earlier."

"What plan?"

Arty didn't answer; his attention was now locked on the three men approaching them. The largest of the three took lead with the remaining two close behind. The leader stood well over six feet and carried significant bulk. His torso was covered in flannel and his thick legs were wrapped in faded denim that ended with a pair of giant construction boots. His greasy hair was long, tangled, and ink black.

"So your girl finally showed up, huh?" the leader asked Arty, his two friends standing behind him, arms folded, grinning at the insult. They were both shorter than the leader but carried similar girth and attire. The one on the left was slick bald with a scar running through his left eyebrow. The one on the right sported the same greasy black hair as the leader in addition to a heavy goatee.

Jim went to stand up, but Arty grabbed his shoulder and guided him back down onto the stool. "We were just on our way out," Arty said.

"No, not yet you're not," the leader said. He gulped the last of his beer then slammed the empty bottle down onto the bar.

That was when Arty and Jim first spotted the ring. It was silver and huge and practically engulfed the man's thick ring finger. A skull was engraved into it.

"Before you leave I'd like you to buy us all a couple of rounds." The man motioned to his friends on either side of him, then to the giggling girls at the end of the bar who seemed to be enjoying every second of the show.

"We're not buying you a round," Jim said.

"No?" the leader said. "Why not?" He extended his arm and knocked over Arty's beer, the remains gradually pumping their way out through the brown neck of the bottle, spreading into a small pool on the counter, then finally a slow drip over the edge of the bar.

Arty glanced down at his spilt beer then looked straight ahead. He had a strange calm over him that didn't seem to fit under the given circumstances. The leader seemed to sense this too; a look of both confusion and anger meshed on his thick brow. The man inched closer, made a tight fist, rested it on the bar so that both brothers could swoon over it in all its destructive glory.

"Nice ring," Arty said without even looking at it. He was still staring straight ahead, still inappropriately cool. "Very original."

The leader's brow furrowed some more. Arty's sarcasm would have been evident to most, but to this man it proved cumbersome. His response was primitive: he opened his fist and closed it again, tighter this time, the skull ring jutting forward like an extra silver knuckle.

A moment followed where no one spoke. A country song was crooning from the speakers overhead. The bartender—who seemed content to keep his back to the affair—clinked and clanked an array of glasses in the square tub of blue liquid next to the bar's sink. The drunken gibberish from the remaining patrons—all aging, defeated men, oblivious to anything around them but the unfair world—periodically rose over the country singer's voice whenever they made frustrated, incoherent shouts to all that might listen.

"Oh for fuck's sake!" Jim finally blurted, kicking back his stool. "You know what? We *will* buy you some drinks. In fact we'll buy you *lots* of drinks. You know why? Because the way I see it, you're gonna need some thick fucking beer goggles in order to fuck those two pigs you got over there."

The leader didn't hesitate. He pummeled his right fist deep into Arty's cheekbone, the sound like a mallet cracking meat. The silver ring cut deep into Arty's flesh and sent him reeling backwards into his brother. Jim caught Arty and quickly tried standing him upright, but Arty's legs were gone from the punch, buckling in all directions every time his feet touched the floor.

Jim opted to drag Arty backward to place him into one of the booths so he could free up his hands for an attack. Arty, however, proved coherent enough to sense what his brother was attempting to do and turned into him.

"*No! Jim, no!*" Arty yelled, gripping his brother's shoulders, stopping his momentum.

"Yeah, Jim," the leader laughed, "listen to your girl."

"*Fuck you, you fucking inbred hick!*" Jim spat over Arty's shoulder.

The leader stepped forward and Arty pushed Jim back towards the door. "We're leaving," Arty said.

The three men were all laughing in unison now. And as Arty gave Jim one final push out the door, he turned over his shoulder and locked eyes with the big man with the silver skull ring. Arty smirked, winked, and was gone. And the big man with the silver skull ring instantly stopped laughing.

3:00 A.M. A battered Ford pickup pulled into an unpaved driveway five miles from the watering hole at which it was recently parked. Loose pebbles crunched beneath the heavy tires before the truck eventually grinded to a stop.

A large man wearing a big silver ring nearly fell out of the driver's side. He righted himself, belched loud, then slammed the car door shut before stumbling around the rear of his truck towards the passenger side. The passenger door flung open and a hefty woman reeking of booze and cigarettes fell into his arms, letting out an obnoxious giggle that culminated with a snort. The two instantly locked lips and exchanged a sloppy kiss that missed more than it connected.

The large man wrapped his arm around the staggering girl and guided her along the short, broken path to the front door of his one-story home—a dwelling that would be aptly described by any passerby as a weather-stained box with a few windows.

Before entering, the drunken couple paused for a second attempt at a kiss, nearly falling over one another in the effort. The alcohol-induced detriment to their equilibrium succeeded in bringing out another sloppy giggle from the female. The big man leered at his drunken catch then turned back towards the front door. He closed one eye (there were now two doorknobs for some reason) and fumbled and scraped his key along the lock's plate until it eventually clicked home. A quick turn of the key, a forceful nudge with his shoulder, and the front door swung open allowing the big man to guide his catch inside. That was the last thing the big man remembered for almost thirty minutes.

The big man felt the headache before his eyes fluttered open. When his vision settled, he made out two men standing in front of him. It took him a few seconds, but he soon remembered who these two men were. One of the men was sporting an impressive wound on his cheek—a wound that he himself had given him.

The large man sprang to attention, but instant resistance seized his entire body, the confines of the ropes that bound him to the chair biting into his skin. He struggled briefly against the binds, but soon quit when he could not detect even the slightest bit of slack in their coiled grip.

"Careless fool," the man with the wound on his cheek said. "You left your wallet open for damn near five minutes when you bought a round for that pig you brought home with you."

The big man blinked several times; nothing this man was saying made any sense. His head ached at its base from where he had been struck upon entering his home, and the more he thought, the more it ached. He went to speak against the wadded cloth that was taped inside his mouth, but only panicked, muffled words escaped.

"Your license, genius," the man with the welt said. "It was sticking out of your wallet like a hard-on. Meatheads like you are so fucking predictable. I knew you'd eventually start trouble with us tonight. I guess you can say I like to plan ahead."

The large man's eyes stopped blinking. He understood now. He struggled again for a brief moment—more a show of bravado than any attempt at escape—and then stopped. He tried another muffled shout, but its futility was heightened more by the pain the effort was causing his head. He resigned entirely and his shoulders slumped, a long strained sigh flapped out of his nose like a snore.

"Now," the man with the welt said. "How 'bout we get a look at that ring of yours? I mean it's such a cool ring after all. A skull. It's just so rebellious and dangerous. Scary even. You must be a real outlaw to wear a ring like that, yeah?"

The man with the welt's accomplice, a stocky man with black eyes and a shaved head, stepped forward, past the man with the welt. He squatted down into a catcher's stance so he could study the ring on the big man's hand that was strapped to the arm of the chair. "This *is* cool," the man with the shaved head said as he fingered the ring. He looked over his shoulder at the man with the welt. "*Very* scary."

"Well I can't see it too well from back here," the man with the welt said. "Can you bring it over to me?"

"I can *try*." The man with the shaved head put on a melodramatic display as he grunted and groaned, trying (but not trying) to remove the ring from the man's thick fingers. "Won't budge, bro," he said. "It's stuck fast."

The man with the welt continued in the vein of his friend's theatrics with an exaggerated frown and sigh. Taking a few steps forward, he squatted down next to the man with the shaved head. "Let me have a try," he said.

The man with the welt took hold of the large man's ring finger and violently jerked it to its left. There was an exceptional crack like a branch being snapped in two. The large man cried out through his gag, the cloth muffling the sound but not the intensity.

"Did that get it?" the man with the shaved head asked.

"Nope. Still on there," the man with the welt replied.

"Better try again."

The man with the welt took hold of the broken finger and now jerked it to its right. No crack this time, just a grinding noise like popcorn kernels being munched. The large man's cries were long drawn-out moans now, the pain shockingly worse than before.

"Anything?" the man with the shaved head asked.

"*Still* nothing," the man with the welt complained.

The man with the shaved head huffed, stood up, and exited the room. He returned moments later carrying a large kitchen knife, a good portion of it coated in dark, wet red. The big man's eyes widened when he saw the bloodied knife.

"Ah, don't worry about her, big fella," the man with the shaved head said. He looked at the knife as he spoke, rotating it back and forth in his hand, studying it. "We made it fairly quick. Still, a pig like that's gonna take a lot of sticking before she eventually stops squealing, yeah?" He laughed and shook his head without a trace of sympathy. "Poor fat slut was just in the wrong place at the wrong time."

The man with the shaved head handed the kitchen knife down to the man with the welt who was still squatting in front of the big man, his calm, almost lazy eyes never leaving the big man's panicked, unblinking pair. His confident smirk never waning. The same confident smirk he'd flashed at the large man before exiting the bar after the fight. Admittedly, that smirk had caused the large man a brief hint of concern as they left the scene. Now it terrified him.

"Okay," the man with the welt announced. He took firm hold of the twisted ring finger in one hand, and tapped the flat of the blade against the big man's forehead with the other, clucking his tongue with each tap like a metronome. "Let's see if we can't get that scary ring off once and for all."

12

Patrick and Amy were awake but still in bed. The sun had just come up.

"How'd you sleep?" Patrick asked.

Amy was resting her head on his chest while he stroked her hair. She waited a few seconds before responding. "About as well as I could given the circumstances. How about you?"

"Okay I guess," he said.

What followed was a brief silence Patrick utilized to prepare for what he felt was the inevitable question to come.

"You *don't* believe me do you?" she asked. Her head was still on his chest, her query was soft.

Patrick hadn't dared voice any of his skepticism last night; his wife's rage would have made arguing his case nigh on impossible. But now, after some sleep, and a chance to reflect without a condescending local sheriff to answer to, Patrick felt that maybe his wife would be a bit more receptive to what he had to say.

"I'll never doubt you, baby," he said. "You tell me the earth is flat and the moon is made of cheese, and I'll stand up in court and swear under oath that my wife is telling the absolute truth." He heard her laugh softly through her nose, her head still resting on his chest. "And I still don't doubt that you saw something in that window." He took a breath, ready to take the leap. "But I do know a few things. I know that what happened at Giant with that perverted asshole was a big deal, and that it upset you big time. I know that we had a bunch of drinks over at Norm and Lorraine's. I know that sometimes the dark can play tricks on our eyes. And I know that since we've been up here we've experienced an odd incident or two to say the fucking least."

Another small laugh through her nose. She wasn't angry yet. That was good. Proceed.

"Am I saying you're lying? Of course not. I believe you saw what you say you saw. However, I think it's possible that maybe, *maybe*, your eyes were just having a little fun with you last night."

Patrick braced himself, expecting his wife to launch herself off of his chest and begin her attack. To his surprise (and relief) she did not. She didn't even flinch. She just sighed deeply and said, "I could have *sworn*..."

Patrick stroked her hair some more, his hand then moving down to her neck where he began kneading it.

"Again, I don't doubt you saw something, honey, I truly don't. When I was about eleven I saw *Friday the 13th Part 2*."

She lifted her head off his chest. "What?"

"Let me finish," he said.

She dropped her head back down.

"This was the one before Jason—the killer—"

"Yeah, I know who Jason is."

He tweaked her ear lobe. "*Anyway*...this is the one before Jason started wearing the hockey mask. Instead he wore a burlap sack over his head with only one eye hole—something I found a *hell* of a lot creepier than a hockey mask. It reminded me of the hood *The Elephant Man* wore over his head—another film that gave me the willies when I was a kid because I couldn't appreciate what a great movie it was at the time. As a kid all I saw was some horribly deformed man wearing a scary hood. And the fact that it was a true story certainly didn't help matters as far as I was concerned.

"But *Friday the 13th*? Scared the absolute shit out of me. Jason wasn't some misunderstood deformed guy like John Merrick, who was as gentle as a kitten. Jason was a ruthless killer who was fucking people up with pitchforks and machetes and whatever the hell else he could lay his hands on. It was as if some evil prick who had access to my young mind had said: 'Hmmm...little Patrick is scared of The Elephant Man. Problem is, the Elephant Man is a nice guy. How 'bout we make a movie with a guy that looks *just like* The Elephant Man, *but*, let's have him be some homicidal lunatic instead. And oh yeah, let's also make it so the crazy bastard can't be killed.'"

Amy gave a short, genuine laugh. Patrick smiled and waited a beat before continuing.

"So to put it mildly, *Friday the 13th Part 2* freaked me the hell out. And you know what? I would have sworn on my mother's life that every now and then I would wake up in the middle of the night and see that burlap sack with the one eye-hole staring back at me through my bedroom window, sometimes even at the foot of my bed. Even when I closed my eyes tight and opened them, he was still there. And as absolutely terrified as I was, something deep down told me he *wasn't* there. Something told me that my eyes were just using that incredibly annoying ability they have to make us see something we just flat-out don't want to see."

Patrick finished his spiel by moving his hand from Amy's neck to her shoulders. Her position on Patrick's chest never changed and her breathing never quickened. He continued massaging her shoulders. After a good minute Amy sighed and said, "I love you."

Patrick brought his hand back to her neck, gave it a gentle squeeze. "And I love ya back."

"I'd turn around kiss you if it wasn't for your morning breath," she said.

"Oh, and your morning breath is an ocean breeze?"

Amy smiled and began drawing circles with her index finger on Patrick's bare stomach. "Should we go over and get the kids?"

"Nah. Norm said he and Lorraine would bring them over. Let's enjoy a little more solitude while we can."

"We could put a movie on if you want," she said, taking her hand off his chest and pointing to the VCR and television in the far corner of the room. "Do you want me to see if my family has a copy of *Friday the 13th Part 2*? You know, the one where Jason wears the burlap sack with the one eye hole just like *The Elephant Man* did? Do you know that one, honey? Not the one with the hockey mask, the one with the burlap—"

Patrick clawed her ribs and she screamed.

13

"Who's ready to go fishing?" Patrick asked his brood.

Caleb looked delighted, Carrie looked mildly amused, and Amy looked repulsed.

"I'm not putting any worms on a hook. And we're not keeping anything we catch," Amy said.

"But what if we catch a beauty? It could be our dinner," Patrick said.

Amy closed her eyes and shook her head. "First of all, I prefer my fish to be served to me on a plate, in a restaurant, thank you very much. I am not about to bring one of those smelly things into our cabin and gut it myself."

"I'll gut it. It'll be—"

"*Second*, I doubt there is anything living in that man-made lake that can even remotely pass as being edible."

Caleb looked up at his father. Patrick looked back down and rubbed the top of his head. "Don't listen to her, champ. We're gonna catch a million of 'em."

"A million of *what* is the question," Amy said.

"Can Oscar come?" Carrie piped in.

"Sure, why not?" Patrick said. "I'm fairly certain *he'll* eat anything we catch. He's like a fuzzy garbage disposal."

Carrie burst out laughing. Patrick leaned over and kissed the top of her head. He then asked, "Who's coming to the bait shop with me?"

"Me!" Caleb yelled.

Carrie shook her head. "I want to play with Oscar some more."

Patrick looked at Amy. "Do you mind staying here with her, honey?"

"Not at all. You go buy your slimy worms. Besides I want to make some final arrangements with Lorraine and Norm." She looked at Carrie and Caleb. "Are you guys excited to go to the movies with the Mitchells tonight?"

Both kids nodded.

"Are they taking us to dinner too?" Carrie asked.

"Yup. Dinner and a movie. Sounds better than the plans your father and I have. We're just doing dinner."

Carrie laughed. Caleb offered his mother and father to come along to the movie. Patrick and Amy exchanged an *our-son-is-so-freaking-adorable* look, and took turns telling him how thoughtful he was to consider them, but, regrettably, they would have to decline.

"Alright, brother-man," Patrick said to his son. "You ready to go buy some worms?"

14

For a brief moment Patrick wished his four-year-old son could read for all the wrong reasons: along the road's edge, leading into the white-graveled lot of the bait shop, a signpost stood tall, announcing one large and crudely painted word to all who drove by.

BAIT.

He couldn't resist saying it anyway. "Think this is the place?"

Father and son locked eyes in the rearview mirror. Caleb shrugged at his father, wide-eyed and innocent.

Patrick smiled back. "Nevermind, buddy. This is the place."

Caleb leaned forward in his child seat in order to get a solid look at the bait shop. Patrick pulled left into the gravel lot, glanced back and caught his son's curious expression. He appeared to be taking his father's sarcastic joke quite literally; Patrick felt sure Caleb's wary brow was declaring that this didn't look like any store *he* had ever seen, Dad.

The place was a weathered one-story home that doubled as a bait shop. A white wooden porch led to a screen-door entrance. On either side of that screen door were two cloudy windows, each displaying an array of lures that dangled and glimmered from fishing line above the window's pane like tiny puppets with jewelry.

To the right of the entrance a rusted porch swing designed for two—likely capable of holding none—swayed lightly from side to side, each sway giving out a metallic groan, as if warning all it would not be held responsible for those crazy enough to deem it fit for sittin' and, God forbid, swingin'.

Patrick had expected nothing less from such a place. In fact he'd counted on it. He loved these rustic mom-and-pop spots, and it was the precise reason they were visiting Crescent Lake as opposed to being stretched out on a sandy beach somewhere, sipping margaritas.

The screen door screeched metal against metal as father and son entered. The interior of the shop had a sharp smell of burnt wood and heavy dust that immediately made Patrick feel like picking his nose. He looked down and spotted Caleb already going at it. "Digging for gold?" he asked his son. Caleb yanked his hand away from his face and shook his head. Patrick smiled and bopped him on the top of the head.

The layout of the shop was basic. To the right were three rows of shelves that held all things fishing, and to the left was a wooden counter top. Behind it stood an old man who Patrick guessed to be at least eighty. He was short, thin, stoop-shouldered, and wrinkled from head to toe. His head was covered with an old baseball cap decorated with fishing lures. Resting on the bridge of his nose was a pair of thick glasses that doubled the size of his green eyes.

Yup, Patrick would have been disappointed with anything less—or actually, more.

"Good afternoon, gentlemen," the shopkeeper announced. His voice was loud and clear despite his fragile appearance. The magnified green eyes were warm and pleasant.

"Good afternoon to you too," Patrick replied.

The shopkeeper leaned over the counter and looked at Caleb. "Hello down there, young man."

Caleb immediately clamped onto Patrick's leg. The old man laughed.

"Name's Edgar," the elder said, extending his hand. "I'm hoping you folks are aiming to do a little fishing today, 'cause I'm afraid I'm all outta surf boards."

Patrick laughed and took the man's hand. "Nice to meet you, Edgar. And yes, my son and I aim to do a little fishing today." He looked down at his son, still wrapped to his father's thigh like a koala to a tree. "Isn't that right, brother-man?"

Caleb looked up and nodded, not ready to commit to a smile just yet.

"So is it some fishing poles you'll be needing?" Edgar asked. "My selection isn't too great I'm afraid, but any one of 'em will get the job done."

"No, no," Patrick said. "We've got poles. All we need is some—"

"Bait!" Edgar said.

Patrick touched the tip of his nose and smiled. "You got it, Edgar."

Edgar turned his back to father and son and shuffled down the length of the wooden counter. Just near the wall's end a large rectangular cooler hummed and lay length-wise along the floor. It reminded Patrick of something you'd find in an old thrift shop, carrying an array of ice cream bars.

Grunting, the old man bent over and slid open the rectangle's glass door. He reached in and pulled out a large Styrofoam container shaped like a cylinder.

"Don't know why I don't store these things in something a bit higher up," Edgar said as he began making his way back down the length of the counter. "I swear every time I bend over to grab something from it I hear the creaks and cracks getting louder and louder. Soon I reckon I'll be able to play a darn good symphony just standin' still."

Edgar placed the container down onto the counter in front of Patrick, adjusted his cap, and pushed his glasses high up onto his nose. The screen door screeched and banged as someone else entered the shop. Edgar gave a quick look towards the entrance.

"Be right with you, sir," he said. He turned back to Patrick. "How do these work for you?"

"Are they night crawlers?"

"Yes, sir. Big suckers too. Fish won't be able to refuse."

Caleb tugged on his father's pant-leg.

Patrick looked down. "What's up, bud?"

Caleb hesitated.

"You wanna see them?" he asked.

Caleb shook his head. His brown eyes looked desperate and he was shuffling his feet as though standing on a hot plate.

"Ah ha," Patrick said. He looked up at Edgar. "Edgar, you wouldn't happen to have a restroom here would you?"

"Sure do." Edgar smiled in Caleb's direction. He turned around and snatched a key off the wall behind him. "Gotta go back out the way you came, then around the shop and to the left, past the porch swing." He handed the key to Patrick.

"Thanks. We'll be right back." He tapped the top of the bait container and smiled. "Keep 'em on ice for us."

"Sure thing," Edgar smiled. "I'm not going anywhere."

The screen door screeched and banged again as father and son left.

"And what can I do for you, kind sir?" Edgar asked his most recent customer.

The customer was a decent-sized man wearing a blue Penn State cap and a white sweatshirt with jeans. He didn't answer Edgar, merely reached out and took hold of the bait container on the counter.

Edgar stuttered. "Is...is it bait you're after, sir? I can get you some from the cooler if you like, but those belong—"

The man in the Penn State hat cut Edgar off by turning his back to him. When he turned back around a moment later, the man placed the bait container back on the counter, held his index finger up to pursed lips, and breathed a gentle shush.

Edgar did nothing in return. He stood rooted, unable to comprehend what was happening. Yet there was one thing he *was* sure about. Nearly three quarters of his eighty years in sales had given him a keen sense for reading people. And something about this man just plain wasn't right.

The screen door called out its familiar screech again as Patrick and Caleb reappeared. Patrick handed the key back to Edgar. The man in the Penn State cap took a few steps back and stood behind Patrick and Caleb.

"Thanks, Edgar," Patrick said. "How much do we owe you for the bait?"

Edgar took the key and looked behind father and son at the man in the Penn State cap. The man smirked at Edgar, put his index finger to his lips again, changed the shape of his hand into a gun, pointed it at Edgar, the back of Patrick's head, and then the back of Caleb's head, each point followed by an imaginary click from the hammer that was his thumb.

Edgar swallowed hard and went pale. His blood ran like ice water and he regretfully acknowledged his previous instincts about the stranger. Should he tell the father and son what was happening? Call the police? No. He was a good Christian. If this man did have a gun he could never live with himself if a father and child lost their lives because of some old fool like him. He wouldn't say a word. He would let the father and child leave peacefully and pray that the stranger didn't have plans for him once they'd gone.

"Edgar?" Patrick followed Edgar's eyes over his shoulder towards the man in the Penn State cap.

"How are ya?" the man asked Patrick.

Patrick nodded. "Good thanks." He looked up at the man's hat. "You a Penn State fan?"

The man nodded once. "Die hard."

"Good man," Patrick said with a quick smile. He thought of Arty for a fleeting moment then quickly shook the thought away. He turned back to Edgar. "So how much, Edgar?"

Edgar said nothing. He was still a pasty white, his magnified eyes skirting and unsteady.

"Edgar, you okay?"

Edgar nodded weakly. "Fine," he said, still avoiding eye contact with Patrick. "Something I ate earlier, I think." He risked a quick look behind Patrick again. The strange man was laughing silently at his feeble excuse.

"Oh, okay," Patrick said. "Maybe pop an Alka-Seltzer when we leave."

Edgar nodded fast. "Yeah, good idea."

Another moment of pause.

Patrick smiled. "So, are you going to tell me how much I owe you, Edgar?"

"On the house."

Patrick frowned. "No, no, come on, Edgar, how much?"

Edgar risked one last peek over Patrick's shoulder. The stranger shrugged back at Edgar, black eyes wide with amusement.

"Threevin," Edgar said fast.

"What?"

Edgar cleared his throat. "Three even."

Patrick raised an eyebrow, handed Edgar a five and said, "Keep the change."

Edgar grunted a thanks and watched Patrick and Caleb leave through the screen door with their container of bait. He waited until their car pulled away before looking at the man in the Penn State cap. He swallowed and steadied his voice. "I have very little cash in the store, mister. But you're welcome to all of it. Please…"

"Please what, Edgar?" the stranger said.

Edgar's next words were a frightened whisper. *"Please don't shoot me."*

The stranger burst out laughing and rapped his knuckles on the counter. "Come on, Edgar, man-up! Has time shriveled away *both* your balls?"

The stranger reached over the counter and gently pulled Edgar's cap of lures off his head. The thin hair beneath was gray and oily. Edgar didn't dare move.

The stranger turned and flung Edgar's hat to the floor. He then took his own hat off and scratched the shaved-bald head underneath.

"I was only having a bit of fun with you, Edgar. Just playing a little game. You like games, right?"

Edgar nodded, still rooted to the floor, still afraid to even breathe.

"How about Penn State? Are you a Penn State fan, Edgar?"

Edgar swallowed, his Adam's apple pronounced like a thick knuckle.

The stranger leaned in and placed his blue Penn State cap over Edgar's head. He left it there for a short moment, smiled, then yanked it down tight over the old man's head causing him to pitch forward, his glasses falling with a clatter onto the countertop.

"You are now, right?"

Edgar's voice was gone.

"*Right?*"

Edgar nodded quickly.

The stranger picked up Edgar's glasses and put them on. "Whoa! Coke bottles!

You're damn-near blind aren't you?" He reached behind his back and withdrew a pistol, held it up in front of Edgar.

Edgar did have poor vision, but his bad eyes knew a gun when they saw one. He thought of his wife, long since gone, and knew he would be seeing her soon.

The stranger pointed the gun at Edgar and aimed it just over his head, targeting a wooden bass mounted on the wall behind him. "Hold still now, Edgar; I'd hate to miss the little fishy and hit you instead."

Edgar managed a plea. "*Please…*"

"*Shhhhh…*I need to concentrate." He adjusted Edgar's glasses. "It's not easy in these ya know."

The stranger slowly lowered the gun off the wooden bass, pointed it directly at Edgar's face, smirked, and pulled the trigger. The gun clicked. The stranger frowned and pulled the trigger again. And then again. More empty clicks.

"Well I'll be a son of…I guess I forgot to load the fucker."

Edgar found his breath; it whooshed out of every pore in his body.

The stranger took the glasses off and placed them on the countertop. He touched the point of the gun gently to Edgar's nose. "I forgot to load it. That means you're either very lucky or I'm very stupid. Which one you think it is, Edgar?"

Edgar felt his bladder fail him. He hardly cared. "I'm very lucky," he said.

The stranger smiled. "Yeah, I'd say you are as well. After all, you've got a brand new Penn State hat now. This weekend is *all about* being a Penn State fan." The stranger dug the point of the revolver into Edgar's nostril. "I'm going to be coming back here in a couple of days, Edgar. I'll be back and I won't forget to load it next time. If you're not wearing your new Penn State hat when I return I'm going to fire a lot of bullets up this wrinkled nose of yours. Sound fair?"

Edgar nodded, the gun barrel digging deeper into his nostril with each nod.

"And you won't do anything silly like calling the police, will you? Because if you did that, well, jeez...I may just have to come back sooner than later."

Edgar shook his head.

"Promise?"

Edgar nodded.

The man pulled the gun away and smiled. "Great. This was fun wasn't it? It's fun to play games like this don't you think?"

Edgar looked down at his soiled trousers. The stranger's eyes followed Edgar's and spotted the stain.

"*Whoopsie,*" the stranger said. "I guess accidents like that happen when you get on in years, yeah? Something about the prostate not working the way it used to?" He took hold of Edgar's neck and pulled him close. "I could check it for you if you like." He brought the gun over the counter and tapped the barrel against Edgar's rear. "Might be a little cold going in, but I'm sure we could make it work. What do you say?"

Edgar swallowed dry and his throat seized up on him. He coughed.

The stranger let go of Edgar's neck. "I'm just kidding, Edgar. I was having some fun again." The stranger then gave a deep, wet snort, and hocked a thick wad of yellow on the counter. "You won't forget your promise now, will you, Edgar?"

"No, sir."

The stranger smiled and dropped his head. He began swirling the wad of phlegm on the countertop with two fingers, seemingly lost in the moment the way an infant might be distracted by a messy toy.

A brief silence passed. Edgar's pulse was in his ears. The stranger just kept his head down, still swirling two fingers in the slime, still in a daze. And then he looked up and casually wiped the phlegm on the front of Edgar's nose.

"Some people spit in their hands and shake on a promise," the stranger said. "I didn't feel like spitting in my hand. That okay?"

Edgar nodded, the yellow slime hanging from the tip of his nose.

"Good." He then gestured to Edgar's nose, the countertop of phlegm, the dark stain on Edgar's paints. "You might wanna get all that cleaned up before the next customer comes in, Edgar. It's gross."

The stranger left, and Edgar collapsed to the floor holding his chest. He wiped his nose then touched the brim of the Penn State cap. He would never take it off again.

15

Back in the Highlander Caleb said, "That old man was weird."

"You thought so, huh?"

"Yeah."

"I thought he seemed friendly at first," Patrick said. "But then he did get kinda weird, didn't he?"

Caleb nodded.

Patrick glanced over at the bait container on the passenger seat. He grabbed it and raised it into the air so his son could see. "You wanna open it up and take a look?"

Caleb quickly shook his head.

"No?" Patrick smiled.

Caleb shook his head again.

"No creepy, crawly critters for Caleb?"

The boy smiled, but the answer was still an emphatic no.

Patrick smirked and set the container back down. "Okay...but we're gonna have to look some time, brother-man."

16

Two wooden docks bordered Crescent Lake, each one extending close to twenty feet out over the water—more than enough distance to cast a decent line into the belly of the lake.

As the family settled in on the dock closest to their cabin, Amy was skeptical but amused by her husband's child-like determination for the afternoon's activity. His enthusiasm for family adventures that held low but harmless odds for success was one of his many charms she loved, finding it irresistibly adorable.

"Wait and see," Patrick told her, head down, fiddling with the crank on his fishing pole. "Just wait and see, my poor pessimistic wife."

Amy snorted. "I *will* see, my dear, dopey, delusional husband."

"Ah—three. Touché. However I got three in the car with Caleb on the way back from the bait shop. All with the letter C. So that's actually *four* if you count his name, which of course I used."

"Sorry, four-year-olds don't make credible witnesses for the absurd, asinine, alliteration affairs you make me take part in," she said.

He cast her a sideways glance, raised an eyebrow, looked at the sky for a rebuttal. His shoulders eventually slumped. "I've got nothing. Kudos, baby."

She took a bow and blew him a kiss.

"Dad?" Caleb said.

"What's up, brother?"

Caleb looked down at the pole in his hands, to the bait container on his left, and then finally up at his father.

"I'ma comin', pal." Patrick started towards Caleb to help him prepare his hook. He looked at Amy first, smirked and said, "Honey, can you hold my rod while I help Caleb?"

Amy tilted her head to one side, bit down on her lip, gave her husband a look that read: *Darling, that double entendre was so blatantly obvious that it would belittle us both if I even attempted to retort with some equally juvenile quip.*

She took his fishing rod from him all the same, but had released the bite on her lip, no longer capable of fighting off a devilish smirk of her own. Patrick's smirk remained, a naughty pumping of the eyebrows joining it, adding to their foreplay, the notion that such actions were limited to the bedroom a foreign concept to the couple.

"Carrie, sweetie, do you want to watch Caleb bait a hook?" Patrick asked his daughter, who was in the process of trying to hold Oscar in her arms for more than two seconds at a stretch before he wiggled out.

"No," she said bluntly as she scooped the dog up again, managing three seconds this time.

"*Women,*" Patrick said, winking at his son. Caleb winked back and smiled. "Alright, brother-man, dig me out a good one so we can bait that hook of yours, okay?"

Caleb walked over the wooden planks and picked up the Styrofoam container. His tiny fingers worked at the plastic lid, eventually peeling it off and dropping it to the ground. He looked at the dirt and the slimy critters therein, then back at his father with an uncertain face.

"They won't bite, pal, I promise. They're just a bit slimy."

Caleb looked back down at the container, closed his eyes, and dug his little digits in.

"That's my boy," Patrick beamed.

Caleb withdrew his fingers from the soil and immediately placed his catch into his father's hand. He would dig and he would grab, but he wasn't about to *hold* just yet.

Patrick laughed and looked down at the worm Caleb had given him. It was exceptionally thick and coated black with soil. He picked it up with his other hand, dusted off the dirt, and spotted a fingernail.

"*Jesus!*" Patrick flung the finger away.

Both Amy and Carrie turned.

"What?" Amy asked.

Patrick pointed at what he had just discarded. It was less than two feet from where Amy stood.

"Is that?" she asked, inching closer, slowly leaning her torso forward to get a better look. "Is that? It is! *It is!*"

"What? What is it?" Carrie asked.

Amy whirled around and blocked her daughter's view with her body. "Nothing," she said, shifting from left to right, stopping her daughter from slipping past. "It's nothing."

Oscar, unfortunately, did not see the discarded finger as nothing. He saw it as an appetizer. With one swift motion he trotted towards it, sniffed once, and then gulped it down.

"*Oscar!*" Amy cried. "*Oscar, no!*"

The dog turned and looked up at Amy with an innocent expression on his face that in dog language would have surely translated to: *It was edible, lady. I'm a dog. What's the problem?*

"Did he eat it?" Patrick asked.

Amy nodded appallingly, one hand over her mouth.

"Eat what?" Carrie asked, now breaking her mother's defense and approaching the dog. "Tell me."

Both Patrick and Amy ignored their daughter. Patrick walked over to his wife and placed his lips to her ear. "Please tell me I'm not crazy," he whispered. "Please tell me that our son didn't just scoop a finger out of that bait container. And *please* tell me that mangy little thing didn't just gobble it up."

"You're not crazy," Amy whispered back. "That was a *fucking finger.*"

Patrick ran a hand through his hair and breathed in. "Okay then—let's go to obvious question number two, shall we? *Why* was there a finger in our bait container?"

"I don't know, sweetheart," Amy replied, her tone exceptionally condescending. "Did the man at the bait shop have all ten of his fingers?"

"Yes, darling," Patrick replied, matching her tone, "I believe he did."

"Well then Jesus, Patrick, you tell me. Was it that stupid lady who tried to sue Wendy's by putting a severed finger in her chili? You didn't happen to notice *her* at the bait shop did you?"

Patrick burst out laughing.

"Are you actually *laughing*? How the *hell* can this be funny to you?" She splayed her hands, let them slap back down onto her thighs. "I mean for Christ's sake, what more can possibly go wrong this weekend?"

"Whoa, wait a minute," he said, patting the air before putting a finger to his lips. Her outburst was creeping out of PG territory and about to introduce the kids to PG-13 or possibly R. "Let's not make too big a deal out of this."

"*No?* Our four-year-old son finding a human finger in your container of worms is an everyday thing?" She was losing the fight at keeping her voice a whisper.

Patrick's smile from his recent burst of laughter was gone. He now wore a look of concern; he knew that when his wife got started, their kids' eager ears and a bus full of nuns armed with rulers would not stop one of her profane tirades.

"Okay, you're right, I'm sorry." He put a hand on her shoulder and she instantly shrugged it off. He sighed. "Alright, I'll go back to the bait shop right now and talk to the owner," he said.

"Don't even bother," she said. "The thing is in the belly of that stupid dog right now anyway. We would have no proof."

"Well *someone* lost a finger. Maybe it's someone else who works at the bait shop."

"It wasn't a stupid employee at the bait shop, Patrick. Someone put that finger in our bait container deliberately."

"*What?* Why would someone do that?"

"Why? I don't know why. Why would a strange man buy us a tank of gas for no reason and then trade candy to a little girl for a stupid doll? Why would a pervert stalk me in a supermarket then look in on us while we had sex?"

The whispering was gone, so was the presence of mind to spell out sex (even though he was fairly sure Carrie knew how to spell it). "I thought we decided—"

"Shut up. Maybe I saw him, and maybe I didn't. But I *did* just see that finger, and so did you."

"So let me get this straight." Patrick was still insistent on whispering. "You're suggesting that one of the two weirdoes we ran into this weekend put that severed finger in our bait container? *How* and *when* would they have done that?" Patrick asked.

"I don't know but they *did*." She turned to Carrie and Caleb.

"Kids, let's go. Fishing's over."

17

"I think this one might be my favorite," Arty said, getting up from his chair and pushing a tape into the VCR. The image on the TV screen went from black to fuzzy to a woman tied to a chair, facing front. Her surroundings were a small white room as bare as a padded cell. In the far left corner, a solitary lamp sat on the floor providing the only source of light save for the modest one pointing directly at her from atop the video camera recording the incident.

"Is this the snake one?" Jim asked.

Arty nodded without taking his eyes off the screen.

"That fucker was heavy," Jim added.

The girl on camera wept softly through her gag. The sound of a door opened off camera. A few labored grunts. The girl's eyes grew impossibly wide as she screeched through her gag like a wild bird. A circle of urine grew on the front of her blue jeans.

Jim appeared on camera now, straining and breathing heavily, his perverse grin never fading despite the weight of the enormous python he carried. A few more grunts and the python was eventually draped over the girl's shoulder and neck, pitching her head forward.

Arty and Jim watched the film with a delight few knew. At times they became hysterical with laughter; other times they fell mute and gaped wide-eyed with a paradoxical awe at the pleasure and torment they had created.

When the girl on screen had finally passed out, and when Jim brought her back around by squirting an old-fashioned seltzer bottle into her face in true *Three Stooges* fashion, the two brothers nearly fell out of their chairs.

"I'd forgotten all about that!" Arty cried.

Jim jumped out of his chair, turned to his brother, and wiped alternating hands down his shaved head while spewing "nyuck" after "nyuck" from the side of his mouth—a spot-on impersonation of the late Jerome 'Curly' Howard that would have been worthy of a standing ovation amongst devoted fans world-wide, all things considered.

Arty had full-fledged tears dripping from his eyes. He wiped them away, straightened his posture, and donned a playful frown. *"Spread out, you knucklehead,"* he said in his best Moe voice.

Jim dropped to the floor, rolled on his side, and began using his legs to spin himself around and around like hands on a clock: a classic Curly Shuffle, complete with *"Woo!"* after *"Woo!"* after *"Woo!"*

Arty wiped away the last of his tears, bent forward and grabbed a second video from the base of the TV. He tossed the cassette to his brother.

"Which one's this?" Jim asked, catching the tape before getting to his feet.

Arty hit eject, pulled the snake tape out and set it aside. "That's the one with the yuppie at the bar who wouldn't shut up about his golf game. The one with the nail gun and the...ahem...new *handicap* we gave him."

Jim smirked before turning his nose up and speaking in a haughty manner. "I'm sorry, Arthur, but that was an absolutely *atrocious* pun. However, that particular gem of a video is easily in my top three, so I'm willing to let it pass."

"Thank you, James," Arty replied, his tone equally pretentious. "Now toss it back so I can pop it in. In fact, if the mood should strike you, I've even got a few more treasures we can peruse after this to *truly* set a fitting tone for the evening's festivities that await us."

"Bravo, Arthur. Bravo."

18

"We're still going to dinner I hope?" Patrick asked Amy.

"I don't know."

"Are you still freaked out about the finger?"

Amy, who was rifling through random drawers in their bedroom as a means to pacify her mind rather than actually pack, replied, "You're not?"

Patrick chuckled. "Not in the slightest. In fact, the more I think about it, the more I question whether the damn thing was real."

Amy turned and left a drawer hanging open. "Huh?"

"Well, we didn't exactly take it to a lab and get it analyzed, honey. The damn thing was probably a rubber prop or something. Some kid at the bait shop probably slipped it in there as a joke."

Amy shut the drawer. "It looked real to me."

Patrick raised an eyebrow. "Oh, I see—and you've seen *how many* severed fingers in your lifetime?"

She folded her arms across her chest and squeezed as if trying to hold onto her convictions. "If it was rubber and not...*meat*, then why did Oscar eat it?"

"Because he's a *dog*. When I was growing up our dog used to go into the cat's litter box and eat its *shit* for Christ's sake. Dogs are loyal and obedient but not too terribly bright, especially when it comes to choosing their cuisine."

Amy looked off past her husband. There was a decent pause before she blinked. "So you think it was a rubber finger then? A stupid prank from a kid?"

To lie or not to lie, Patrick thought. Amy had a good point about the dog eating meat. Dogs will eat anything, but rubber would have likely been chewed up and spat out. Maybe. Still, the rubber finger theory had come to him in a flash, and if he could, he would have literally patted his own back for thinking so quick on his feet. So for the time being, he would nurture that spontaneous gem he'd concocted, convince his wife it was a rubber finger. A harmless prank.

As for him? Just ask the hairs on the back of his neck—the ones he was constantly patting down and giving zero chance to rise up and speak freely. Those hairs felt the finger was real. Very real and very fucking mysterious. *Because if you suspect the damn thing was real, Patrick (and deep down you do), then we must now address the next two obvious questions, regardless of how hard you're trying to shove them into the back of your mind:*

Whose finger was it, and how the HELL did it get inside your bait container? It's not like the Styrofoam had been packed on an assembly line, where quality control might miss a small rodent, some broken glass, the odd finger...

Did Edgar do it? He would have certainly had enough time to plant the thing when you took Caleb to the bathroom. But hold on, dummy—he had all the time in the world to plant it before you even GOT to the store. So that makes no sense.

The guy with the Penn State hat? How fucking ironic would THAT be? No. Edgar was there the whole time. I think he would have spoken up if someone put a goddamn finger in our bait container while we were in the bathroom.

But wait...Edgar WAS acting strange when we returned.

No. Stop it, dummy. This is absurd. You don't have any answers and your paranoia is getting the best of you. Certainly understandable given recent events, yes? Yes. You're being paranoid.

But there is one thing you do know, isn't there? You WILL keep sticking with the rubber finger theory, won't you? You'll stick to it and make it damn good for Amy's sake. Solve the mystery on your own time if you want, but for right now, ignorance will be today's special. In fact, why not take a big serving of what you've been feeding Amy? All this crazy shit so far…it has to be nothing but good old-fashioned bad luck, right? HAS to be. Things like this just don't happen on purpose. No way. So swallow it down and try not to choke, Sherlock.

"I'm certain it was, baby," he said. He patted the back of his neck, walked towards Amy, kissed her lightly on the lips. "We have a wonderful night ahead of us. Let's not let a silly thing like this ruin it."

She hugged him tight. "It was a sick joke?"

He squeezed her back and replied, "It was."

"Whoever did it should be beaten."

"They should."

"We won't let it ruin our night."

"We won't."

"I feel better," she said.

"I'm glad."

She lifted her head off his chest, looked up and kissed him. "I love you."

"You should."

Amy was wearing a white, form-fitting dress that flaunted every curve of her impressive figure. Her long dark hair was still damp from her recent shower and gave off the combined scent of flowers and fruit.

She leaned forward at the waist, her stomach flat against the edge of the sink, applying makeup with a critical eye in the bathroom mirror.

Patrick walked by the bathroom in dark slacks and a white button-down that was neither tucked nor buttoned just yet. He paused when he got a good look at his wife.

"Sweet mother of…" he drooled. He entered the bathroom, stood behind his wife, and wrapped his arms around her waist.

Amy put her eyeliner down and smiled at her husband's reflection. "You like?" she asked.

"Me *love*."

"I'm gonna blow my hair out the way you like," she smiled.

"Mmmmmm…" Patrick leaned in and kissed her neck. "Perhaps we should skip dinner altogether."

"What, you didn't get enough last night?"

"I will *never* get enough of you." He dropped down and sunk his teeth into her butt.

She let out a yelp, giggled, turned and punched him in the chest. "Get out of here, I need to get ready."

As Patrick turned to leave, Carrie and Caleb appeared at the bathroom door. Caleb was holding two flat rocks. He went to hand them to his father but Carrie pushed him aside.

"I can't find Oscar," she said.

"Carrie, please don't push your brother like that," Patrick said.

Caleb attempted a return shove but Carrie shrugged him off as though he wasn't there. Her eyes stayed fixed on her father. "He's been gone since we went fishing. I keep calling for him…"

Probably off somewhere, barfing up the finger he ate this afternoon, Patrick thought.

Amy, who had gone back to attending to her face in the mirror said, "He'll come back when he's hungry, honey. You and your brother need to get ready to go to the Mitchell's."

Carrie looked down at her attire—a faded Hannah Montana T-shirt and a pair of dirty jeans—then back up at her mother with an odd look. "I *am* ready."

Amy kept one eye on the mirror while the other stole a quick glance at her daughter. "Wouldn't you rather wear something nicer for the Mitchells?"

Carrie looked at her clothes again. "No."

Patrick stepped out of the bathroom (giving his wife a subtle pat on the bottom as he passed), and approached his son. "Whatcha got there, bud? More rocks for skipping?"

Caleb nodded eagerly and handed them to his father.

"Whoa, take a look at *these* beauties."

Caleb beamed.

"Come on," Patrick said. "Let's go out to the lake and skip them before your mom and I take you over to the Mitchell's."

Father and son raced outside. Amy put the eyeliner down and tilted her torso out the bathroom door. "*Don't get dirty!*"

19

The silver Highlander glided along the main road, north of Crescent Lake. As promised, Amy had blown her hair out in the style Patrick liked so much, and he found it damn difficult to concentrate on the wheel.

"Edible, baby," he said, stealing his umpteenth glance. "You are looking absolutely *edible*."

She leaned over and kissed his cheek while he looked out onto the road. "You're not lookin' too bad yourself there, sexy." She ran her fingers down the buttons of his collared shirt.

Patrick's white button-down was covered with a jet-black sport coat that accentuated his broad shoulders. His top two buttons were undone (a tie was simply out of the question for Patrick Lambert), and his slacks and polished shoes were the exact color of his sport coat. Even his hair, which usually had the uncanny ability to face all four directions of the globe, was gelled and parted in a neat, trendy fashion, making him look the equal of his wife's thirty-three years instead of his own thirty-eight.

"I'm thinking we might stand out once we get to the restaurant, we look so good," Amy added.

"We'd stand out *anywhere* we went, hotness," he said. "However, both Norm and Lorraine insisted this place was pretty snazzy.

Of course that won't change anything. We'll still be the sexiest couple there."

She smirked, kissed his cheek again, then sat back in her seat. "How far?"

"Twenty minutes, give or take. It shouldn't be too bad. It's more than likely we'll be back before the kids are," he said.

Amy instantly leaned back over and squeezed her husband's shoulder, excited. "Ooh, then you know what we should do? We should take a moon-lit stroll around the lake as soon as we get back."

"In these clothes? They'd get filthy," he said.

"Since when do you care about something like that?"

"Thought I'd try and earn some points."

"Nice try. We can stop by the cabin first and change."

Patrick put a hand over his mouth and gasped. "You mean...get *naked*?"

Amy shook her head. "My poor horny husband—so desperately guided by his rampant hormones."

"I know all about hormones, you know," he said.

"Stop."

"I even know how they're made."

"*Stop.*"

"Do you know how to make a hormone, honey?"

She took her hand off his shoulder and sat back in her seat. "You've told me this one a million times."

"*You refuse to pay her.*" Patrick grinned at his wife like a schoolboy, always pleased with himself after delivering one of the classics.

Amy turned away, but smirked out her passenger window. She loved every inch of him.

20

Carrie wanted chicken fingers. Caleb wanted a cheeseburger. Lorraine and Norman would eat anything put in front of them if it meant appeasing the Babysitting Gods and keeping the children happy. So the primary goal was as straightforward as straightforward gets: locate a restaurant that serves both chicken fingers and cheeseburgers.

"I think Charlie's will have chicken fingers and burgers," Norman said.

Lorraine nodded. "I'd bet on it."

Norman clapped his hands together. "Alright then. Charlie's it is."

"Who's Charlie?" Caleb asked.

Carrie turned to her brother. "He's the one who makes our food, stupid."

"Hey, hey—no name-calling when you're with us," Norman said. "Charlie is the *owner*. The restaurant is named after him."

"So then who's going to cook our food?" Carrie asked.

"I'm not sure," Norman said.

"So it *could* be Charlie," Carrie said.

"I doubt that, sweetheart. I'm sure Charlie hires people to cook *for* him."

"But it *could* be."

Norman chuckled and waved the white flag. "Yes, I suppose it's possible."

Lorraine sipped the remainder of her tea then placed the empty cup on the coffee table. "Are you two excited for the movie?"

Only Caleb nodded. Carrie decided it wiser to test the pocketbooks of their temporary guardians first. "Can we get popcorn?"

"Of course," Norman said. "Can't have a movie without popcorn."

Carrie smiled, tested a bit more. "Can we get candy too?"

"No candy," Lorraine said, settling back into the sofa. "It's bad for your teeth."

"That's what Mom always says."

"Well Mom is right. Popcorn will be enough."

"Popcorn and *soda*," Carrie said firmly. "My mouth will get dry."

Lorraine glanced at her husband. He winked at her.

"We'll see," Norman said. "No promises."

Carrie seemed to find this response acceptable, wandering out of the Mitchell's den and into their kitchen. Caleb headed over to the sofa and jumped onto Lorraine's lap. She let out an unavoidable "*OOF!*" as soon as the four-year-old landed.

Caleb appeared to find her slapstick response quite amusing and immediately began flight-preparations for a second launch. Lorraine quickly latched both hands onto his little shoulders, smiled and said, "No, no, sweetie—you're going to make Mrs. Mitchell pee her pants if you do that again."

21

The same pair of binoculars that had watched the silver Toyota Highlander back out of cabin number eight before exiting Crescent Lake was now watching a light blue Volvo station wagon back out of cabin number ten. Two adults and two children could be identified inside the Volvo.

"The Volvo folks are the neighbors," Jim said as he handed the binoculars to Arty. "I'm assuming the kids in back…?"

Arty took the binoculars and peered through them. Dusk had arrived, but the binoculars were top of the line. "Yup—that's them." He motioned for them to move, but stopped suddenly. He turned to his brother, a devilish grin curling upwards onto his face. "Should we say something?" he said. "Should we say something cool, like the guys in those espionage movies do?"

Jim grinned back. "You mean like, '*the hatchlings have left the nest.*'"

Arty threw his head back and barked out a single laugh. He then straightened his posture, and, in a similarly deep and serious voice, "*The bacon is in the pan.*"

Jim shoved Arty back a step while barking his own laugh. Arty rolled with the shove, invigorated by his brother's physical exuberance. Arty's demonstrative love for the game had always been kept on a more composed leash in contrast to Jim's, who often slipped his leash entirely, Arty the one to catch him before Jim was lost for good—more so lately due to the state of their mother.

But not tonight. Tonight, Jim's contagion fueled Arty. Discretion was still paramount of course, always would be; it was what separated them from the rest of the sheep. But tonight Arty and Jim celebrated this stage of foreplay as one, not as individuals. They laughed and shoved one another with equal vigor on that wooded hill above Crescent Lake. Roughhoused and joked like drunken teens on prom night, their dates waiting in the cabins below, virginities ripe for the taking. All they had to do was go down and take it.

"Come on, my brother…" Arty eventually said, placing one hand on Jim's shoulder, the other fanning across the darkening landscape. "Let's go have some fun."

22

The restaurant known as The Walnut Creek Grille had been recommended highly by both Lorraine and Norman, who claimed it was easily the nicest and most romantic place in the area. Amy had embraced their friends' recommendation without pause, but now grew skeptical as Patrick pulled the Highlander into the strip mall just off Walnut Creek Road.

"This can't be it," she said, ducking down, looking hard through the windshield.

Patrick drove slowly through the crowded lot. "This is where Norm said it was."

"We're in a strip mall," she said.

"You knew that."

"Yeah, but I didn't think it was *part* of the strip mall. I thought it was detached— like next to it or something."

Patrick continued cruising the length of shops. The strip was long and common: a pharmacy; a book store; a pizza place; a barber shop; a video store. So far no Walnut Creek Grille.

"What does it matter?" he asked.

"Well, I didn't get this dressed up so we could eat at Dairy Queen."

"Come on, honey," Patrick said, eyes still fixed on each passing shop as he spoke. "Norm and Lorraine wouldn't have recommended it if it wasn't any good."

Amy shrugged. "I guess."

The rows of shops began bending towards the right. They appeared close to the end.

"Maybe this *isn't* the right place," Patrick admitted. "I didn't see it anywhere, did you?"

Amy said, "Huh, uh."

Patrick hung a right and rounded the strip mall's corner. Both he and Amy shouted: "*There!*"

The Walnut Creek Grille was the very last shop, a useful detail Patrick felt Norm could have mentioned earlier.

"Jinx," Patrick said after their simultaneous blurt. "You can't talk until you buy me a martini."

"Gay."

"Hmmm...already breaking the rules *and* bigoted?"

"I have a gay brother. I can say what I want with immunity."

"I'm gonna call Eric and ask."

"Go ahead. He'll call you gay himself."

Patrick grumbled.

An empty parking spot was right in front of the restaurant.

"Ooh, look at this," Amy said, pointing. "Rock star."

"They obviously knew we were coming."

Patrick parked the Highlander and the couple got out. Their spot was practically on top of the entrance.

"You sure this isn't a handicap spot?" Patrick asked, checking the ground beneath the SUV, searching for even the tiniest hint of blue paint.

Amy took hold of his arm with both hands and pulled him towards the entrance. "We're fine, come on."

Patrick's first words when they entered the restaurant were, "Whoa." He looked at Amy. She looked back, a delighted smile on her face. "Deceptive isn't it?" he said.

The exterior of the restaurant was modest. The interior was extravagant, but hardly overt in its accomplishment. It was subtle with its décor and ambience, choosing to embrace the patrons with a sense of warmth and comfort as opposed to flaunting its stature by making them feel privileged to bathe in its presence.

The restaurant was small and concise. To the right was a bar whose back mirror was lit with a dim, pleasant glow that illuminated rows of top-shelf liquor and cast a faint shine down onto a smooth marble top.

To the left was the dining area. The surrounding walls held appreciable art and small lamps shaped as ornate candles, lighting the room with a soft touch as if they were the real thing. Waiters and waitresses dressed in posh garb weaved deftly between tables covered in fine cloth and silverware, pouring wine and delivering silver trays of cuisine.

Directly ahead an attractive male and female host stood behind a wooden podium. Both smiled genuinely as Amy and Patrick approached.

"Hi," Patrick said. "Lambert? Party of two?"

The female glanced down at the appointment book, smiled again and said, "Follow me."

Their salads had come and gone—Patrick's a Caesar, Amy's a garden with fat-free Italian.

"This place is so nice," Amy said. She sipped her glass of Pinot and sighed a deep, contented sigh.

Patrick smiled with his eyes. "Feeling better?" he asked.

"Much," she replied. "I had no idea it would be this nice."

Patrick sipped his martini. "No, I mean do you feel better about…everything."

Amy took another sip of wine. "I don't think I'll ever feel better about that."

"But you're feeling a *little* better, right? A bit more at ease?"

Amy set her glass down and stared at it for a few seconds before replying. "I don't think I'm ever going to feel a hundred percent about all that's happened. On a scale of one to ten, I'd say this sojourn has been a two thus far—this restaurant being the only thing keeping me from rating it a one."

Patrick nodded slowly and now it was his turn to look at his drink. He played with the toothpick, spearing his olive multiple times, searching for levity. "Yeah. Still, it'll make a pretty outlandish story to tell when we get home, won't it?"

"Maybe in time we can find the humor in it, but at the moment I'm afraid I just don't see it," she said.

Patrick quickly shook his head. "No, I'm not saying it's *funny*, I'm just saying...it's *over* now, so..."

Amy raised an eyebrow. "*So?*"

Patrick stopped torturing his olive, plucked it and ate it. "Forget it," he said, chewing. "I don't know what I'm trying to say."

And he didn't. He wasn't even sure he should have brought the whole thing up— the last thing he wanted to do was ruin their evening. It just seemed appropriate to mention for some reason, the way somebody asks for an update involving a terminally ill loved one. You know the news will be bad, but if it's discussed more than ignored, perhaps it may ultimately lose a bit of its impact, become a therapeutic way of coping.

"It doesn't bother you at all does it?" she asked.

Patrick first thought about Arty and the gas and Carrie's doll. It was indeed bothersome, but confusing took more of a lead between the two. In fact, the more he thought about it now, the more he decided that *bizarre* had won the race. Bothersome and confusing had finished and earned their respected spot, but bizarre was indeed the clear winner.

The man who had crudely propositioned Amy in the supermarket before leaving the rice on the car was different. That was truly upsetting, but it was something that could have just as easily happened back home. As for that same man looking into their window while they made love? Yes. Of course that had initially angered him. Angered the hell out of him. He still wasn't sure if Amy's eyes had betrayed her or not, but the mere possibility that she'd truly seen what she claimed boiled his blood.

And finally there was the finger in the bait. That bothered him. It did. But the whole incident seemed so random, so unrelated to all the bizarre goings-on that had already transpired. Logic simply had no say on that one. So what choice was there but to ultimately laugh at the absurdity of it all?

"You don't think it bothers me?" he said.

Amy shrugged. "It doesn't seem to. At least not a whole lot."

"I think it's too surreal," he said. "Everything that's happened…it's just so absurd. I don't know. Maybe I'm just not digesting it all yet. Call it a defense mechanism. Call me a stubborn dummy."

Amy took another sip of her wine. She smiled at Patrick, weak and small, but there. "I know you want everything to be okay, baby," she said. "You're like Chevy Chase from the *Vacation* movies in your quest to showing your family a good time—nothing's more important to you."

Patrick smirked at her wit.

"And I'm willing to write off the whole weird experience with that Arty guy. But the other guy I just can't let go of," she said. "Even if I didn't see him in our window; even if my eyes were playing tricks on me, the whole incident at the supermarket and in the parking lot with the rice is enough to stay with me for a bit."

Will she mention the finger? Patrick wondered.

"And let's not forget about the finger," she said.

Patrick sipped his martini, kept his eyes down and chose silence. Amy reached across the table and took hold of his free hand. "Don't get me wrong—I'm enjoying myself tonight, I really am. But I wonder if we should even *be* here."

"Out to dinner?"

"Crescent Lake."

Patrick asked something he already knew. "Do you want to leave?"

She looked at her wine again. There was a small sip left that she swirled in her glass with two fingers on the base of the stem. "No," she said. "I don't. But don't expect me to suddenly forget everything that's happened. That finger *could* have been made of rubber, been a prank from a kid. And I *could* have been seeing things when I looked out the window and saw the supermarket guy last night. But it still doesn't put my mind at ease, Patrick. You can't expect otherwise."

"I don't. You know I don't. And if I was in your shoes I'd feel exactly the same way." He picked up her hand and kissed it.

She smiled, a stronger one this time, then gulped the remainder of her wine. "I think I need another."

"Then another you shall have."

Another good smile. "Why did we even start talking about all this crap again?"

Patrick shrugged. "Beats me. Small talk until the main course arrives?"

She pursed her lips. "Oh right—that conversation definitely qualified as small talk."

Patrick laughed and kissed her hand again. The waiter came by and cleared their salad plates and Patrick used the opportunity to drain the rest of his drink as well.

"Would you folks care for another round?" the waiter asked.

"Yes please," Patrick said.

When the waiter brought their next round, Amy said, "So is the plan to keep drinking until we forget about everything?"

Patrick raised his glass. "Works for me."

23

Arty and Jim squatted in the backyard of the cabin they'd selected, their bodies cloaked by the surrounding black the woods provided. The cabin was close to the Lambert's, making it an ideal transitional spot for them to prepare.

"Could be on a timer," Jim whispered, motioning to the lit windows of the transition cabin.

"Doubt it," Arty said.

They shuffled side by side, to the left of the cabin. There was a car in the driveway. Arty pointed to it. "Somebody's home."

24

On the ride home, Patrick said, "Such a great meal. Lorraine and Norm have discovered a little gem in that spot."

Amy leaned back against the headrest and sighed. "It was good wasn't it?"

"Very. Duck was amazing."

"Better than Nicola's back home?"

"Pretty damn close."

Amy curled to one side, closed her eyes but asked, "So what now?"

"What do you mean?"

"I mean do you want to head back or do you want to go somewhere for a drink?"

"I thought you might ask that." Patrick released the sneaky smile he'd been fighting since leaving the restaurant. "Your wonderfully thoughtful husband happens to have a bottle of Cristal chilling comfortably at the cabin as we speak."

Amy opened her eyes. "What?"

"Oh yes. Your man can be quite the devious fellow."

Amy leaned to her left and planted a big one on the side of Patrick's mouth. "I *love* Cristal," she said.

"I know you do."

"What about our little moon-lit stroll around the lake?" she asked.

"We can do that after."

"After what?"

"After the champagne and..."

Amy looked at her husband with an accusatory, albeit playful eye. "The champagne *and*...?"

"Well, honey, if the champagne happens to put you in a certain mood, then I can't be held responsible for that, can I?"

Amy laughed. "You are absolutely shameless."

Patrick shrugged. "Cozy cabin in the woods? Cristal waiting for us? Kids occupied with good friends? Call me the world's biggest perv if you must, but I'm just lookin' to engage in some hardcore lovin' with my sexy wife as often as humanly possible."

"Big perv..." And then, leaning to her left once more, she pressed her lips to his ear, kissed and licked the lobe. Whispered, *"But you're forgiven."*

Patrick stomped the accelerator.

25

Lois Blocker had just finished packing away the kitchen. Her husband Maury was making the rounds throughout the cabin's interior to ensure nothing would be left behind when they left for the winter. Unlike many other residents who were often gone after Labor Day, the couple enjoyed the bracing months of October and November at Crescent Lake. This year, however, the Blockers were leaving early. And for good reason: their children had surprised them with a trip to the Virgin Islands. Just the two of them. Late autumn at the lake was indeed an enjoyable tradition, but sipping margaritas on a sandy white beach in St. Croix sounded pretty darn good too.

"You sure you want to leave tonight?" Lois asked when Maury joined her in the kitchen.

Maury pushed his rimless glasses further up onto his nose and brushed a hand through his thinning gray hair. "Are you forgetting the sandy paradise that awaits us?"

"I mean *tonight*—this late."

"I've already switched the heat and water off, sweetheart. Might as well just get going."

"But it's dark now. I don't like you driving at night."

He stood behind her at the sink and wrapped his arms around her waist. "Would *you* rather drive?" he smiled, reaching around and tapping her glasses, far thicker than his.

She turned and faced him. "Wise guy. I'd rather *neither* of us drove."

He brushed a strand of salt and pepper hair out her face. "I want to get home; I'd like to get settled in and unpacked before we start having to *re*-pack for St. Croix."

She patted him on the butt. "You know darn well that we'll both be in bed as soon as we get home. There's nothing that can't wait until morning."

"But if we leave in the morning we won't be home until noon."

"Oh and I suppose that means our whole day will be shot?" She kissed him. "Come on, honey, you can leave the water off; just switch the heat back on and we can have a good night's sleep, start bright and early tomorrow."

He groaned.

She kissed him again. "Perhaps I'll make tonight worth your while."

He pulled his head away and feigned shock. "Lois Blocker! Act your age."

She giggled. "This is the new millennium, dear husband. Sixty-five is the new forty, you know."

He smiled. "I am indeed a lucky man."

"I'll tell you what; you go switch the heat back on. I'll be in the bedroom to see if I can't…set the mood." She winked.

"Believe me, you've already set it."

She patted his butt again. "Go on. I'll be waiting."

"Did I say I wanted to leave *tonight*? I don't know what I could have been thinking."

Lois had initially intended on attacking her husband the second he walked through their bedroom door. She was wearing the silk nightgown she knew he loved so much and had been giddy with anticipation. But he was taking longer than expected. She now sat on the corner of the bed, her legs crossed, palm bracing her chin. She looked at the clock on the nightstand. He'd been gone twenty minutes. Switching the heat back on should have taken no more than five, ten tops.

"Maury?"

No answer.

She stood, walked to the door, called his name again.

Nothing.

Had he taken a spill in the cellar? She was worried now. She pinched the lapels of her gown together and went to the closet to get her slippers. When she turned around Maury was at the door.

"There you are. I was getting worried."

Maury was pale.

"Maury?"

Maury flew forward into the room, falling to his knees. Lois cried out. A man with a shaved head appeared in the doorway. He was holding a gun.

"Hi," the man said.

26

The clink of the champagne glasses was an hour ago. A near-empty bottle of Cristal sat in a small puddle of its own condensation on the kitchen counter. Patrick and Amy were taking their time getting dressed in the bedroom. Actually, Patrick was; Amy was keen on dressing and going for that moon-lit walk.

"I'm gonna put on some sweats," Amy said. She went to roll out of bed and Patrick hooked her at the waist and pulled her back.

"Not yet," he said, his lips going up and down her bare back and shoulders. "Just a little longer."

Amy wiggled free and hopped out of bed, her naked body casting a dim, but enticing profile in the moonlight.

"Jesus, baby," Patrick said, "if you want to get out this bedroom, I suggest you dress quickly."

She laughed and hiked up a pair of blue sweatpants followed by a gray sweatshirt. "Think I'll be warm enough in this?"

"If you wear a jacket."

"Duh."

He threw a pillow at her. She caught it and dropped it to the floor. "Now you're pillow-less. Get up."

He slapped his hands over his face and moaned.

"God you're worse than Carrie on a school day. My sneakers are in the kitchen. I'll be right back. *Get up.*"

Patrick groaned and got to his feet. He scanned the perimeter of the bedroom for discarded clothing that would suffice for a second round; the idea of rifling through drawers for new attire with champagne and recent sex still sapping brain cells was far too daunting.

"What should I wear?" he yelled into the kitchen. "Should I just throw on what I wore at the Mitchell's last night?"

"No."

"It was just jeans and a button-down."

"No."

He sighed and slumped down onto the corner of the bed. "Is the path around the lake muddy?"

"Huh?"

"*Muddy.* Are we gonna get dirty or something?"

"Patrick, just find something else to wear please."

He rolled his eyes at no one, stood again, trudged towards the dresser. He tugged the middle drawer open. "Dog shit?" he called.

"*What?*"

"Think there'll be dog shit?"

Amy re-appeared in the bedroom an inch taller, her sneakers snug to her feet. "How the hell should I know?"

"Well I'm sure Oscar isn't the only dog around here," he said.

"Well let's just hope the people around here have enough decency to clean up after their pets. Besides, if you just look where you're stepping you'll be fine."

"It's dark out," he said as he pulled on his own pair of sweats.

"The lake will have decent lighting from the surrounding cabins. I'm sure you'll be able to detect the odd pile of poo if we happen to stumble across it."

Patrick yanked down a blue sweatshirt, then ran a hand back and forth through his hair—a futile attempt at keeping his cowlicks from behaving after the earlier assault with hair gel. "Yeah, well, if I *do* step in some I'm gonna scoop it up with a stick and chase you around the lake with it."

"Grade school reminiscing are we?" Amy pulled her hair into a ponytail and fastened a band around it. "What am I thinking? You need to graduate before you can reminisce."

Patrick started putting on his sneakers. "And yet you married me."

"I lost a bet."

Patrick finished tying his shoes and stood. "I wonder where our dumb dog is anyway. Carrie said she couldn't find him earlier. I haven't seen him either. Have you?"

Amy was frowning.

Patrick said, "What?"

"*Our* dog?"

"He's been great with Carrie. She loves him to bits."

Amy's frown was going nowhere. "There is no way on earth that dog is coming home with us. You know that right? Please tell me you know that."

Patrick looked away and nodded.

"*Patrick?*"

"Alright, alright. I guess I'm just thinking about what to say when Carrie inevitably asks."

"How about 'no'?"

"Okay fine, but you're the one who's telling her."

"Okay I will. But you know she'll run right to you afterwards and try again. So prepare yourself, buddy boy." She ended her spiel with a *good-luck-with-that* slap to his chest.

"Ouch—stop abusing your husband. He's very delicate."

"Well bring your delicate butt along—I want to get a romantic stroll in before the kids come back."

"Patience, my darling. You can't rush romance."

"You can when you've got a four- and six-year-old headed back from the movies with sugar in their blood and cartoon animals bouncing around in their heads."

"Good point. Let's go."

27

Maury and Lois Blocker lay next to one another in bed. Lois wept silently. Maury's pale complexion was now a sickly white. The couple was too scared to even hold on to one another.

"You need to get off the fence here, bro," Jim said to Arty. "We're wasting time."

Arty stood at the foot of the bed. He held an aluminum baseball bat along the length of his leg. Jim was to the right of the bed, a pistol pointed at the couple.

"I'm still thinking," Arty said.

"What's to think about?"

"Leaving too big a mess is what. You feel like cleaning up?"

"No, but our choices were pretty fucking limited from the start. Either someone was home or they weren't."

Maury Blocker cleared his throat. "Please," he said. "If it's money—"

"Shut up," Arty said. He spoke to the couple as if they repulsed him. "This has nothing to do with you."

"Tick tock, bro," Jim said.

Arty nodded. "I'm just thinking about efficiency. The less mess, the sooner we can get started."

Jim shrugged. "I'm open to suggestions."

"Well we gotta get rid of their car, right?"

Jim nodded.

Arty tapped the bat against Lois Blocker's foot. "How tall are you?"

Her fear meshed with a confused frown. "What?"

"*How tall?*"

"I don't...five-two?"

Arty tapped the bat on Maury's foot. "You?"

"About five-seven, I guess."

Arty brought the aluminum bat down onto Maury Blocker's head once, then twice. Lois Blocker screamed after the second hit, immediately prompting her turn. Arty crushed her skull with the first swing.

Panting, Arty turned to his brother, bat in both hands. "Sometimes you just get up to the line of scrimmage and need to call an audible, James my boy."

Jim started laughing. "The fuck are you talking about?"

Arty threw the bat into the corner where it landed with a distinctive twang. "They're short little fuckers. We can stuff 'em in the trunk before we ditch the car. I *really* didn't feel like digging any holes this weekend." He tapped the side of his forehead. "Efficiency."

"I've got the smartest big brother in the whole wide world."

Arty held out a fist. "Rock, scissors, paper to see who strips the sheets?"

28

Patrick and Amy were barely down the length of their driveway when Lorraine called to them from next door.

"*Shit,*" Patrick whispered.

"*Told you,*" Amy whispered back.

"You guys back so soon?" Patrick called over to her.

The couple met Lorraine halfway, on the strip of lawn between the two cabins.

"Norman decided to take the kids for ice cream after the film. The parlor is a bit out of the way, so you two still have a good deal of time left to yourselves." Lorraine winked at them.

"Perfect," Amy said. "We were just about to take a moon-lit walk around the lake."

"Romantic stuff, ya know?" Patrick said.

Amy elbowed him. Lorraine smiled and looked up at the sky. "Well you couldn't have picked a better night for it. It's a beautiful one."

Amy looked up with her.

Patrick asked about the kids and Norman again. "So wait, what happened? Did Norm come back and drop you off *before* heading back out with the kids?"

Lorraine nodded. "I was getting tired. Glad I'm a grandmother now and can give them back at the end of the night. I forgot how exhausting it can be."

Amy gripped her husband's forearm with both hands and began dragging him away from Lorraine. "Hence the reason we treasure *every* minute."

Patrick pretended he was being dragged harder than he actually was and gave Lorraine a silly look. "I guess that means we're going. Thanks again Lorraine, we'll be back soon."

Lorraine laughed and headed back inside.

They had just finished their stroll around the lake.

"I don't see Norm's car in the driveway yet," Patrick said, squinting towards the Mitchell's cabin. "We can do another lap if you want."

"Oh, so you're liking this now, are you?" Amy asked.

Patrick looked out onto the lake before answering. The smooth black surface of the lake reflected hypnotic patterns of moonlight that held his gaze like a shiny pendulum.

While the serenity of the cabin and its remote surroundings were the primary motives for their sojourn west, Patrick only just realized, to his own surprise, that it was his wife's suggestion of observing the lake at night that proved to be the most tranquil and soothing element of the entire vacation thus far.

"Yeah," he sighed. He pulled her close and looked out onto the lake again. "It really is beautiful." A shimmer of moonlight reflected off the lake and caressed the contours of Patrick's face as though it appreciated the compliment.

Amy rubbed his chest. "I've got such a big, sensitive man."

"Sensitive but tough, right?"

"Oh of course, baby—the toughest."

"Good. Because I can be macho too you know. I can belch or fart or punch an animal if you want."

"Please don't." She pulled away and took hold of his arm to start lap number two.

They strolled a good twenty yards more, periodically glancing left at the lit cabins before shifting their gaze east to become entranced once more by the lake's reflection of the moon.

"Beautiful night for a walk," a male voice said to their left.

They stopped. Patrick smiled and said, "Sure is."

Amy squinted and leaned forward towards the voice. When her eyes settled she recoiled as if a bug had flown in her face. She spun into Patrick.

"*It's him,*" she said.

Patrick looked down at his wife, then up at the wooden porch from where the man had greeted them. The porch was roughly ten feet away, three small stairs leading up to it. The man who had addressed them was leaning against a banister and periodically flicking a metal wind chime that hung just above and in front of his face. The man's head was shaved and he was leering, not smiling, at the couple.

"Who?" Patrick asked.

"Him from the store. From Giant. *From the fucking window in our bedroom!*"

Patrick stared at his wife in disbelief. The man flicked the wind chime again, the ding lifting Patrick's head towards him once more. He spoke to Amy but kept his eyes on the man on the porch. "*What? Are you sure?*"

Amy held on to Patrick's hand with a death-grip and stepped forward, her husband's arm like a rope while scaling down a mountain. She squinted again. The man with the shaved head took a step forward, took a bow, and blew her a kiss.

Motherfucker.

Patrick ripped his arm away from Amy and charged the porch, only to stop instantly on the first step. The man had drawn a gun, Patrick's head the target. Patrick stood frozen in mid-stride, like a child playing a game of Red light, Green light.

"Whoa, easy there, stud," the man with the shaved head said. "You've got an awfully mean look in your eyes. I'd hate to have to shoot them out."

Patrick remained still. Amy's heavy breathing could be heard behind his back. The man with the gun shifted his head to the left and looked past Patrick, towards the heavy breathing.

"Hey, lover," the man said to Amy. "I take it you remember me then?"

Amy said nothing. She had chosen, like her husband, to stay frozen and silent while the gun was still up and pointed in their direction.

"Of course you do," the man continued. "I mean a woman who gets *that* worked up over a few harmless words in a supermarket isn't likely to forget so easily." The man kept the gun up, turned his head and wiped his mouth on his shoulder. He'd started to salivate. "But if you ask me, that was nothing to how worked up you were last night when this stud right here was pumpin' away between those sexy little legs of yours."

Patrick clenched his jaw. His body was twitching now, begging to let his common sense disappear so he could rush forward at all costs. The man with the shaved head cocked the gun's trigger, his leer becoming a laugh.

"Am I pissin' you off, big man? Is it pissin' you off that I saw your slutty little wife riding your pole, her beautiful titties bouncing up and down like—" He moaned. "—like two scoops of *fuck yeah?*" He wiped his mouth again, continued leering. "Because I know it would piss *me* off. I mean if some guy hit on my woman in a supermarket, then returned later that night to watch her get *fucked?* *Jeeeesus* would I be pissed."

Patrick, slow and deliberate, took two steps backwards and stood upright. He paused, then chanced a few more steps until he was beside his wife. He maneuvered Amy behind him to shield her.

"Well maybe you're not so pissed after all," the man said after Patrick backed off. "Me? I would have ran up on this porch and taught me a lesson."

The words were out of Patrick's mouth before he could snatch them back. "Put that gun down and I'll show you how pissed off I am."

The man with the shaved head held the gun up to his face, gave it a curious look and said, "What? This? Is *this* the reason you won't grow a pair and come on up to defend your wife's honor?"

Patrick said nothing.

"You're thinking I'd *shoot you* if you came up here?" the man continued. "I couldn't shoot you, pal. I could never hurt anyone. Just isn't in me."

The man walked towards a wicker table in the center of the porch and set the gun down. "There." He splayed empty hands. "All gone."

The man then turned those open hands into fists and put them up in a classic 19th century boxing stance, one fist behind the other, chin ludicrously high. "Come on then, stud. Let's do a bit of fisticuffs, yeah?" He made small circles with his fists as though ready for the opening bell. "Come on, you don't want your wife to think you're a pussy, do ya? Because no matter what they might tell you, it's always the knight-in-shining-armor shit that gets 'em wet. You see, a woman will make love to a pacifist..." He smirked. "But she'll *fuck* a knight."

Patrick twitched again.

The man exaggerated his stance, raised his fists high. "So what's it gonna be, stud? You gonna be the knight or the pussy?"

Patrick started forward.

Amy lunged after her husband, grabbed his arm with both hands. "*No!*" She fronted Patrick and placed both hands on his chest. "No, Patrick, he'll grab the gun as soon as you go up there. *He's* the pussy!" She turned and faced the man, one hand still on her husband's chest. "*YOU'RE the pussy!*" She turned back to Patrick. "We'll call the police. We'll go home right now and call the police." Back over her shoulder again at the man, "*WE'RE CALLING THE POLICE!*"

The screen door to the cabin opened, a metallic bang declaring it shut once the porch's newest occupant appeared. He was a man with dark hair, dark eyes, and a welt on his cheek. He was holding a doll. "What the *hell* is going on out here?" the man asked. "Can't a guy play with his doll in peace?"

Patrick's mouth fell open.

Amy leaned forward and squinted. "Is that…?"

"*Arty*," Patrick whispered.

Arty held up Josie the doll. He made one of the plastic arms wave at the stunned couple. "Howdy, Penn State fans."

29

"We're leaving *tonight*," Amy said. "The second the kids come back, and the second the sheriff arrests those assholes, *we-are-leaving.*"

Patrick sat at the kitchen table, gripping a glass of water. Frequent jabs of ire flooded his limbs and tempted him to squeeze until the glass shattered in his hand.

"They know each other," he said. "They *fucking know each other.*"

"It makes sense," Amy said. She was pacing throughout the kitchen. "Arty knew which car was ours from the gas station. For all we know he was there with the bald guy at the supermarket."

"They're fucking with us," Patrick said with a pitiful laugh. "They've been watching us and fucking with us this whole time."

"They couldn't possibly *live* in that cabin could they? I mean there's no way, right?" Amy asked.

"No," Patrick said. "No way."

"Well how does *that* work then? If they don't live there—"

"I don't know, Amy. Maybe they broke into the place."

"Well if that's true, then what about the people who *do* live there? What happened to them?"

Patrick pinched the bridge of his nose hard. "I have no idea. We need to let the sheriff go and check the place out."

Amy paced some more before taking a seat at the table. "It was all too weird—all this bullshit in such a short period of time."

Patrick nodded. "It's how they've managed to stay ahead of us—working together the way they were."

"You still think that finger was a prank from a kid?" Amy asked.

Patrick took a drink of water. "I don't know."

"You still think it was a *rubber* finger?" Her tone was condescending.

Patrick shot her a look. His wife was frustrated and scared, and Patrick knew an outburst on his part would solve little. He swallowed his anger, steadied his breathing. "I really don't know, Amy. Right about now I would have to say the damn thing was probably real."

Amy snorted a disgusted smile and began massaging her temples with both hands.

Patrick looked away. He didn't look at her when he spoke. "I should have listened to you." His voice was softer now. "We should have left when you said."

Patrick was surprised how quickly his wife said, "No." She took both hands away from her temples, sat upright in her chair. Her face was apologetic for her snide remarks. "No, I didn't want that. I wanted to stay. And you knew that…"

Patrick kept his profile to her; eye contact didn't feel right yet.

"I just needed you to convince me, to tell me everything would be okay." She reached across the table and took one of his hands. "It's what you do. It's why you're my rock."

In a matter of seconds, Patrick went from wanting vengeance to wanting to cry. He still found it hard to look at his wife. If he did he was certain his eyes would leak.

"It *is* what I do," he said. "But I do it out of necessity *and* sincerity." He took her hand into both of his, finally looking at her. Tears did come, but sorrow was only a fraction of their makeup. Intense resolve was the remainder. "I've said the same things to you a million times over the years. But I know you don't mind. I know you want to hear them. You want to hear me tell you that you're beautiful in your new dress even after I've told you twice already.

You want to hear me tell a funny and romantic story about us at a dinner party that you've heard a thousand times before. You want me to stop running the lawnmower and look over at you, hard at work in the garden—stained jeans; dirty hands; sweaty face—and hear me tell you that I love you, and that you're the most beautiful woman I've ever seen in my life, even though I'd said it just ten minutes before.

"You want to hear these things again and again because they make you feel safe and cherished. And that's something you only realize when those words aren't spoken for a while.

"So my repetition may appear to be a necessity, but it's always genuine, always sincere. And I'll never get tired of telling you. And I'll never let you feel what it's like to miss those words.

"So I'll say it again; and my sincerity with this one is stronger than anything my soul can possibly manage. I love you with all my heart, Amy. And I'd die a million deaths to protect you and our children. You call me your rock—well you guys are mine."

Amy started to cry. She stood up and walked to her husband's chair, sat on his lap and hugged him tight. "I love you so much, honey." She kissed him hard, her nose and tears wet against his face. "When the sheriff gets here, we take him to that cabin and have him arrest those guys. We then wait for Norm and the kids, pack, and be on the road and back in our own beds before we know it. Far, far away from here."

He kissed her. "God damn right, baby."

"Two nights in a row," the sheriff said as he strolled up the Lambert's driveway. "At least you caught me a little earlier this time."

The sheriff made no attempt whatsoever in hiding his cynicism, but Patrick was past caring; he wanted no time wasted. "We'll take you to the cabin," he said immediately.

"Whoa, slow down, son. Let's clear some things up first," the sheriff said, hoisting his belt, belly bouncing. "You said on the phone that you walked passed a cabin here that was housing the man who

harassed your wife in the supermarket? The same man who *allegedly* looked in your bedroom window as well? That right?"

Patrick nodded quickly. "Yes."

Amy flashed a look of contempt when the sheriff over-emphasized *allegedly*.

"And this other man?" the sheriff asked. "The other man you claim was at the cabin?"

"He's the one who's been following us. He has our daughter's doll," Patrick said.

"Come again?"

"It's...it's hard to explain. But the guy is bad news, and he's *with* the man from the supermarket. That's not a coincidence," Patrick said.

The sheriff stayed quiet.

"I told you on the phone he pulled a *gun* on us," Patrick said. "That counts for something doesn't it? I mean that has to carry some impact with you."

The sheriff cleared his throat—a wet, gravelly sound. "It could. When and why did he pull it on you?"

Patrick went to answer but stopped, something suddenly occurring to him. He had attempted to charge the man's porch—to set foot on his property. Patrick was not too sure about the laws around here when it came to home security and guns, but perhaps the man had been legally justified to pull the gun the moment Patrick's foot touched that first step of the front porch. But this begged another question: whose front porch was it? It couldn't be theirs. It *couldn't* be. All this time? To have them be so close?

Patrick did something he would have never done in any other circumstance. He lied to an officer of the law. "I don't know why he pulled the gun. He just pulled it and began taunting us."

Amy acknowledged her husband's lie and never flinched. They were sharing more than the same page; they were sharing the whole damn book.

"Taunting?"

"Yes!" Amy piped up. "*Admitting* that he had been watching my husband and I make love last night. Admitting that he was peeping through our bedroom window like some sick—"

Patrick took his wife's hand to stifle her outburst.

The sheriff's expression made a sudden shift from skepticism to surprise. "A confession?" he asked.

Amy gave a pathetic chuckle. "And then some."

"So he pulled a gun and confessed to being on your property last night."

"Yes."

"And this other man—you say he stole your daughter's doll?"

"Not exactly," Patrick said. "He bribed her with candy at a restaurant. He'd been following us."

The sheriff's chin retracted. "What would a grown man want with a child's doll?"

"Well you know what, sheriff? We've been asking ourselves that very same question," Patrick said, his sarcasm impossible to suppress.

The sheriff stroked his long gray moustache. He swallowed the sarcasm silently, appearing to let it pass for now.

"Does it matter though?" Patrick continued. "We could care less about the doll. The point *is,* is that these two men have been playing games with us the second we got up here, and it's escalated to the point where we now fear for our safety. Hell, I'd be willing to bet that the cabin we saw them in wasn't even *theirs.*"

"You believe they broke into someone's home in order to antagonize you?"

"*Yes, I do.*"

"Well if that's the case, then maybe we've got something serious going on here. But then we've got to ask ourselves, where does that leave the true owners of the cabin?"

"I don't know...*in danger?* I'm telling you there's something very bad about these two men, sheriff. I mean for Christ's sake we even found a finger in our bait container this afternoon."

The sheriff turned an ear to the couple and leaned in. "Say that again?"

"We went fishing today, and there was a severed finger in our bait container," Patrick said. "Right about now I'd bet good money those two men were behind it somehow."

The sheriff leaned back, raised one of his gray, bushy eyebrows. "A finger in your bait container? Why on earth didn't you call me then?"

Patrick glanced at his wife who returned an equally frustrated look. "A dog...he..." Patrick sighed. "He ate it."

"A dog ate it?"

Wait for it, Patrick thought.

"Are we talking about a finger here, or some homework, Mr. and Mrs. Lambert?"

Ta-Da!

The sheriff delivered his remark with subdued delight, his huge gray mustache failing to mask a smirk.

Amy's face reddened, her hand squeezing Patrick's. The couple chose silence, hoping the sheriff was finished with his questioning and was now ready to take action.

"Well alright then," the sheriff said, hoisting his belt, the belly bouncing again. "Why don't I go check out that cabin?"

"We'll take you," Patrick said.

"Oh no," the sheriff said. "No, you folks are staying right here. Lock your doors and stay put. I'll come back to you once I've checked—"

"Do you even know which cabin it is?" Amy blurted.

The sheriff tilted his head and gave a patronizing smile. "No I sure don't, Mrs. Lambert. And if you'd given me a chance to finish my sentence I might have gone and asked." He turned and spit on the driveway, a dark, heavy wad the size of a quarter. Patrick realized he was dipping tobacco. "So...let's try this again." He wiped his mustache clean with his thumb and index finger. "Do you think you folks would be so kind as to point me in the direction of that cabin?"

30

The time that passed before the sheriff returned to the Lambert's cabin after his search had been agonizing. Every click or crack heard from outside caused Amy and Patrick to flinch. Worse yet, Norman had yet to return with the kids.

"I'm sorry, Mr. and Mrs. Lambert, but there isn't a soul in that house," the sheriff said. "No signs of forced entry either. Truth be told, it even looked as if they cleaned up and shut down for the season."

Patrick, Amy, and the sheriff stood on the Lambert's front porch. The sheriff's previous skepticism to the whole ordeal (which, for a fleeting moment earlier, Patrick hoped was gone; he and Amy had finally managed to convince the sheriff that something foul was indeed afoot, and perhaps Sheriff Holmes might actually find something beyond the tip of his whiskey-reddened nose) was now back. Back and seemingly fixed in steel, going nowhere.

"Shut down?" Amy said.

"Sure," the sheriff said. "Summer's gone, autumn's here, and more than half the folks around the lake will disappear until decent weather returns. Gets cold and dark up here sooner than you'd think."

"Did you go inside the house?" Patrick asked.

"Yep."

"How?"

"*How?*"

"Yes. How did you get inside the house?"

"Through the cellar 'round back," the sheriff said.

"It was unlocked?" Patrick asked.

"That's right."

"Well doesn't that tell you something?" Amy said.

"Like what?"

"Well if these people were leaving for the winter as you suggested, then why would they leave their home unlocked for six months?"

The sheriff smiled. "This isn't the city, Mrs. Lambert. People tend to be a bit more trusting up here. It's one of the advantages of living out here in the *sticks* I suppose."

Patrick believed the sheriff had enunciated "sticks" as if the man felt he was a minority amongst bigots—seemingly certain that Patrick and Amy had frequently used such terminology in jest to describe the place he called home.

"Besides," the sheriff continued, "it's not uncommon for families to leave a door unlocked to have a service come through for maintenance during the winter months. Leaving a cellar door open is actually quite common. In fact, it was the first door I checked before entry. To tell you the truth though, I even wondered if it was necessary—I didn't even spot a car in the driveway."

"Maybe it was in their garage," Amy said.

The sheriff snorted. "Closest thing you'll find to a garage at Crescent Lake is a carport, Mrs. Lambert. And you can see right into those. Of course it doesn't matter much cuz these folks didn't even have one."

Patrick's frustration was now past courtesy. He spoke from the hip with zero concern for subtleties. "You searched that entire house?"

"Sure did."

"And found absolutely nothing?"

The sheriff pursed his lips, breathed deep through flared nostrils. "*Yes, sir.* Like I already said, that house is empty, whether you want to believe it or not. I even called in a little background check. Place belongs to a Maury and Lois Blocker—older couple in their sixties. There were positively *no signs* of them in that house whatsoever."

"Then they left. They knew you'd be coming and they left. We told them we'd be calling you," Amy said.

"Looked to me as if they left a long time ago," the sheriff said.

"I'm not talking about the *owners*; I'm talking about the two assholes we saw. They knew you'd be coming, so they ran."

The sheriff glanced around, bored now.

"These guys are *smart*, sheriff," Patrick said. "They're having fun with us. With you too." Patrick's last comment was a desperate attempt to bring the sheriff onto their playing field. The sheriff, unfortunately, took the comment the way Patrick feared he might. He looked as if someone kicked his ego in the nuts.

"Nobody's having fun with *me*, son. If I'm telling you there's no one in that house, then there's no one in that house. Got me?"

"Well you can't possibly think we're making this up can you?" Amy asked. "What in God's name would we have to gain by doing something like that?"

The sheriff shrugged. "I never accused you folks of making anything up. But you asked me to check the place out and I did. And like I'm telling you now for the *third* time, there were absolutely no signs of forced entry, or of persons recently occupying that cabin."

"I don't believe this." Amy threw up her hands. "So what are you going to do?"

The sheriff spit more tobacco and adjusted his hat. He was back in control, bored again. "I can send my deputy down to patrol the area if that will help you sleep better."

"Don't bother," Patrick said. "You said you'd do that last night, and a hell of a lot of good it did. Besides, we're not *staying* the night. We're waiting for Norm to return with our kids and then we're getting the fuck out of here."

The sheriff raised an eyebrow at Patrick's language. Patrick continued undeterred.

"And I'll tell you something else, sheriff. I'm not quite sure how you got your badge, but I wouldn't be a bit surprised if you ordered it off the back of a fucking comic book."

The sheriff's flicked the tip of his hat up with his middle finger. His bushy gray eyebrows were now a sharp V. He took a step towards Patrick and got in his face. Patrick smelled the tobacco and cheap after-shave.

"I'll tell you this much, Mr. Lambert. Maybe you and your wife made this whole thing up; maybe you didn't. I can't be sure. Maybe it's something you city folks like to do to entertain yourselves way out here in the sticks with us ignorant country folk…"

Oh we're going there again, are we? Patrick thought.

"But what I *can* tell you, Mr. Lambert, is that us country folk have jail cells that are just as uncomfortable as the ones you got in that big city of yours, and you're about one more wrong word away from finding yourself spending the night there instead of headin' on home with your wife and kids."

Patrick stayed quiet. He was angry but not stupid. The sheriff continued.

"Now, my suggestion is to go back inside, pack your things, and wait for Norm to come back with your kids. Once that's done, I suggest you do exactly as you said, and *get the fuck out of here.*"

Patrick took a step back and swallowed his rage. He waited until the sheriff had walked back to his cruiser, out of earshot, before saying, "You got it, dickhead."

He guided Amy through the front door then slammed it.

31

"Where *are* they, Lorraine?" Amy asked.

All three sat around Lorraine's kitchen table, each with a mug of tea.

"They should be back soon. Like I said, the ice cream parlor is a bit out of the way. That's why I wanted Norm to drop me at home first."

"And he's got no cell phone?" Patrick said.

Lorraine gave an apologetic shake of the head. "Sorry. We may be the only couple on the East Coast now without one."

"Fuck," Patrick said, to which he immediately followed with: "Sorry."

"That's okay, Patrick," Lorraine said. "Given the circumstances, I would say 'fuck' sums things up rather well."

Patrick forced a quick smile.

Lorraine sipped her tea and added, "To tell the truth, I'm more than a little unsettled myself. The thought of having horrible men like that roaming around our community isn't sitting too well with me. Perhaps Norm and I will leave *with* you tonight—stay away from the lake for awhile until those men are put in jail."

Patrick nodded hard. "Not a bad idea at all, Lorraine. Although I wouldn't hold my breath about those men being put in jail. That sheriff is about as useful as a mesh condom."

"I'll tell you what's strange," Lorraine said. "I'm nearly certain I saw the Blockers only a couple of days ago."

"What do you mean?" Patrick asked.

Lorraine's face scrunched with uncertainty. "I thought I spotted them taking a stroll around the lake. They were a good distance away, but if I had to bet, I'd say it was Maury and Lois."

"And when was this?" Patrick asked.

"The day before you arrived maybe?"

"Is it possible they've since packed up and headed back for the winter?"

"It's possible…" Lorraine began tracing a finger along the rim of her teacup, her mind elsewhere.

Amy asked her, "What is it?"

Lorraine's eyes flicked up from their trance. "Just remembering something." Her brow furrowed as she tried recalling events. "I can remember driving back here with Norm a few years ago, a couple of days before Thanksgiving. I'd forgotten a picture album we were planning to show the family. Took me all summer to put the darn thing together and I went and forgot it." She paused, the furrow in her brow etching deeper, the culprit now mystery instead of recollection. "But the Blockers were still here; they hadn't left yet. I distinctly remember Norm making mention of it now. He'd said he'd spotted them on their front porch. He wondered if they'd chosen to stay put for the holidays that year."

Patrick and Amy said nothing, their silence prompting Lorraine to elaborate.

"Some folks around here do that. They're year-rounders. They don't mind the cold."

Patrick went to speak, but as if reading his mind, Lorraine spoke and answered his question. "Except the Blockers aren't year-rounders. They do leave for the winter season. I know that for a fact. I guess that year Norm spotted them they'd gotten a late start, or, as Norm wondered, they decided to stay put for the holidays."

She shrugged. "Maybe they had family coming to see *them*. Had their holiday at the cabin."

Patrick stood from the kitchen table and began to pace. "Okay then, having said that, what are all the possibilities we're looking at here? I mean, to be brutally honest, I only see two. Either that douche bag sheriff was right and the Blockers *did* leave for the upcoming season, which would mean those two assholes somehow broke into their empty cabin and left without a single trace, or..." He looked at the two women. Their eyes met his gaze for only a second before skittering away, "possibility number two" realized, yet neither woman willing to say it aloud for fear that once spoken it could, and would, be a likely certainty.

To Patrick's surprise it was Lorraine and not Amy who eventually finished his thought. "...Or the Blockers were still home when those two men entered their cabin."

"Exactly," Patrick said without a trace of satisfaction. "And if that's the case, then the Blockers..."

Neither woman finished his sentence this time, the superstition of voicing fears at its pinnacle when murder was the implication.

Amy stood and walked to the window. "I want to leave." She turned her head towards Patrick. "Do you think we should go back to our place and start packing so we can go the second they get here?"

"No," Patrick said. "No, we're staying here together. When Norm comes back we'll *all* head over to our place and pack. Then we'll *all* head back here so Lorraine and Norm can pack." He looked at Lorraine. "I think you we're right; it's a damn good idea if you guys took off for awhile. I'm sure Norm will agree."

Lorraine nodded. "I'm sure too."

Amy and Patrick both took their seats again.

Patrick thrummed his fingers across the surface of the table.

Amy dropped her head and started massaging her neck with both hands. She stopped suddenly, head popping up. "Do you hear that?" she asked.

Patrick stopped thumping the table top with his fingers and held them up for Amy to see. "That was me. Sorry."

"No," she said, standing up. "Something else. Listen."

The room went quiet. Nobody breathed. In the distance there was the faint sound of chimes.

"Do you *hear* that?" Amy asked again.

"Bells?" Lorraine said.

"Chimes," Amy said. "Do you and Norm have wind chimes?"

"No."

Patrick stood and went to the window. He put a hand over his eyes to cover the glare from inside the house, and squinted towards their cabin. The back porch was dark, but he could still make out the silhouette of something small hanging from its canopy. Something new. He cracked the window and stuck an ear out. The chiming was definitely coming from their cabin.

Patrick's mind suddenly flashed on the man with the shaved head. His finger flicking chimes on the Blocker's porch...

Patrick pulled his head inside and shut the window. "Stay here," he said as he headed towards the front door. Amy went after him but he turned and thrust out his palm. "*Stay here*," he said again. She did.

Patrick went out the Mitchell's front door. He did not walk cautiously to his back porch. He ran, almost hoping to collide with his antagonists. In movies everybody slinks slowly, gives the bad guys time to hide and wait. Patrick wanted to rip the goddamn Band-Aid off quickly. Wanted to run feverishly towards his tormentors, shock them and catch them by surprise as they tried to scurry away after setting their trap.

Arriving at his back porch, Patrick instantly reached up into the dark to snatch the chime. His intent was to rip it down and hurl it as far away as possible, hoping to maybe hear a definitive splash should it reach the lake.

Except he didn't. Instead, Patrick jerked his hand away from the chime as though it had scalded him. He jerked his hand away because when he touched the chime, he felt something furry.

Patrick reached into his pocket and fumbled for his key. He opened the door, reached inside, flicked on the porch lights, and froze.

It *was* the same wind chime that had been hanging on the Blocker's porch.

It *was* the same wind chime that the man with the shaved head had been flicking with his fingers.

But that wasn't what froze Patrick.

What froze him was the furry something he had touched. It was hanging dead center in the middle of the surrounding chimes like a rope-handle to a bell. It was a tail. A tail that looked like it belonged to Oscar the dog.

32

Patrick reappeared at the Mitchell's front door with a rifle gripped tight in both hands. Both Lorraine and Amy took several steps back, Lorraine involuntarily raising her hands in a submissive gesture.

"*What?*" Amy said. "*What's wrong?*"

"They're still here," Patrick said. He gripped the rifle with such intensity it looked as though he meant to break it.

The rifle had always been at the cabin. The Lamberts were not hunters, but Amy's father was. He kept the gun locked away in the cabin for the rare times he still went on hunting trips. Patrick knew where he kept it, never approved of it, always ignored it, and was now grateful for it.

Amy looked at the rifle in her husband's hands with frightened eyes. "What are you talking about? Why do you have my dad's gun?"

Patrick ignored his wife and turned his attention on the front door. He locked it then twisted and pulled at the handle, testing its stability. Satisfied, he whirled around and took powerful strides towards the back door where he repeated the same ritual.

"Patrick."

He returned to the living room, slid the rifle open, double-checked the ammunition he'd loaded at the cabin, nodded to himself, slammed the metal bolt home.

"*Patrick!*"

Patrick's frantic trance broke, eyes wide, looking as if he'd been shaken from a nightmare. "The *chimes*," he said. "The wind chimes that maniac was flicking on the Blocker's porch...they're dangling from our back deck with Oscar's fucking *tail* hanging in the middle of them."

Lorraine gasped and put a hand over her mouth.

"They killed the dog?" Amy asked.

Patrick snorted and tightened his grip on the rifle. "My guess would be yes. Either that or they held the poor bastard down and sliced off his tail. Either way, I think it's safe to say that things have gone from bad to exceptionally fucking worse."

Lorraine lowered her hand from her mouth and said, "Oh that poor little thing."

Patrick hurried back to the front door, cracked the blinds on one of the adjacent windows. The driveway was empty. No headlights in the distance. "Where are they, Lorraine? Is the ice cream place *that* far away?" he said.

Lorraine shook her head in quick bursts and said, "Yes. I mean, no. I mean *yes*, it's kind of far, but *no*, I would have expected them to be home by now."

Patrick faced Amy, the rifle tight to his chest. "*Please God no,*" he said in a breathless whisper.

"Please God no *what?*" Amy said. "What are you thinking?"

Patrick swallowed hard, his mouth drying up on him. "I'm thinking that if these bastards have been three steps ahead of us this whole time, then how the hell do we know they don't have Norm and the kids?"

Now it was Amy who put a hand to her mouth.

"But when could they have done that?" Lorraine asked. "*Someone* had to recently put that wind chime up on your porch. The parlor is far. The distance and timing doesn't add up."

"Maybe they never *made* it to the parlor," Patrick said. "Did you watch them leave?"

"What?"

"After Norm dropped you off, did you watch them *actually* back out of the driveway and *leave* Crescent Lake?"

Lorraine thought for a brief moment, her eyes dropping to recall. When she eventually looked up, she could not meet Patrick's stare. "No. No, I didn't. I didn't think I'd have a reason to. I didn't think…"

Amy rubbed Lorraine's back.

Patrick lowered his head. "So there's a chance they never even left the lake."

Amy asked, "So what exactly are you suggesting?"

"I'm suggesting those two fucks might have grabbed them before they even had a chance to leave."

"Doesn't that sound like a big risk?" Lorraine asked. "Suppose someone saw them?"

"And suppose someone didn't?" Patrick said. "Or suppose they didn't even use force to get hold of them. These guys are *smart*, Lorraine. Norm's one of the nicest guys in the world. For all we know these men could have tricked him; said they had a flat, needed directions…who the hell knows?"

Amy made a face of horrific possibility. "Are you saying its possible Carrie and Caleb were there? They were being *held captive* in the Blocker's cabin while we were dealing with those guys?"

"Maybe," Patrick said. "I don't know."

Amy looked like she wanted to punch things and cry.

"The sheriff said he searched that cabin," Lorraine said.

"That sheriff is fucking useless," Patrick said. "If you ask me he probably didn't even go inside the damn place. Probably just peeked in a few windows."

Lorraine walked carefully towards the kitchen table as though she was a bit drunk, grabbing at nearby things for balance. She sat gingerly, took a long breath, wiped her face. Her skin was near white.

"Lorraine, are you alright?" Amy asked.

She closed her eyes and nodded. She kept them closed when she replied, "Yes—I'm just very scared."

Amy walked over and put a hand on Lorraine's shoulder. Lorraine rested her own hand on top of Amy's and squeezed it. Amy looked at Patrick. "What do we do? Do we call the sheriff again?"

Patrick scoffed, his jeer for the sheriff and not for the intent of belittling his wife's suggestion. "Are you joking? At this point I don't even think he'd show up if we did." He started towards the kitchen. Placed the rifle on the counter and ran both hands under the faucet, splashing cold water onto his face. Finished, he grabbed the gun again and faced both women. "Here's what we're going to do," he said. "You two are going stay here. You're going to turn off the lights; keep the doors and windows locked; and stay out of sight. I'm going—"

"No!" Amy screamed. "You're not going anywhere! You're not—"

"*Shut up!*" he yelled. There was a twinge of guilt for his outburst, but now was not the time for tact. He would apologize later. And there *would* be a later.

Patrick spoke his next words slowly and methodically. "I am going to the Blocker's house. I will have the gun with me. I am going to search *every inch* of that house. If I find *anything,* I will deal with it. If Norm and the kids come back, you tell Norm what's been going on, and *all of you* stay locked up tight until I return."

Amy's attempt at controlling her tears had failed. They were flowing freely now, her voice wet and strained. "And if you don't return?" she said.

Patrick looked at his wife with desperate intensity. "I'm going to return."

Amy cried harder. Lorraine stood and hugged her, then looked over her shoulder at Patrick. "I'm not too sure this is wise, Patrick," she said. "If these men are as dangerous as they seem…"

Patrick's gaze was unflinching. "Well then think about this, Lorraine: what if these dangerous men have got a hold of *your* husband and *our* children? What do you suggest we do? Sit here and wait? Excuse me, but fuck that."

33

The moment after Patrick kissed his wife, hugged Lorraine, and walked out the front door armed with a loaded rifle, the two women sprang into action. They did exactly as Patrick had said: locked every window and door, turned off all lights, then hurried to Norman and Lorraine's bedroom where they both took a spot on the floor, against the wall, out of plain sight, knees bent to the chest, arms wrapped tight around them, not daring to speak for the first few minutes they sat huddled together.

"What do we do if Norm and the kids show up?" Amy eventually whispered.

"What do you mean?" Lorraine's whisper was even softer.

"Does he have a key, or will we have to get up and let him in?"

"He has a key," she said. "But I'm sure he'd think it odd if I locked the door. I never lock the front door."

A short pause.

"I'm scared," Amy said. "I want my babies to be okay." And then quickly, she added, "Norm too of course."

Lorraine smiled. "I know, sweetheart." She wrapped her arm around Amy and pulled her in tight. "We just have to do as Patrick said. We need to stay out of sight and wait for him to return."

"Oh God, but what if—"

Lorraine squeezed Amy's shoulder hard, cutting her off. "Stop thinking like that. We have to stay positive. We need to be strong."

"I am positive; I am strong." She stopped, her eyes, lit only by moonlight, re-living something dark.

"But those men...they've been following us. Watching us. They know—"

Lorraine squeezed harder. "Stop it, Amy. We need to keep quiet for now and listen for Patrick and Norm. Focus on it, okay? Focus. *We are* going to see my husband and your family very soon. *We are.* I promise. Just focus on that and be strong, sweetheart, okay?"

Patrick held the rifle vertically, hidden along the length of his body as he walked towards the Blocker's cabin. The last thing he wanted was a nosy neighbor reporting a strange man walking the perimeter of the lake with a rifle in hand, looking as though he meant to shoot anything that blinked. Or maybe he *did* want that. It might be the only way for the sheriff to show his face again. No—the dumb bastard would probably shoot him by mistake.

Speaking of said dumb bastard, Patrick had no difficulty recalling the sheriff's words and did not even try to enter the Blocker's cabin through their front door. Instead he immediately headed around back and started for the cellar.

Two heavy wooden doors lay on a slight angle up from the ground. Patrick bent over and tugged at them. They opened with a slow creak like something out of a horror film, and despite his focus, he could not help but snort at the appropriateness of it all.

Patrick took slow crunchy steps down each bug- and leaf-encrusted stair until his nose was inches from the steel door that led inside the cellar. He found out (but had no time to swallow any pride) that the sheriff had indeed been correct. The cellar door was unlocked.

With the rifle held firm in his right hand, Patrick gripped the knob on the cellar door with his left and turned it slowly. He eased the door open and stepped into darkness. It smelled of dust and mold. A damp chill found Patrick's skin immediately. He shuddered involuntarily and used his free arm to rub the other in a bid for warmth.

Eyes wide, Patrick was desperate to adjust to the blackness that was enveloping him with each step. He knew that in time his vision would become accustomed to the dark, but his anxiety and fortitude did not afford him any patience. His goal for now was to locate some source of light, and he immediately cursed himself for allowing his bravado to override a more efficient game plan back at the Mitchell's. If he'd allowed his common sense to get a word in, he might have remembered a flashlight.

Lorraine and Amy had not moved. They remained huddled together in the dark, moonlight from the window their only source of light. They prayed they would soon hear the jingle of Norm's keys in the lock, or Patrick's fist rapping on the door followed by the echo of his voice, assuring them that he was okay and to let him inside.

They listened hard. They heard an owl's incessant hoot. They heard tree branches crackle, each one a possible footstep. They heard the occasional gust of wind palm the glass of the bedroom window, rattling the frame. And that was all they heard. There was no jingling of Norm's keys. No knock on the door, the echo of Patrick's voice following. And each moment that passed without those hopeful sounds their unrelenting fear grew deeper.

Patrick had fumbled blindly throughout the cellar like a one-armed mummy, the rifle still tight to his side. He had managed to locate the railing of the staircase but questioned whether or not he should ascend without a credible source of light. Suppose it was equally dark upstairs? If his attackers were up there waiting, their eyes would be well adjusted; he would be a sitting duck.

He had done his best to peruse the surrounding areas of the cellar, and with the exception of some damp boxes, many spider webs, and a wall of tools, he had found no flashlight. Not even a lighter or a box of matches. His only choice was obvious, and it was as unwelcome as any. He would have to climb the stairs in darkness.

Patrick gripped the railing with his left and steadied the rifle with his right. He was hesitant on his first step for fear of the wood giving out a groan under his weight. If his attackers *were* behind the door above, waiting, he would need every conceivable advantage. He would need the element of surprise. Old wooden steps that complained with each foot you placed on them would be akin to announcing your arrival.

He placed his toes gingerly on the first step, pushed on it, then allowed his heel to come down. No creak. He put his full weight on that one foot and then tried the other. Still no creak. Stair number one had passed the test.

Stair number two would get the same treatment—one foot, toes first, and then the heel. When silence was the reward, the second foot would get its turn.

Stairs three through thirteen all proved worthy to their first two counterparts and passed each delicate test with muffled brilliance. Fourteen was Patrick's final hurdle. It was all that stood between him and the door leading into the Blocker's home.

He decided, on the spot, to bypass fourteen entirely. Instead he would brace his right foot on twelve, his left on thirteen, and keep the rifle fixed on the door the whole time. He would then lean forward with his left hand, turn the handle, and push the door open with as much strength as he could muster from his angled position. The moment *asshole number one* appeared in the doorway, he would be primed and ready—a solid, stable position to gain the upper hand. Or if worse came to worst, blow their heads clean off their fucking shoulders.

Patrick's right foot stepped gingerly back to twelve, his left taking a firm spot on thirteen. Rifle gripped tight in his right, his left hand stretched slowly towards the knob until his fingertips grazed the brass. Another small lean and he was there. He gripped the knob and turned slowly. When he could turn no more, Patrick held his breath, steadied the rifle, and shoved open the door.

It was dark upstairs. Not as dark as the cellar, but dark. Patrick gripped the rifle with both hands now. His heart pounded in his ears. He wanted to shout, to taunt his enemies into appearing in that doorway so this could be done. Let their brazen silhouettes appear even for a second and I'll blow a goddamn hole in them, he thought.

And then step number ten creaked behind him. Patrick spun into a white light, his vision instantly gone. Two hefty blows followed: one to the groin when he raised his arm to shield his eyes, a second to the back of the head when he doubled over. Patrick slid down steps twelve through one face-first.

34

Amy Lambert and Lorraine Mitchell were both close to experiencing a full-body cramp. The tight bundles they'd wrapped themselves into had been taut throughout their wait, however the jingle of Norman Mitchell's keys in the front door, or the knock and call from a safely-returned Patrick had yet to occur, so the two women had no such intentions of relocating just yet. Fear kept them rooted tight.

"I need to pee," Amy whispered.

Their conversations thus far had been shared worry and desperate reassurances things would work themselves out, reassurances they prayed they would one day reminisce about: Norman *was* actually with the kids and just happened to be behind schedule. Patrick searched the Blocker house and found nothing. Or better yet, Patrick searched the Blocker house, found Arty and the man with the shaved head, and kicked the living crap out of both of them before they were hauled off to jail.

"I know, sweetie," Lorraine whispered back. "I need to go too."

"Should we try?"

"I wouldn't."

"Dammit," Amy said. "I'm scared and I have to pee. Great combination."

"At least we haven't been drinking."

"Patrick and I were earlier."

The mention of her husband's name conjured up his image. At the restaurant, smiling adoringly at her from across the table. Now her kids, laughing and playing with Oscar behind the cabin. Now Oscar. Likely dead. Patrick holding the rifle, his expression of frantic conviction contagious. The man with the shaved head on the porch, pointing a gun, taunting Patrick. Arty appearing, holding the doll, waving its arm, smirking at them. The possibility that these men had her babies...

"This can't be real," she said. "This..." The grim images flashed again. "This can't be real."

Lorraine's face turned equally somber. Amy continued.

"I keep thinking I'm going to wake from a dream at any moment, you know? I mean this is the kind of stuff that you see in the movies, not real life."

"In the movies the good guys always win," Lorraine said.

Amy glanced at Lorraine, then looked away when she said, "It depends on what movie you're watching."

Lorraine didn't reply.

Amy looked out the bedroom window. The moon was full and strong. She stared up at it as she spoke. "You see stuff in the media about all these horrible things going on all over the world. You see people murdering for something as ridiculous as a pair of shoes. You see the constant violence and struggles in the Middle East, and it's tragic and horrible, but there's still a sense of righteousness over there, a belief in what they're doing. The result is terrible and violent, but the *motive* is there. Even the man who murders for shoes has a motive. No matter how ludicrously asinine, he still has a motive. He wants the shoes."

"Amy—"

"You see that's just it, Lorraine. A motive. There's no motive here. No reason for this to be happening. These men...they're having fun with us. Playing with us like it's some kind of game. That's not a motive, is it?"

Amy took her eyes off the moon and looked at Lorraine. She didn't want a response from her neighbor, just an ear so she could vent. But Lorraine responded anyway. And the response frightened Amy.

"Maybe having no motive *is* their motive. They torment others because they enjoy it. Nothing more."

Amy fell silent. She saw despair in Lorraine's eyes and she immediately touched the woman's knee and rubbed it. "I'm sorry. I shouldn't have brought all this crap up. I guess in some weird way it's therapeutic for me to talk about it. In retrospect I guess it's kind of like talking about all the gory details of your impending surgery before they slice you open, huh?"

Lorraine produced a tired but genuine smile. "I suppose that would be a somewhat competent analogy. Although I could have done without 'gory' and 'slice you open.'"

Amy now genuinely smiled herself and rubbed Lorraine's knee again, keeping her hand there. "Time to change the subject?"

"Please."

Amy kept smiling. "Maybe when this is all over we'll all go on a trip together. Somewhere warm maybe?"

Lorraine put her hand on top of Amy's. "Norm and I haven't been to Florida in awhile."

Amy closed her eyes and leaned her head back against the wall. She took the first peaceful breath she'd taken in hours. "Patrick and I used to rent this amazing place in Clearwater before the kids were born."

"Clearwater? Norm brought me there once to watch the Phillies during spring training. It was absolutely lovely. Such a beautiful—"

Amy clamped down onto Lorraine's knee with a sudden jolt. "*SHHHHH!*"

Lorraine jumped then gaped at Amy. "*What?*"

Amy's hand stayed locked on Lorraine's knee. She held her breath, refused to even blink, afraid the wet click of her lids would impede her hearing. She eventually spoke in a dramatic whisper. "*Did you hear that?*"

Lorraine pecked her head forward, listened intently. She turned back to Amy and shook her head no.

"*The back door,*" Amy mouthed. Their previous conversation of vacations and Florida had risen pleasantly upwards into a semi-normal tone. Now it was a minute decibel above lip-reading. "*I heard something at the back door.*"

Lorraine tilted an ear upward, listened again. A light rapping echoed from somewhere outside. A moan followed, low and pained.

"*What is that?*" Lorraine said.

Amy shook her head.

The rapping was louder now, the moan longer, desperate.

Amy released her grip on Lorraine's knee. "*There's someone at the back door.*"

Lorraine snatched Amy's hand right back. "*Don't you dare.*"

"*It sounds like someone's hurt.*" She pulled her hand free from Lorraine's. "*What if it's Patrick?*"

"*Amy, NO.*" Lorraine's eyes held panic. "*We don't know WHAT that is. It could be a trap. We need to stay here.*" She reached for Amy's hand again. Amy wouldn't take it.

"What if it's not a trap? What if it *is* Patrick? What if he's hurt?" Amy's whisper was louder now, her voice raspy.

"Amy…"

"I'm going to look," Amy said. "I'm not going to open the door, but I'm going to go look."

"*Amy…*"

"I'll stay low to the ground and out of sight. When I get close to the door I can peek out through the window and get a quick look. No one will see me."

"Amy, please…"

"Lorraine, goddamnit, if it *is* my husband then I'm going to fucking help him." Amy's eyes were strong and unbreakable. Lorraine's chest sunk and she hung her head. Amy leaned in and hugged her hard. "I'm sorry. But you'd do the same for Norm, right? You'd do the same." Lorraine lifted her head, closed her eyes and nodded. Amy nodded back and repeated, "I'll stay low to the ground and out of sight."

35

Jim rocked impatiently from one foot to the other like a boy needing to pee. He even squeezed his groin a few times. But unlike a boy who might squeeze to stifle back the sensation to pee for fear of wetting his pants, Jim squeezed because it tickled hot with anticipation.

He thought of a familiar song. Something about waiting being the hardest part. Tom Petty. Was it Tom Petty? Yeah—that's who it was. Well Tom was right. Waiting was fucking excruciating.

He squeezed his groin again.

36

Amy slowly uncoiled from her ball. Her legs were tight and cramped and she gratefully extended them outward, rubbing both vigorously to get the blood flowing.

Rolling flat onto her stomach, she then began inching along on her belly. She reached the bedroom door and rolled to one side, straining an arm upward until her fingers touched the knob. She strained an inch further and gripped the knob tight. She managed a look over her shoulder before turning it. Lorraine was wincing at her, as if expecting the turning of the knob to trigger an alarm. Amy brought her head back to the door, gently turned the knob (she heard Lorraine's breath catching behind her), and then opened the door just wide enough to maneuver herself out into the living room. She looked back at Lorraine one last time. Lorraine stared back with terrible apprehension. Amy gave a weak nod and an even weaker smile, then slithered out of the bedroom.

Amy was flat to the ground. She slithered slowly towards the back door, using muscles she never knew she had. She stopped, strained both eyes upward, and could now see the window to the back door—about ten feet ahead.

There was another groan, but weaker now. *Failing?* she thought. *Was his health failing?* Amy was filled with a dreadful sense of urgency. She slithered faster, desperately trying to resist the urge to pop up onto all fours and crawl to her target.

She was close now. A foot tops. The window was high and to the left. If she timed it right, she could snatch a decent look despite the lack of light. If it *was* her husband, she would recognize him instantly, dark or no dark.

With a swift but cautious burst, she made the extra foot to the door and propped up onto her knees. Now both feet under her butt in a catcher's stance.

Rise slowly and ease your head up just enough to get a peek. Just a peek. Strain your eyes until they bleed if you have to, but just take a quick peek for now, then right back down again. Just a quick peek.

Amy rose slowly. Her thigh muscles burned. Inexplicably, she quickly thought of doing squats at her gym back home. She hated squats, and she hated the Nazi fitness instructor that made her do hundreds in class. Right now she would happily do a million and *kiss* the Nazi instructor afterwards if it meant being back home.

Her head was an inch from the window. She could feel the cold radiating off the pane of glass as she neared it. She could look up and see the black sky.

Another inch. She was level with the window now.

Quick peek.

Amy popped her head up and looked down. Patrick was there. Flat on his back, eyes closed.

Amy jumped to her feet and cried out his name. She unlocked the back door, ripped it open, fell to her knees at her husband's side.

"Patrick!" she cried again as she frantically checked his body for injuries. She bent over and pressed her ear to his chest. A powerful hand snatched hold of Amy's ponytail from behind, jerking her backwards onto her butt. The hand yanked the ponytail down like a handle, forcing Amy's head skyward where she was greeted to a hard, wet kiss.

The man with the shaved head licked his lips and grinned. "Hello again, lover."

37

Norman Mitchell had the patience of a saint. He therefore stressed little when Carrie, who had insisted she was capable of eating the *large* ice cream sundae, projectile-vomited the entire contents of her tiny stomach into the back seat of the Volvo station wagon on the ride back to Crescent Lake.

A rest-stop-cleaning job later and they were back on the road, windows down, Carrie donning a ghostly complexion, and Caleb holding his nose from the smell of curdled cream that still polluted his memory.

"How're you doing back there, sweetheart?" Norman called to the back seat.

Carrie was too afraid to open her mouth. She could only nod, hoping Norm would catch the quick bob of her head from the rear-view mirror.

"We're almost home, just hang on."

"It stinks!" Caleb yelled over the rushing wind from the open windows.

Carrie, who would have ordinarily responded with an immediate swipe in Caleb's direction, remained motionless. Nausea was in town, and gulping air and staying exceptionally motionless was the courtesy. Still, she did manage to cast a sinister glare at her brother. The second she felt better she would bop him a good one for sure.

When Norman pulled his blue Volvo station wagon into the driveway of cabin ten, his first words were, "What the heck?"

This prompted both Carrie (whose nausea was now all but gone) and Caleb to lean forward in their car seats and simultaneously ask: "*What?*"

The interior of the Mitchell cabin was dark, yet the front door was wide-open. Norm kept the car idling, his headlights the only source of light on the cabin. He clicked his high beams on hoping to get a better view of the cabin's interior via the open front door. He also hoped the extra glare from his high beams would be a silent honk of his horn and prompt his wife, or maybe the Lamberts, to appear in that open doorway, hands shielding their eyes, waving him in.

When Carrie asked why they weren't going up the rest of the driveway, Norman gave the little girl an honest, albeit useless answer. "I don't know," he said.

Carrie was eager. "Are we gonna—"

"Kids," Norm began, "I'm going to leave the car running here, then go inside. I'm going to lock all the car doors and I want you to *keep* them locked until I come back outside. Okay?"

"Why?" Carrie asked.

"Can you just do that for me? Please?"

Both kids nodded.

"When I come back out, *then* you can unlock them. Okay? Do you understand? Keep them locked until Mr. Mitchell comes back out."

They nodded again.

And then it was Caleb who asked, "What's wrong?"

Norman forced a smile. "Nothing's wrong, buddy. Silly Mrs. Mitchell just left the front door open. I want to go in first and make sure no animals got inside and started gobblin' up all our food."

He made a silly face and pretended to nosh on something the way a squirrel might a nut.

Caleb smiled.

Carrie did not. "Where are Mommy and Daddy?" she asked.

"They're probably next door at your cabin, sweetheart."

Carrie looked out her car window towards their cabin next door. It was black. "I don't think they're home," she said.

Norman noticed it too. *Oh please, God, let them be screwing each other,* he thought. *Please let the worst of our problems be catching them in the act.* And why not? It made sense. It made perfect sense. Time away from the kids. Romantic cabin to themselves. They've probably been at it all night.

But his *own* house? Pitch black with the front door wide open? His stomach swirled with adrenaline. He did not want to waste time making excuses anymore. Norm moved with an urgency that he prayed would not contaminate the children.

"Kids, can you just do as Mr. Mitchell says and wait here in the car please?"

The children didn't nod this time; they stared back with uncomfortable wonder.

Norm took it as a regrettable yes. "Great. I'll be *right* back. Just hold tight okay?"

Norm opened his car door and stepped out. He clicked the tiny black switch on the driver door's interior and all four locks thumped as they shrunk into their holes. He closed the car door, waved and forced another smile at the kids, then jogged to his open front door, the high beams of his idling Volvo lighting his path.

"Lorraine?" he called the moment he was inside. He took two more steps, each one slow and delicate as though the floor might give under his weight. "Lorraine? You in here, honey?" He heard nothing but the distant idle of the Volvo outside.

Norman began to imagine the worst. He thought of the man who had accosted Amy at the market and then peeked into her bedroom window last night. Had he come back? And if he had, was he dangerous?

Norman felt his pulse thumping all over. He *was* imagining the worst. But better to imagine the worst and be prepared than to be ignorant and caught off guard, right? He scanned his surroundings, searching for a potential weapon. A sharp metal poker was leaning up against their fireplace to his left. He hurried over and grabbed hold of it. He steadied it in his hand like a fencer about to duel. *Am I really going to have to use this?*

"Lorraine?" he called again. His voice cracked this time, the adrenaline sapping his saliva.

Norman took cautious steps towards the bedroom, the tip of the black poker leading the way. The bedroom door was open a crack. He placed the tip of the poker against the door and pushed slowly. The door felt heavy on the end of the poker as he pushed it open.

He took in every inch of the dark room, squeezing the handle of the poker for all he was worth. He twisted his left arm and blindly patted the wall to his left, feeling for the light switch. He found the switch and flicked it upward. The room came alive with light, and Norm blinked quickly so his eyes would adjust.

The bed was made. The closet doors were shut tight. The room looked as if he may have been the first to visit that day.

Norm let out a long, slow breath. Yes, the room was empty, and yes, he would still need to search the rest of the cabin, but the morbid thought of finding his wife murdered in their bed (a thought that had *refused* to leave his mind the second it crawled in there) had not come to fruition; and for that he felt a relief like no other.

Norm took another couple of steps into his bedroom, gave one last grateful look at their empty bed, then turned back towards the door. It was then he realized why the bedroom door had felt so heavy on the end of the poker when he pushed it open. His wife Lorraine was hanging on the back of it. Her head hung to one side, eyes open and lifeless, sagging lips already blue. Below the blue mouth her throat was slashed ear to ear, her entire torso soaked in red.

Norm dropped the poker to his side without realizing it. He didn't cry and he didn't scream. He could only stare. If he had found his wife dead in bed as he had feared, he would have rushed to her side and wept. After the weeping he would have righted himself and began cursing and screaming vengeance while thrashing around like a wild man with that poker as his equalizer. But this? *This* image? How could he have possibly evoked such a thing? The shock was brilliant. It made him certain his vision was a hoax, a ludicrous trick that projected a false image of his dead wife hanging before him like a giant flesh-puppet stored away on its hook.

His shock had made him deaf, too. He didn't hear the closet door open behind him. Didn't hear the footsteps approach his back. And he didn't hear the aluminum bat whistling down onto his skull.

The Volvo's headlights continued shining on the open front door of the Mitchell's cabin. Carrie and Caleb waited anxiously in the back seat for Norman to reappear.

Norman never did reappear; but someone else did. It was a man who looked very familiar to Carrie. He had dark hair and dark eyes (except he was wearing a big white Band-Aid on his cheek now for some reason) and was smiling brightly as he approached the car. It was also evident that he was carrying something behind his back.

As the man came within a foot of Carrie's window he leaned forward at the waist and, still smiling brightly, sang, "*Look who I've got...!*"

Josie the doll was whipped out from behind the man's back and pressed up against the car window.

Carrie's eyes jumped with delight and her squeal of "*Josie!*" reverberated through the car window and above the idling car.

"Hi, Carrie," the man said loudly through the glass. He over-annunciated each word. "Your mommy and daddy are at *my* house. We're having a *big* party and they asked me if I would come pick you and your brother up and bring you over there."

He held the doll up against the window again and moved it from side to side as though it was dancing. Carrie giggled and the man laughed. He then asked, "Do you think you could unlock the door for Josie and me?"

38

Maria Fannelli usually didn't bake cookies this time of night. On any other evening she would have been finishing the last drop of her chamomile tea, switching off the television, and making her way upstairs to prepare for bed.

But there would be an exception tonight. A very special exception. Her grandchildren were on their way over.

Her son had phoned ahead and told her to expect the children soon. Maria had no sooner hung up the phone before she began gliding from one corner of her kitchen to the other, snatching the necessary ingredients from both her cupboard and refrigerator. Her smile, the kind of smile only a grandmother awaiting the arrival of her grandchildren is capable of producing, never waned for an instant.

Once the cookies were in the oven, Maria returned to her den. She was too excited to sit, so she stood, waiting in front of her recliner—pink house-robe from neck to ankles, red fuzzy slippers on the feet, warm, welcoming blue slits beneath a pair of thick lenses, and shoulder-length white hair that was just slightly tangled and unkempt.

Ask five people to draw a lion and you'd get five different lions. Ask those same five to draw a grandmother and you'd get five Maria Fannellis.

Maria waited in front of that recliner, wringing her soft white hands together as though she had four winning lottery numbers, the impending knock on her front door the official announcement of the fifth and final.

When the knock arrived she found herself moving with a speed that surprised even her. She opened the front door and those blue slits behind the lenses stretched wide and that grandmother-smile took up half her face.

She bent forward and hugged her grandchildren with as much love and vigor as her body could muster. When she was finished she stood upright, smiled adoringly at her son, and gave him a hug of equal love and vigor.

Arty Fannelli hugged his mother back and said, "Hi, Ma. Are those *cookies* we smell?"

39

Arty drove the Volvo Station Wagon towards his mother's house. Carrie and Caleb were silent in the back seat, Caleb's eyes getting heavy, and Carrie over the moon, pre-occupied with Josie's return.

It was imperative that Arty call his mother before their arrival, but first he needed to touch base with Jim to ensure their prior arrangements were moving along as planned.

Arty flipped open his cell phone and dialed his brother's number. Jim answered on the first ring.

"What's up?"

"So far so good," Arty said.

"You call Mom yet?"

"Not yet. I wanted to get hold of you first—make sure things were moving along okay."

"Everything's fine here. I'm at Mom's now."

"You're there *now*?"

"Yeah, no worries though; she didn't hear anything. I've got them fixed up tight in the basement. Lights are all off. It's black as coal down here. We're good."

Arty lowered his voice and said, "Well you'll need to wait until I can get Mom and the kids into the family room before you try and move them upstairs."

"But you haven't called Mom yet," Jim said. "We don't have much of a plan B if she's having an *on* day do we?"

"I told you she'll be off. She was spacey when I was there earlier setting up the camera. She didn't even ask any questions when she saw me running wire through the floor. Kills me to say it, but she'll be off. She'll be off."

"Okay," Jim said. "But call her now."

"Fine. If there's a problem, I'll call you back. If not, then you know we're good to go and I'll send you a text to let you know when you can start moving them."

"Alright."

Arty snapped his phone shut and turned to the kids in back. His mouth was barely open when Carrie beat him to the punch.

"Where's Mr. Mitchell?" she asked.

Arty turned back towards the road. "He'll be there; don't you worry."

Carrie frowned. "I don't get it."

"You don't get what?"

"How will Mr. Mitchell get to the party?"

Arty smiled. "He's going to *drive* sweetheart. How else would he get there?"

"But this is *his* car."

Clever little bitch, Arty thought.

"I know it is, sweetheart. Mr. Mitchell is going to be getting a ride with *Mrs.* Mitchell. He's back there at the cabin now waiting for her to pick him up with a different car. Okay?"

"No—I still don't get it."

Oh how he wished he could tell the truth. To watch the expression on her little face when he told her that Mr. Mitchell was very dead. That his bald head was split open like a ripe melon. *Would you be as inquisitive then, you little shit? I don't think so.*

"I'll tell you what, honey," Arty began, "Why don't we let Mr. Mitchell *himself* explain it to you when we get to the party? How does that sound?"

Carrie didn't answer, and that was just fine with Arty. He treasured the silence for a moment before bringing up something crucial to the game. He spoke slow and concise like a schoolteacher.

"Hey, kids? You're going to be meeting my mother at the party tonight. She's a very friendly lady who loves to play silly games." He shot a quick smile over his shoulder. "Her favorite game is a goofy one where she teases and pretends to be everybody's *grandmother*. It's a game she loves to play, and she takes it *very seriously*. And you know what the best part is? If you play along I'm sure she'll bake up some *cookies* for us." Another quick smile over the shoulder. "How does that sound? You think you can play along? Because I can tell you right now; my mom makes some *pretty tasty* cookies."

"Will she pretend to be my Mommy and Daddy's grandmother too?" Carrie asked.

"Probably," Arty said. "She can be pretty silly sometimes."

Carrie laughed. "That's funny."

Arty grinned. "It *is* funny isn't it?" He flipped open his phone again, dialed, waited a tick, and then, "Hey, Ma! Guess what?"

40

Jim Fannelli was in the basement of his mother's house waiting for a text message from his brother Arty. The basement had a ground-level entrance via sliding glass door that Arty had left unlocked during his earlier visit when he was installing the camera. Jim used it to bring both Amy and Patrick Lambert through unobserved.

Husband and wife were both gagged, then bound at the wrists and ankles. The exertion of moving them (especially a man Patrick's size) annoyed Jim, and he was only too happy to drop them hard onto the basement floor like bags of laundry—Patrick first, and then Amy. When Amy hit, the heavy impact brought out a cry and a whimper. Patrick instantly growled and fought his binds.

Jim laughed. "They should be here soon, tiger," he said. "I just spoke to Arty a few minutes ago."

Patrick lay on his side to Jim's right, Amy flat on her back and to the left. Both bodies were vertical silhouettes on the floor as Jim didn't dare offer up any light for fear of alerting his mother to his presence so soon.

Amy tried screaming through her gag once, but this resulted in a resounding stomp to her solar plexus that curled her body into a breathless, agonizing ball. Patrick went berserk the instant the blow landed and flailed desperately against his binds. He received an equally debilitating blow in the form of a hefty boot to the head that all but knocked him unconscious.

"Jesus, you guys aren't making this easy on yourselves are you?" Jim said. "I mean all you have to do is lay here and shut the hell up and I'll leave you alone." He spit on the concrete floor. "I mean no one's gonna rescue you out here in Mayberry. We might as well be on another fucking planet."

He laughed as softly as he could before adding, "And don't think Arty and I don't know about your little buddy the sheriff. I'm sure it'll kill you to agree with me here, big guy, but you gotta admit he's a useless old fucker, isn't he? Couldn't catch cold wearing undies in a snowstorm." He paused, liking to think he was about to answer the questions they would have undoubtedly asked had they not been gagged.

"Yeah, he searched that cabin we were at," he said. "Did a bang up job too." He laughed again, a little louder now. He put a hand over his mouth for a few seconds to catch himself, eventually whispered, "At one point Arty and I were standing no more than three feet from him, I shit you not. The old fart was in the kitchen poking around, and we were pressed up against the opposite wall doing our best not to piss ourselves laughing.

"He didn't even check the bedroom where Arty hit a homerun with those old folks' heads. We were stressing about that—worrying that we might have missed something, ya know? Like a spot of blood or whatever. But the dumb fucker *didn't even check the room.*" He couldn't help it; Jim barked out a single laugh before instantly slapping a hand over his mouth and whispering, "*Shit.*"

Amy started to cry.

"Aw, don't start doing that, lover," Jim said. "We've got a long night ahead of us. I don't want you drying up on me…" He squatted next to her, wiped away the tears, guided his fingers down her body, stopping at the crotch of her sweats, grinned and added, "…In more ways than one."

The sexual innuendo resonated with Patrick instantly; he went berserk against his binds again.

"You're right, Patrick," Jim said, turning towards him. "God dammit, you're right. If she does start drying up on me I could just use a little something to keep the cylinders running smoothly, yeah? A nice lube job? With an average catch I usually just spit on my cock. But your wife?" He wheeled back around to Amy, patted her on the ass, then stood. "She'd get the good stuff. Maybe some of that expensive shit that gets all warm and tingly the faster you fuck…" He started pumping his hips back and forth, both hands miming a grip onto an imaginary ass in front. "Give us *both* a little pleasure, yeah? What do you say, lover?"

Patrick gargled something loud into his gag.

Jim froze his sexual mime in mid-thrust. Slowly turned towards Patrick. "Okay, that was a little *too* loud, Patrick. You're leaving me few options. I know you're pissed off—and I don't blame you one bit, tiger—but still, *way* too loud.

"So it seems like my only option is to just keep on beating you until you eventually shut up. But something tells me you're a pretty stubborn guy. So why don't I just say this, so we can put an immediate end to everything and have some peace and quiet. Here goes: if you don't shut the fuck up, *right now*, and *stay* shut the fuck up, I will be sure that your little angels—who are due to arrive here at any moment by the way—will experience fear and pain beyond anything you can possibly imagine."

Jim paused and licked his lips. "Do I make myself clear, stud?" He turned to Amy. "What about you, lover? Am I clear with you too?" He took a step back. "Am I clear with the *both* of you?"

The basement was still as dark as ever, and husband and wife were still silhouettes, but the shocked whites of their eyes managed to penetrate the gloom the instant their children were mentioned. Stone silence followed.

"Good," Jim said. "Good mommy. Good daddy."

41

The light shuffling of footsteps from above had been a constant the entire time Jim held the Lamberts captive in his mother's basement. When the smell of baked cookies floated their way down the basement stairs, Jim's heartfelt smile nearly gave way to tears.

"Bless her heart," he said after a strong sniff of chocolate and cookie dough. "Listen to her scurrying around up there. She's so excited."

And then the light shuffling above became hurried shuffling. The sound of a door opening. Muffled voices, enthusiastic in pitch. More footsteps, both heavy and light.

Jim looked at the ceiling, his eyes widening with excitement, mouth hanging open before curling upward into a smile. "You hear that?" he whispered, still looking at the ceiling. "Hundred to one they're here." He brought his attention back to the bound couple on the floor. "My brother and your kids are here."

42

Arty Fannelli, 27, and Jim Fannelli, 25, wanted to stand, not sit, when the neurologist came in to give them the diagnosis.

"Dementia?" Arty said. "You mean like Alzheimer's?"

The doctor, a tall middle-aged man with thinning blonde hair and small rimless glasses, held up a hand and shook his head. "No, no," he said. "Dementia is a rather generic definition, for lack of a better phrase. We ran a CAT scan and gave her several cognitive functioning tests. She *did* exhibit a few of the symptoms you had expressed concern about earlier, however I believe it's far too early to give a diagnosis of something specific like Alzheimer's."

"So what does that mean?" Jim asked. "Does that mean she can get better if she takes medication?"

The doctor took a deep breath. "Well…sort of. There are medications we can try that may help her condition, however I feel obligated to be very frank and honest with you here. Your mother is only sixty-three years old. That's a relatively young age to start showing the symptoms she's been exhibiting."

"Which means she'll get worse," Arty said.

The doctor looked at the floor for a moment before looking back up and saying, "Yes. But the point I am trying to get across is that because of the early onset—"

"It'll come on faster and be more severe," Arty said.

"Well, I wouldn't have necessarily put it so succinctly, however—"

"It's true though, right?" Arty asked. "I mean we're all men here, doc. You don't need to baby us." Arty's expression was ice.

The doctor's face reddened. He nodded quickly. "Of course...I...it's just that some people prefer more subtle ways of delivering this kind of information. You obviously prefer a more straightforward approach. "

"Yes."

The doctor nodded quickly again.

Jim and Arty exchanged looks. Jim looked on the verge of angry tears. Arty was still ice.

"I am assuming your father is no longer in the picture?" The doctor asked. His tone was like a feather.

"He passed away," Arty said.

The doctor tried on a look of professional sympathy. "I see."

"So what happens now?" Arty asked.

"Well, as I mentioned earlier, we should definitely try medication; but I would also consider looking into some sort of long-term-care community."

"A rest home?" Jim blurted.

"In a manner of speaking," the doctor replied. "A home where she can be watched and assisted as needed. At the moment she seems perfectly capable of performing most tasks, but there is a good chance her recollection of *time* and *place* will become distorted. She may also begin to struggle with remembering certain rudimentary domestic skills.

"Now keep in mind, this may happen soon, or it may not. It could be years from now before her symptoms progress to that point. But of course if they begin to develop sooner rather than later—which, as we just discussed, may be likely—it's nice to have peace of mind to know she's being looked after."

"*We're* going to look after her," Arty said.

Arty's tone made the doctor take a step back. "Great." He swallowed and cleared his throat. "That's even better. It's obvious you care very deeply for your mother. Having family look after a loved one is always—"

"We'll look after her until the day she dies."

The doctor took another step back, turned and hurried towards a stack of papers on the white counter-top. Without turning back around he said, "How about I write that prescription for you now?"

Maria Fannelli wanted to know what the doctor had said. The boys lied to her.

"That doctor is full of shit, Ma," Arty said. "He was going on and on about this and that, and none of it was making much sense. Right, Jim?"

Jim sat in the back seat of the car looking out the window, his mind somewhere else entirely.

"James?" Maria said.

Jim turned away from the window and looked at his mother. She stared at him from the passenger seat.

"Are you alright? Is Arthur telling me the truth?"

"Everything's fine, Mom." Jim spoke with no affect.

"There, you see?" Arty said, reaching out and rubbing his mother's knee. "Now, the doctor gave us a prescription for some medicine he wants you to try."

"Medicine for what?" Maria asked. "I thought you said he was full of s-h-i-t?"

"It's no big deal, Ma; it's just a precautionary thing. Jim and I will drop you at Alberta's house, and you two can chat for a little bit while we get your prescription filled. Okay? Sound good?"

Maria turned and looked at Jim again, then back towards Arty in the driver's seat. There was a look of uncertainty in her eyes. "Do you boys promise you're telling me everything?"

Arty looked in the rear view mirror without moving his head. He caught Jim's stare and the two shook hands with their eyes.

"Yes, Mom," Arty said. "We promise."

Jim began crying seconds after they'd dropped their mother off at Alberta's house. Arty reached his right arm over towards the passenger seat and rubbed his brother's shoulder. Jim punched the dashboard twice.

"Whoa, easy, bro," Arty said. "We'll get through this. I meant what I said in that office. We'll look after her until the day she dies."

Jim wiped his tears away and fell silent. He stared out the window, his eyes glazed, the passing view the visual equal of white noise.

"Hey," Arty said. "Hey, you still with me?"

"I'm here," Jim replied.

"What are you thinking?"

He said nothing.

"Jim?"

Still staring out the window he said, "I'm thinking someone else needs to hurt the way I hurt."

"Will that make you feel better?"

Jim turned away from the window and looked at his brother. He didn't have to say anything.

Arty nodded.

"But I want something different," Jim said. "I don't want any transients or whores."

Arty raised a brow. "Careful, Jim," he said. "Don't lose me."

"No one's losing anybody. Just drive for a bit, okay?"

Arty had done as his brother had asked and drove for a bit. They headed west on route 30, venturing further away from the city until they began entering the affluent strip of the Philadelphia suburbs.

"Jim, this is the Mainline," Arty said. "Rich assholes with a neighborhood watch for their neighborhood watch. We should turn around."

"Get off 30," Jim said. "Turn down one of these streets or something, I don't care."

Arty made a left off 30 at the next stoplight.

"Jim, it's the middle of the afternoon in fucking suburbia. If someone goes missing around here people *will* give a shit." He paused, studying his brother's profile to see if his words were having an effect. "If you want to do what I think you want to do, then we need to turn around and head back—"

"Stop," Jim said. He didn't shout the command, just spoke it aloud as though reading from a book.

Arty thought his brother was trying to shut him up. "*Stop?*"

"Stop the *car*."

Arty silently obeyed and slowed to a stop alongside a long strip of residential curb. Enormous houses with lawns big enough to host professional soccer games stood regally in the distance.

"Jim, what are you thinking?" Arty asked. "Tell me what you're thinking."

Jim looked past his brother and out the driver's side window. Arty followed his gaze. A young couple was walking ahead of them along the opposite side of the road. The answer was now clear.

Arty said nothing. Jim kicked open his door and ran across the street. The couple couldn't have been more than seventeen—high school kids walking hand in hand, treasuring summer love.

Jim punched the boy to the ground before the young man was even aware of what was going on. The girl screamed in horror but was instantly silenced by Arty who snuck up behind her and placed a hand over her mouth and an arm around her throat.

Jim was now mounted on top of the boy and punching into his face, shredding it with each sickening crack of bone on flesh. Arty looked on as he held the writhing girl in his arms, knowing a simple beating would not be enough for his brother—he would need much more.

Jim, as though homing in on his brother's intuition, exceeded the mere beating and jammed both thumbs deep into the teenager's eyes. The boy squealed in a pitch that was only matched by the girl being held by Arty.

"Jesus, Jim!" Arty laughed, his previous apprehension now gone as the violent contagion took hold of him, a common occurrence when his younger brother's hysteria grew to epic proportions.

Jim pushed off the young man's chest and leapt to his feet. He brought his foot high into the air and stomped down hard onto the blinded boy's face, knocking him unconscious. A second and third stomp deformed the boy's face and took most of his teeth out.

Jim looked up and grinned at Arty, his eyes wild, saliva dripping from his mouth—a pervert watching a porno.

The young girl in Arty's arms was in absolute hysterics. Jim approached her with wet thumbs and wiped the gore from her boyfriend's eyes onto her face.

"Time to go," Jim eventually said with a breathless calm, the porno now finished, his load shot, the ritual nap after calling his name. Arty nodded, spun the girl around, and head-butted her square in the face with the force of a bowling ball down a laundry chute. The girl dropped to the ground as though her legs had been cut from beneath her, and the two brothers ran to their car and drove back to the city to meet their mother.

43

"Of course they're cookies!" Maria Fannelli said. "I couldn't very well see my own grandchildren without filling their bellies full of cookies could I?"

Carrie looked up at Arty, a giggle close to breaking loose. Arty looked down and met the child's gaze. He winked, then out of the side of his mouth whispered, "*See what I mean?*"

Jim stared at his cell phone, willing it to beep. He wanted things to start so badly. He could hear Arty, his mother, and the two children above him, moving around and chattering back and forth, his mother's laughter echoing above all else. He wanted to be a part of it. Waiting and listening down in the dark was agonizing. Yes, it was a vital part of the game, and yes, the next time it would be Arty's turn to do the laborious bits behind the curtain while he got to work center stage, but those thoughts gave little comfort. Now was all that mattered. And right now he was anxious and annoyed.

Jim walked over to Patrick and kicked him hard in the center of the back. When Patrick grunted and Amy whimpered for her husband, Jim said, "Sorry. I was just seeing if you guys were still awake."

Once Arty was fairly confident his fictional brood had settled into the family room, he explained to his mother about the wound on his cheek (a silly accident he told her, nothing more), then took out his cell phone.

"Are you going to call Mommy and Daddy to see when they're coming back to the party?" Carrie asked.

Maria looked at her son, her confusion evident. Arty smiled and walked towards the sofa. Caleb was at Maria's feet munching on a cookie, and Arty ruffled his buzzed hair before leaning into the sofa, close enough to kiss his mother's ear. He whispered, "*It's a little game we play, Ma. She's just being silly.*"

Maria looked over at Carrie, then back at her son. Her face held the same look of innocence and wonder as Carrie's did, and Arty found it hard to stomach the ironic similarity between the two.

"Yes, honey," Arty said. "I'm giving them a call now." He looked at his mother and winked. Maria smiled and laughed. Caleb leaned his head all the way back into Maria's lap and asked her what was funny. She responded by leaning forward, kissing Caleb's forehead, and then offering up more cookies from the plate to her right. Caleb happily took another (the combo of more sugar and a four-year-old attention span kicking his query to the curb), and began to hum as he munched away, crumbs sprinkling the front of his shirt after each bite.

Jim's cell phone beeped and his heart jumped. He flipped the small device open, casting a tiny green light in the black basement. The message read:

in family room. move now. be quick n quiet

Jim snapped the phone shut and jammed it into his pocket. He squatted down next to Patrick and said, "Okay, big man, you're first."

Carrie looked disappointed when Arty returned to the family room with his cell phone shut in hand.

"Why didn't you let me talk to them?" she asked.

"They're going to be here shortly, honey. They said they'll talk to you then."

Carrie still looked displeased. Maria patted the spot next to her on the sofa and said, "Carrie, come on over here and sit next to me."

Carrie looked at Arty first: an uncertain look a child might give their parent before braving a swimming pool for the first time. Arty stood by the doorway of the family room; it gave him a reasonably clear view through the adjoining den and into the foyer that held the stairway. He was stood there for a reason, and Carrie's look of uncertainty threatened a journey towards him.

"Go on," he said as he nudged her over with a quick flick of his head. "Don't be rude."

Carrie took a big bite of her cookie then headed toward the sofa. Arty let go of the breath he was holding and smiled inside. Carrie flopped up onto the sofa seat causing Maria to bounce.

"Whoop!" Maria laughed. "Such a big girl my granddaughter is!" She wrapped her arm around Carrie, pulled her in and squeezed.

Carrie allowed the hug, but when she withdrew the little girl's expression made Arty hold his breath again.

"Why do you do that?" Carrie asked.

"Do what?"

Arty's voice was sharp and firm. "*Carrie.*"

Carrie ignored him. "Pretend to be my grandmother."

Maria's face was like a child's again. "*Pretend?*" she said.

Arty, who had no intention of leaving his post by the family room door anytime soon, risked a quick walk over to the sofa and bent forward so he was eye level with Carrie. His eyes held a threat, but hers returned no fear; they were stubborn and unblinking. She simply turned her head back to Maria (if she wasn't sitting on a sofa, Arty was *certain* the willful little brat would have turned her entire back to him) and continued.

"Yeah," she continued. "You like to pretend you're everyone's grandmother."

Maria put a hand to her chest. She then slid the hand upward, squeezing both lapels of her robe together, a habit of hers when she got confused, tightening up her armor to keep the bad out.

"I do?" she eventually asked. She looked at Arty with another expression he was all too familiar with:

Am I forgetting things again, Arthur?

Arty burned with rage. He wanted to break his own rules of the game and whack his palm across the side of Carrie's defiant little face. He wanted to grab the little girl by her ear and tell her what he and his brother had planned for her and her family later this evening. He wanted to tell her so badly his stomach cramped and his head throbbed.

And then his own voice, like a hand on his shoulder, counseled him—as it always did.

This is a big part of the game, Arty. You need to harness this feeling. Bottle it up for now. Uncork it on the little bitch at the appropriate time. This is one of your many gifts. What makes you and Jim so special. What separates you from the rest of the rabble: the pathetic fools with grandiose delusions of malevolent superiority, who ultimately fall flat because they lack the control to truly excel. And you do excel, Arty. If you could leash your rage with those hillbillies at the bar, you can certainly do it with a six-year-old child. All part of the game, Arty…all part of the game.

The red in Arty's skin drained away. His breathing steadied and the tight fist at his side slowly unclenched. He laughed hard and loud, and with a smile that was all teeth said, "She's *teasing* you, Mom! The little stinker is *always* doing this kind of thing."

Both Maria and Carrie stared at Arty, confused, but each for different reasons. Maria ultimately decided to shake off her confusion and return to giddy, albeit anxious, laughter. And to Arty's delight, Carrie had lost interest in the practice of grilling fake grandma; she was soon crunching on another cookie, her eyes apathetically fluttering all over the room's décor.

Confident the crisis had been thoroughly averted, Arty returned to his view by the family room door. Upon arrival, he immediately saw his brother Jim, carefully trudging up the stairs with the bound and gagged Patrick hoisted over his shoulder like a giant duffel bag. Arty became so excited he nearly pissed himself.

44

"I think I might need to use the little boy's room," Arty said to the group, patting his belly and making a bloated face. "Too many cookies."

Carrie said, "That's gross."

Maria said, "*Arthur.*"

And Caleb helped himself to another cookie.

"Well *excuse me*," Arty said with a silly face. He walked casually out of the family room, began walking faster through the den, then sprinted up the stairs like a child eager to wake his parents on Christmas morning.

"Glad you could join us," Jim said as Arty entered the room. "The three of us have been getting acquainted. I believe you know Patrick and Amy?"

Arty tipped an imaginary hat towards Patrick and spoke with a western drawl. "Sure do. Howdy, sir." And then towards Amy with a second tip of the imaginary hat. "Ma'am."

Jim said. "So what do you think? Are we good?"

Amy and Patrick were still gagged and bound, but now sat upright, tied to two wooden chairs pushed flat against the wall furthest from the door. The room was empty (recently emptied) save for a television atop a large metal stand placed directly in front of the captive couple. Behind the television a bundle of cords and wires snaked their way down the length of the stand and off to the side where they disappeared into a small hole through the wooden floor.

"Yeah, I think we're good for now," Arty said, then, motioning towards the television, "Can you guys see okay?"

Both Amy and Patrick did nothing. Arty stepped forward and slapped Patrick's face hard. Patrick's arms instantly jerked against the binds that held them to the arms of the chair.

"*Can you guys see okay?*" Arty repeated.

Patrick felt his wife's stare on him. Her protector was useless now. Could he look at her? What would his eyes say? I'm sorry? He felt bile in his throat and willed it away. The pain was beyond anything physical he had ever experienced or could imagine. But he knew he'd have to look at her eventually; he'd resisted since the moment they were thrust next to one another in the bedroom.

Patrick bit down hard on his gag and forced his head towards his wife. He looked at her feet first. Then her lap. Then her face. But still no eyes, he couldn't meet the eyes. His whole body quaked like a small seizure. When he finally did look into his wife's eyes, she instantly cried and so did he.

And Arty threw his head back, opened his mouth as though a laugh was imminent, but began clapping his hands instead. "Bravo. Fucking *bravo*," he said. "I mean this is what it's all about, isn't it?"

Jim nodded his approval, his grin matching his brother's. "I think they can see the TV just fine, bro. They're just being a bit overly dramatic with all the tears and stuff."

"I agree," Arty said. "Bunch of crybabies these two."

Patrick's head ripped towards Arty. The tears were still there, but now they burned his bulging eyes like acid. His skin was purple, his crazed breath machine-gunning out his nose, the nostrils big then small, big then small.

Arty pointed at Patrick and turned to his brother. "Look at the look he's giving me right now. What the hell is that all about you think?"

Jim shrugged and leaned against the wall. Arty turned back to Patrick.

"You're scaring me with that look," he said. Arty stepped forward and jammed his index finger into Patrick's eye. Patrick's head shot back before dropping towards his chest where he began shaking it vigorously from side to side.

Jim pushed himself off the wall with a wild look in his eye. "That shit *hurts* doesn't it?" he said. "The dirty fucker did the same thing to me the other day!"

Arty bent forward and kissed Patrick on the top of his head, began petting his hair like he would a dog's. "Okay, you know what? I'm sorry. You were just scaring me there for a minute." He gave Patrick's head a final stroke that finished with a gentle pat. "Why don't we watch some TV? You can use the other eye for now. Jim, you mind turning the television on?"

Jim did as he was told, and the black screen came to life. The image was from above and slightly angled, but it was a clear shot of the family room. Maria Fannelli sat with Caleb at her feet, and Carrie next to her on the sofa. The impact of seeing their children on camera caused both parents to cry out through their gags.

Both brothers ignored the muffled wails as though they never happened. Arty spoke over them with an even tone, like a teacher to a noisy classroom, refusing to resort to shouting in order to regain control.

"Our mother," Arty said. "And your kids of course."

Amy and Patrick both gaped at the screen. The silent movie showed their children entertaining the older woman, blissfully ignorant to the goings-on above their heads.

"Look how happy she is," Arty said. "She thinks they're her grandchildren."

The couple's heads turned simultaneously towards Arty, their confused frowns neon signs.

"The doctor called it *dementia*," Arty said. "It's not a specific diagnosis really— kind of like calling a flower a flower when it could be a rose or a tulip or something else I guess.

"We tried medicine but all it did was make her want to sleep. And when she'd wake up she'd forget where the hell she was half the time. It's weird too, this dementia. Unpredictable. She's got no problem remembering Jim and I, or shit she did when she was a kid, but recent stuff…" He made the motion of something spiraling down a drain. "There one second, and then…*pfft!* Gone."

Arty walked in front of the television and stopped, blocking the couple's view. "My brother and I love our mother. Deeply. And before you start running weird thoughts in your head, I can assure you there's no Norman Bates shit going on here. We had a father, and we loved him a great deal as well. They were wonderful parents; a blessing to any child."

Arty switched off the television and shuffled over to the opposite wall from where his brother was leaning. He took a seat on the wooden floor, his knees up, both arms resting on them.

"I'm an avid reader. Always have been. Being educated is unquestionably the single best weapon in one's arsenal." He paused. Waited for some reason. Then, "I read a lot about psychology. Especially the whole *nature versus nurture* thing when it comes to naughty people in the world.

"Some folks will tell you bad people are made through their environment. And then some folks will tell you it's a hereditary thing—bad people give birth to *more* bad people. Makes sense right? It's genetics; it's in the bloodline."

Arty paused, looked up at the ceiling for a moment. A wicked smile then slowly curled his lips, a light-bulb moment evident. He lowered his head, face alive with revelation. "Are you two *Three Stooges* fans?" he asked. "Jim and I are. Diehard. Absolutely *love* The Boys. We even like the Shemp episodes; Larry's character was much more developed in those, and Shemp definitely had some serious skills—his ability to improv was brilliant.

"But *Joe?* Don't even get me started. The pussy had some kind of clause in his contract stating that Moe was never allowed to slap him too hard." Arty pursed his lips, rolled his eyes. "And never mind what a whiny little bitch he was on screen. Guy held the distinction of watching legends like Moe and Larry all but impossible. I swear if the fucker wasn't already dead, Jim and I would find a way to pay him a visit."

Jim grunted in agreement.

"I'm getting carried away, aren't I?" he asked. "Okay. Anyway, there was an early short—one with Curly called 'Hoi Polloi.'" He thought for a second. "1935, right, Jim?"

Jim nodded.

"Yeah, it was done in 1935," Arty continued. "Over *seventy* years ago. You know what that means?" He chuckled. "Of course you don't; I haven't told you what the episode was about yet."

Jim chuckled too.

"You see in 'Hoi Polloi,' two rich guys are having an argument. One guy says that environment is the most crucial factor in social distinction. The other guy scoffs at him, claiming that heredity is far more relevant. They go back and forth for a bit until they finally decide to make a bet for ten grand."

"Environment Guy bets that he can take any man and turn him into a gentleman after three months of proper environment. Heredity Guy is hesitant to take the bet, because back then ten grand was a shit load of money, right?"

Arty looked at both Patrick and Amy as if they might actually answer him.

"So, Heredity Guy asks to make the bet for *three* men instead of one. You know, to make the bet a bit more fair. Environment Guy accepts, and of course we *know* who those three men are gonna be right?"

He looked at the couple again, a silly grin on his face, then back to the show in his head.

"So The Boys are exposed to all this fancy, ritzy crap for three months. They're learning to eat properly, speak properly, dance properly. Everything.

"The final scene is at this big dinner party with all these snooty rich folks. The Boys have to pass the final test by making their big debut into high-society; to prove they're changed men so Environment Guy can win his bet." Arty paused. "So what do you think happens?" A keen smile teased his face before finally erupting into a cheer.

"They blow it of course! They start breaking shit, slapping each other, just flat-out doing what they do best."

Both Arty and Jim were laughing now, hands periodically going to their mouths to keep the noise at bay. Arty continued.

"So Environment Guy admits he lost and hands Heredity Guy a check for ten grand, *but*...as soon as Environment Guy hands over the check to Heredity Guy, all hell breaks loose at the party. It seems The Boys made quite an impression on all the *proper* people in attendance. The boys' violence towards one another became contagious, and soon people are slapping faces, poking eyes, bonking heads, and loving every single second of it.

"The snobby pricks who were born into their perfect little environment only needed a whiff of violent behavior from The Boys for them to go completely ape-shit, and start *mimicking* that violent behavior by beating the hell out of each other. It's funny; its slapstick; but that final scene tends to shadow the *true* message that everyone seems to miss..."

A deliberate pause.

"There *was* no true winner! While the Stooges' heredity may have been too steeped in ignorance to be changed by environment, their primitive acts of carnage were enticing enough to make even the snootiest of dinner guests resort to naughty behavior! Who would have thought a fucking *Three Stooges* episode would carry such a message?"

Both Arty and Jim were laughing hard again, hands mashed over their mouths.

"And here we are now," Arty continued. "Seventy years later and there's *still* no definitive answer on the subject. One argument will hold true to the environment theory I just mentioned. That's *nurture*. Bad people are made from bad parenting; bad environment. Parents who fucked them, beat them, or just plain neglected them; sent them off to fend for themselves in a cruel world. And trust me, there's a shit load of studies to support those theories."

Arty took a deep breath, exhaled and continued.

"So just when it starts to make sense, and you're thinking, *Yeah, that seems pretty logical,* some other hotshot will come along and make a damn good case for the heredity factor. *Nature.* Serial Killer Stanley's father was a fucking whack-job, the father's father was a fucking whack-job, and *his* father's father was a fucking whack-job..." Arty spiraled both hands around as if trying to hurry up his own story.

"And even though Serial Killer Stanley may have been raised by good-old-loving mom—and whack-job dad was out of the picture from day one—the kid *still* has daddy's naughty genes, which explains why little Stanley used to like to torture animals and start fires when he was an aspiring psycho.

"And of course more case studies would follow to support this theory, making you go, 'Hmmmmm...that makes damn good sense too.'"

Arty then jumped to his feet, suddenly and remarkably excited.

"And when I stopped and took all of this in—the countless case studies; the countless theories; the fact that there *is* no definitive answer—and I digested it, it made me feel like my brother and I were so...special. We were something that actually *breaks* the rules of nature and nurture. *Exceptions* to the rules." He looked as if he might squeal before his next comment. "And there are *two* of us! Not *one* exception, but *two!* What are the odds? I mean really, what are the *fucking odds?* We had perfect parents and a perfect environment. Mom and Dad never beat us, or raped us, or neglected us. Hell, we were never even grounded. If anything, they were *too* nice."

Arty walked back to the wall he had leapt from and leaned against it. He scratched his head and cleared his throat before continuing.

"So we weren't *born* to bad people and we weren't *raised* by bad people. But *it* was there. *It* was always there. *It* was..." He stopped for a moment, took a sharp intake of breath, seemingly overwhelmed by his own admiration. He shook his head quickly. Regrouped.

"After Dad died our school shrink tried to analyze us. Find out why Jim and I were in denial about the whole thing. Why we refused to show emotion and mourn and weep and sniffle and sulk and blah-fucking-blah-blah.

"But I guess it was safe to say that it was after Dad's passing that we knew there was something different about us. We couldn't quite put our finger on it, but we sensed it. Sensed something remarkable. *Exceptions to the rules.*" He whispered the phrase now, as if it appreciated in value whenever spoken.

His posture then changed. He straightened up. "And Mom? Mom's our anchor. Our blessed anchor that keeps us from drifting into a place we could probably never come back from. Without her innocence and love to keep us grounded I couldn't even *begin* to imagine how far my brother and I could drift." He then frowned and instantly added, "Don't get me wrong; we *have* the discipline; we *have* the control. We've proved that countless times. But Mom…she just sews it up tight; makes it perfect…"

Arty trailed off again with that last word. There was a moment of silence where subtle sounds were loud. Sniffles from Amy's nose. Heavy, labored breathing from Patrick. The muffled, unmistakable voices from the children below.

Arty eventually blinked and came back. "We get no pleasure out of just killing. Hell, we didn't even want to kill that old couple you were hanging out with back at the lake. We just kind of… *had* to." He walked over to Amy. "You see this…" He wiped her tears with two fingers and gazed at the wet pads of his fingertips. "This is what we truly love." Arty stuck both fingers in his mouth and sucked gently. When he pulled them out he licked his lips and said, "And we've never regretted a single day in our lives."

45

Sam Fannelli cut the engine on the small fishing boat and used the oars to guide him and his two sons into the spot he was aiming for.

"What do you think, boys? This good?" Sam's thinning brow was already beaded with sweat as he put a hand up to shield the sun.

Arty and Jim looked out across the giant body of water that was Marsh Creek— smooth green water held together by a strong perimeter of trees and more trees.

"Will we be able to catch fish here?" Jim asked.

"I hope so," Sam replied. He stood, causing the boat to sway and both boys to grip the sides of the boat. "Should have brought a baseball cap," he said, bringing his hand over his eyes again before looking off in all directions. "Still, it looks like we've got a nice stretch to ourselves. I had a feeling it would be more peaceful on a weekday. You boys are lucky you've got such an awesome dad who takes a day off work to go fishing with his boys."

Arty rolled his eyes. Sam caught it and laughed at his son. "Oh, I see—fifth-graders are too cool to hang out with their old man?

How 'bout you Jimmy? Are third-graders too cool to go fishing with their dad?"

Jim shook his head no.

"Well one out of two ain't bad," Sam said. "Trust me, Arty. You're gonna enjoy this more than you do blowing things up on that Nintendo of yours."

"I'm having fun, Dad," Arty said without a smile.

"Good," Sam said. He was smiling enough for both of them. "I'll tell you what, why don't you boys crack yourselves a soda from the cooler, and I'll bait our hooks for us."

The boys were now shirtless save for the orange life jackets strapped to their torsos. The parts of their shoulders that were exposed had reddened considerably from the relentless sun.

Empty soda cans and potato chip packets were scattered about the wet wooden floor of the boat, and all three fishing rods were cast and left floating nibble-less for the past two hours.

"Should we go somewhere else, Dad?" Jim asked.

Sam propped his rod up along the edge of the boat and slid over to where his youngest son was sitting.

"We can if you like," he said. "But catching fish isn't really the point is it?"

Jim looked blankly at his father.

"Well the point is to spend time together. Father and sons. Male bonding stuff in the great outdoors and all that. Living in the city, we don't get to do this kind of stuff too often. I thought it would be a nice change of pace." He put his arm around Jim and squeezed, then turned and smiled at Arty.

Arty smiled back because it felt like the thing to do.

"I love you boys you know."

"We love you too, Dad."

Sam Fannelli then slapped both hands down onto his thighs and said, "Well! Having said that, I think we've been doing the 'great outdoors thing' long enough, don't you? What do you say we pack it in and head back to the city for a late lunch full of grease?"

Jim's eyes lit up. "Yeah."

"Sound good, Arty?" Sam asked.

"Yeah," Arty said.

Sam clapped his hands together. "Let's do it."

Jim bent to pull his fishing pole free from the wooden plank he'd nestled it under, but gave up after a few tugs and grunts.

"Stuck?" Sam asked.

Jim gave it one more useless tug then glanced at his father. "Yeah."

Sam removed his life jacket and got down on both knees to get a good look beneath the plank. "You got it jammed in here pretty good, pal," he said.

After a few jerks and grunts of his own, Sam managed to wrench the pole free from beneath the plank, nearly tumbling backwards from the effort. "Eureka," he breathed.

Sam got back to his feet and stretched his back before noticing his rod twitching at the opposite end of the boat. "Hey!" he yelled. "Hey, I think I've got one!"

Sam's enthusiasm launched him towards the rod before consideration for the boat's stability under his sudden shift in weight had a chance to register. Before he could even make an attempt to right himself, he'd plunged face first into the lake.

When Sam Fannelli gasped to the surface, the look of panic on his face was exceptional. He was a man who had been raised in the city his whole life. A man who had never had a single swimming lesson in all his forty-seven years.

And a man who had just recently removed his life jacket.

"Boys!" he coughed, spitting out green water. "Boys, *help me*!"

When Sam had fallen overboard his momentum had pushed the boat back several feet. In Sam's condition, it may as well have been a mile.

Both Jim and Arty were on their feet, balancing themselves on different sides of the boat. Their expressions were equal to that of their father—fear and panic.

Sam went under for a second then fought to surface again. Between sputtered gasps he cried, "*ARTHUR! THE OAR! THE OAR!!!*"

Arty spun, grabbed the long wooden oar along the edge of the boat's floor, whipped back around, looked at Jim…and then froze. His younger brother's expression was different now. It had gone from fear and panic to something else entirely.

And it only took Arty a few seconds to recognize that his younger brother was trying his absolute hardest not to laugh.

Arty, oar still firm in both hands, looked away from Jim and towards his drowning father. Sam Fannelli was bobbing up and down, choking wildly when he surfaced, eyes impossibly wide with fright.

Arty looked back at his brother again. Jim had succumbed to full-on laughter now, his father's dread a feather tickling his bare feet.

Arty didn't join his brother in laughter just yet. Instead he extended the oar out to his father, touched the top of his head with it, and pushed him under.

What the two brothers witnessed next caused them both to fall backwards into the boat where they laughed until their stomachs cramped and their cheeks ached.

It was the look of absolute horror on the face of a father who had suddenly realized that his two sons meant to drown him for their own amusement.

46

"Maybe it's time Carrie and Caleb met Uncle Jim?" Jim asked.

Arty looked at Amy and Patrick first, smiled, then faced his brother. "I think that's a great idea." He turned back to the couple and pushed the television stand a useless half-inch closer, clicked it back on, winked and said, "Want to make sure you guys have a great view. I contemplated giving you some popcorn but..." He pointed to their gags, their binds. "Probably wouldn't have worked out too well."

"Arty?" Jim called from the door.

"Patience, my brother. Patience."

The two brothers left the room, shutting the door softly behind them. When they arrived at the bottom of the stairs Arty took Jim by the arm and pulled him close. "Carrie, the little girl, can be a pain in the ass," he whispered. "She already made Mom doubt some things. Try and steer clear from her. Dote over the little boy more often if you can. He's a good kid. Quiet and harmless."

Jim nodded and Arty let go of his arm. The two brothers walked through the den and into the family room.

"Look who I found," Arty announced to the room, his mother in particular.

"James!" Maria cried. She nudged Caleb gently to one side and stood up to approach her son.

Jim hugged his mother hard and kissed her on the cheek. He held her by the face when he asked, "How you doing, Mom?"

She nodded fast, patting his shoulder with the same speed of her nods. "I'm good, I'm good. How are you, sweetheart?"

"I'm doing just fine, Mom."

Maria patted her son's shoulder again then returned to the sofa with Caleb back at her feet. "Oh this is so wonderful—everyone here like this. Sit, James, sit."

Jim went to take a seat, but was instantly questioned by Carrie before he had a chance to settle.

"Who are you?" she asked.

Jim glanced over at Arty. Arty returned the glance with raised eyebrows and a *See what I mean?* expression.

Maria's stint with earlier doubts had left her self-conscious, and she seemed to feign indifference to Carrie's question towards Jim. Arty spotted it all the same and took control. "This is Uncle Jim," he said.

"Where are Mommy and Daddy?" Carrie asked him again.

Her confident manner seemed to amuse Jim as he smirked at the little girl's grit. Still, he ignored her and followed his brother's advice by leaving his chair and stepping over to Caleb. He loomed down over the little boy at his mother's feet. "How's my big man doing?"

Caleb craned his neck as far back as it would go in order to take Jim in. His mouth hung open in a tiny O, cookie crumbs still flecked around the sides.

"Fine," he said softly.

"Fine? *Just* fine? You look better than fine to me, my man. You look strong enough to fly!"

Caleb continued staring, seemingly unsure whether he should be excited or completely freaked out.

"Have you ever flown before?" Jim asked.

Caleb shook his head, his mouth still dangling open, his eyes still looking through the top of his head.

"You *haven't*? Well what do you say we get going then, pilot Caleb?"

Jim bent over, scooped up Caleb, and swung him over one shoulder like a man carrying a log. Caleb's body was rigid, but Jim's enthusiasm seemed to pique the little boy's interest enough to keep him in the game a little longer before crying out.

"Okay, pilot Caleb," Jim began. "Hold your arms out straight like Superman."

Caleb did.

"Good. Now…" Jim grinned. "Are you ready?"

Caleb nodded hesitantly.

"Come on, pilot Caleb. I said, *are you ready?*"

Caleb nodded again, stronger this time, but still with a hint of doubt.

"Well then let's get ready for takeoff…"

"Be careful, James," Maria said.

"Here we go…3…2…1…*BLAST OFF!*"

Jim raced throughout the family room with Caleb over his shoulder, the man making wild airplane sounds that changed pitch every time they dipped, rose, and swooped around a corner.

Caleb's uncertainty became a thing of the past; the boy giggled wildly with each sudden spin and buzz throughout the room.

The occupants of the entire family room lit up as they watched Jim with Caleb. Maria looked on in absolute delight; Carrie was close to asking for a turn herself; and Arty wished more than anything that he could be upstairs to see the expression on Patrick and Amy's faces as they watched.

Patrick and Amy sat next to one another in their holding room, unable to take their eyes off the television. They watched in helpless horror as a psychopath raced around a room with their four-year-old son over his shoulder.

There was no sound on the television, but they could hear Jim's hooting and their son's faint giggles from below.

At one point Jim and Caleb went off camera, leaving the family room to go elsewhere. It was only seconds later before the couple realized that the sounds of the man and their child were becoming more distinct, and they were in fact, climbing the stairs towards the very room they were being held captive in.

They could hear Jim's heavy footsteps pounding up the wooden stairs towards them. They could hear their son's giggles rising. And before long, they could hear Jim's voice right outside the bedroom door.

"*What do you say, pilot Caleb? Should we venture inside?*"

The excruciating irony the couple felt just then was surreal:

They did not want their son to enter the room. Did not want him to see his Mommy and Daddy battered and helpless. Did not want him to see that they could not protect him, could not save him from the boogeyman.

And yet it was only the boogeyman *himself* who had the ability to make that wish come true. That realization was an explosive punch to the sternum that stole their breath and gave them no other option but to sit and hope for a madman to obey their deepest wish.

"No!" Caleb's little voice echoed, the sound of it making tears instantly pour from Amy's eyes. "*Downstairs! Go back downstairs!*"

"*You sure?*" Jim asked, and Patrick was certain the man was grinning fangs with fire-red eyes at the door when he spoke.

"*Yeah! Yeah!*"

"*Okay, pilot Caleb, you're the boss. Hold on!*"

The voices and thumps started to fade, and as they watched Jim and their son eventually reappear on the TV screen, husband and wife regretfully thanked the boogeyman.

They did another quick loop around the family room before Jim flew Caleb right up to his mother's bookshelf. Jim stuck Caleb's face close to a row of books. "There's a secret camera in the bookshelf, pilot Caleb! Wave to the secret camera! Wave to the secret camera, pilot Caleb!"

And there was a secret camera. A small, portable camera that Arty had installed deep into the shelf earlier that day.

Caleb couldn't see it. *Nobody* could see it. But it was there. And the little boy waved and smiled. Carrie jumped up onto the arm of the sofa, and, following her brother's lead, gave a hearty wave and a smile into the "secret camera" as well.

"Kisses!" Jim grinned. "Blow *kisses* into the camera!"

Carrie immediately did, blowing several of them, posing like a movie star. Caleb balked.

"Come on, pal," Jim said, "I'll do one first." Jim puckered up and brought his lips as close to the hidden lens as possible. Both kids then giggled as Jim added an exaggerated wink for the benefit of his audience above.

Caleb finally gave in and blew a kiss at the secret camera before giggling and turning away.

Upstairs, the silent movie Patrick and Amy were watching had turned the explosive punch to the sternum into a shotgun blast.

47

Maria Fannelli held a look of both contentment and fatigue. She had her boys and her grandchildren with her, but it was late.

"You getting sleepy, Ma?" Jim called to her, Caleb sitting on his lap in the big recliner.

"A little," she admitted. "I'm okay though." She reached over and stroked an equally tired-looking Carrie's hair.

"You *do* look tired, Ma," Arty said. He was leaning against the bookshelf that held the secret camera.

"Oh, but I'm not ready to go to sleep just yet," she said. "I don't get moments like this too often."

"I know you don't, Ma, but we did get a late start." Arty pointed at Carrie and Caleb. "And the kids are looking a bit sleepy too; it's past their bed time."

Caleb jumped in Jim's lap. "I'm not tired!"

Jim gave him a squeeze on the shoulder and said, "Good for you, champ."

Carrie's eyes drooped, yet still she asked the question that had been her theme throughout the night. "When are my Mommy and Daddy coming?"

Arty shook his head, smiled and said, "You are one insistent piece of work, kiddo." He walked to the sofa, squatted down so he was eye-level with her, and said, "Why don't we go find out what's keeping them?"

Carrie's droopy eyes lifted and she hopped off the sofa.

Arty held up a hand. "Give me a second first, kiddo. Why don't you play with Josie?"

Carrie turned towards the doll that had been lying beside her on the sofa. She picked it up and began whispering to it.

Arty went to an antique wooden desk in the far corner of the room and pulled a white iPod from one of its drawers.

"Mom?" he said. "Why don't you listen to your sounds for awhile? Jim and I are going to go do something with the kids for a bit."

Maria took the iPod from her son and gave the device a look of resentment. "Oh Arthur, I'll fall asleep."

"The sounds are good for you, Mom, you know that. Jim can get you one of your pills." Arty turned and looked at his brother. Jim immediately picked Caleb off his lap and went towards the kitchen.

"James, wait," she called.

Jim was already in the kitchen; there were sounds of cabinets opening and a glass of water being filled.

Maria sulked. "Arthur, I really don't want to go to sleep just yet."

Jim returned with a pill in one hand, a glass of water in the other. He played his part. "We won't let you sleep through the night, Mom. Promise."

Arty leaned in and kissed his mother's forehead. He then helped her out of the sofa and guided her towards the big recliner. "Just a little rest, that's all," he said.

Maria sat and Jim handed the pill and water to her. He too then leaned in and kissed his mother's forehead.

Maria placed the pill in her mouth and drank from the glass.

"Just for a little while, Ma," Arty said again.

"You won't leave before waking me?"

"No, of course not," Jim said.

Arty took the iPod out of his mother's lap and fiddled with a few buttons before handing it back to her. "I put the ocean sounds on. I know you like those."

"They remind me of when your father and I would visit Avalon," she said.

"I know they do, Ma."

She nestled the headphones into her ears, leaned back and closed her eyes.

"Good?" Arty asked. His tone was very loud—for a reason.

Maria opened her eyes and pulled one of the headphones from her ear. "Did you say something, Arthur?" she asked.

"No, Ma," Arty smiled. "Go back to your sounds. I love you."

Maria plugged the earphone back into her ear, blew a kiss at her two sons, and waved to the two children standing by the family room's entrance.

Both kids waved back—Caleb's sincere, Carrie's an impatient courtesy.

Maria smiled, leaned back in the recliner, and closed her eyes again.

Arty whispered to Jim, *"She won't hear a thing."*

Both brothers turned away from their mother and approached Carrie and Caleb. Arty squatted down in front of the kids and asked, "Okay—you ready to go see what Mommy and Daddy are up to?"

48

Patrick and Amy Lambert watched Arty and Jim attend to their mother on the TV. They watched them move her to the recliner. Watched them give her a pill and a glass of water. Watched them give her the iPod. And they watched her wave to their children before leaning back and drifting off to sleep. One might have surveyed the scene as two sons doting over their elderly mother.

Patrick and Amy saw two sick men showcasing ulterior motives.

When the two men and their children left the family room—and the TV screen—the sounds that followed for the couple were akin to the executioner loading his rifle.

Heavy footsteps climbing wooden stairs.

Tiny footsteps climbing wooden stairs—their babies' footsteps. Closer now...

The footsteps stopped. Shadows slid back and forth beneath the bedroom door. A sudden knock to the tune of "Shave and a Haircut" followed by a voice, deep and friendly. *"Anybody home?"*

49

Joanne Lynch, the school psychologist and guidance counselor at Hamilton Elementary, was young for her accomplishments at just over thirty, and was as passionate about her job as an artist to his craft.

Today she would be taking a shot at the Fannelli brothers. Three months ago their father died in a horrible boating accident in Downingtown, Pennsylvania. The reason Joanne Lynch was taking time after school hours to sit down and talk with these boys was because in the two months since they'd returned to Hamilton, the boys had exhibited no signs of children coping with the loss of a parent. No signs whatsoever.

This behavior concerned their teachers, and more notably, their mother. And it was only their mother's concern that made the brothers agree to stay after school and listen to what this woman had to say.

"Can I get you boys a soda or something?" Joanne Lynch asked once the brothers were seated.

The office was blatantly inviting. Posters were wallpaper, most inspirational, a few showcasing the current teen celebrities being worshipped worldwide. Shelves held books in addition to popular toys—Transformers, a Cabbage Patch Doll, stuffed animals, games—strategically placed for all to see. A bowl of *good* candy (Joanne Lynch knew what the kids currently liked) was on her desk. *This is not a dull place*, the room pleaded. *This is a cool place, kids—a place you can "chill" and "rap" with me whenever you want.*

In front of Joanne Lynch's desk were four cushy chairs positioned in a semicircle. Arty and Jim did not sit next to each other. They took a chair on each end of the half-circle so they could face one another. Arty had suggested this to Jim beforehand so that Jim could take cues from his older brother during the course of the session.

Jim looked at Arty as soon as the soda question was asked, and Arty shook his head with a subtlety that was invisible to anyone but Jim.

"No thank you," Jim said.

Joanne looked at Arty. "Arthur?"

"*Arty*," Arty said. Now, only one person on Earth was allowed to call him Arthur.

Joanne looked genuinely sorry. "I'm sorry. *Arty*. Would you like a soda?"

Arty shook his head slowly and said, "No thank you."

Joanne smiled and took a seat behind her desk. She started to dig with a delicate blade. "So how does it feel to be back in the swing of things now?" she asked.

Both boys mumbled affirmative replies.

"Are you doing well in your classes?"

More hollow affirmatives.

"Arty, you're the big man on campus now. A fifth grader. How are you liking it?"

"It's fine."

"Jim? How about you? You liking third grade?"

"Yeah."

Joanne looked down at her desk and rubbed the nape of her neck. She was chipping at granite with a toothpick.

"Okay, boys…" She raised her head, breathed in. Time for a different approach. "I'm sure you know that your mother asked me to speak to you. And, well…that's why we're here. Your mother, and myself for that matter, are a little concerned about your behavior as of late."

Arty frowned, and then Jim frowned.

"Were we bad?" Arty asked.

"No, *no*." Joanne's eyes widened, her hands waving in front of her. "My goodness no. You've both been fine. Please don't think you're in trouble here. In fact, the problem has been that you've been a little *too* fine…considering all you've been through."

The brothers gave the woman a blank stare.

"Boys, you suffered a very serious loss, yet you've exhibited no signs of anguish or grieving whatsoever. You're showing *classic* signs of denial and suppression—" Joanne quickly stopped, shook her head as though scolding herself, then repeated her words with more juvenile clarity. "What I mean is, you don't seem to be bothered by your father's death at all. Your mother and I think you might be holding it all in, and that maybe you're afraid to let it out."

Arty knew what to say. Even at the age of ten, he knew what this woman wanted to hear. He fed her. "I don't think we understand."

Joanne Lynch looked almost too eager to explain. "Well, you see, boys, it's not uncommon for people—children especially—to hold very sad memories deep down inside so they can go on with their lives. It's something called suppression."

She paused a moment. When Arty realized she was gauging a response, he feigned interest and nodded understandingly. Joanne continued.

"I think witnessing your father's death was so upsetting for you boys that you've almost pretended it never happened. You might even be thinking that your father may return someday."

Arty envisioned his dead father reappearing on their doorstep, soaking wet and asking his sons why they decided to drown him with a large wooden oar. He bit the inside of his cheek to keep from laughing.

A minute of silence followed. Joanne Lynch had said her bit and seemed content to wait in that silence, perhaps hoping that tears would soon follow—a sure indicator that she had not only scratched the surface of the Fannelli boys, but made a sizeable crack to boot.

Arty knew the next move. He shot a quick glance at Jim that carried flared nostrils and a clenched jaw. *Do as I'm about to do, Jim*, it read.

And Jim took the cue perfectly. As soon as Arty dropped his head into his hands and started to cry, Jim did exactly the same.

Joanne Lynch hurried from behind her desk and pulled both boys in for the hug. As each boy took a shoulder, pretending to sob, they periodically exchanged goofy faces behind the woman's back. Arty even pretended to squeeze Miss Lynch's butt.

When Joanne released her hold on the boys, they *did* have tears in their eyes, but the culprit was hardly suppressed feelings of loss.

When the sniffling died down, Joanne spoke first. "How are you boys feeling?" she asked.

Arty nodded and muttered, "Fine."

Jim did likewise.

"I think we might have had a real breakthrough here today," she said. "I would really like it if we could meet again. We can talk about anything you want. Anything at all. What do you say?"

Jim looked at Arty who said, "Okay."

"This meant a lot to me, boys. I hope it did to you too."

Arty and Jim walked slowly out of Miss Lynch's office, heads down. As their distance accumulated, so did their speed. When they rounded the corner and saw a clear path towards the boys' room they started to sprint, ultimately bursting through the bathroom door where they fell to their knees in hysterics.

They laughed at how "concerned" Miss Lynch was. They laughed at the mention of Dad ever returning (Arty shared the image he envisioned in the office and Jim nearly wet himself). And they damn near laughed their lungs out recalling how Arty pretended to grab Miss Lynch's ass.

But mostly, they laughed at the absolute absurdity of it all. Why aren't you sad boys? Why aren't you doing poorly in class, sulking up and down the hallways, being antisocial? How about this, lady: why do you give a shit? Because we sure don't.

The two boys were still snickering when they walked outside and into the school's parking lot. When they saw the gray Toyota pull up, any and all laughter stopped. Their anchor was here. The one whose unconditional love and purity had given them—and would continue to give for many years to come—the necessary social skills needed to behave…normally.

They didn't truly know it just then, but they sensed it. They sensed that their mother, their bedrock, would play that pivotal role in the development of their lives, and at that moment the love and devotion they felt for her was almost paralyzing.

Both boys climbed into the Toyota, kissed their mother a big hello, and told her how well things had gone. More than a little pleased, Maria Fannelli drove off thinking she had done some serious good for her beloved boys.

50

The bedroom door swung open. Arty entered first and pulled the TV cart to one side so that both parents were in plain sight.

A few things happened then as the two children entered the room:

Carrie looked at the condition of her parents and blinked a lot.

Caleb looked at his parents, and then immediately turned towards his older sister to gauge her reaction.

Arty and Jim stepped back and watched the scene with fervent anticipation.

Both Amy and Patrick looked at their children with desperate expressions that managed to transcend the comprehensible limitations of age, instantly resonating in both children with the explosion of a thousand nightmares.

Carrie burst forward towards her parents, Caleb close behind.

Jim and Arty shut the bedroom door behind them and began taking witness to the start of what they'd created. They witnessed the Lamberts struggle desperately against their binds in an attempt to hug their children. Witnessed the children sob and take turns hugging each restricted parent, their innocent faces wrought with fear.

And they witnessed it with a satisfaction few could ever know.

"Carrie?" Arty said. His gentle tone was a whisper among the hysterical cries. He called louder. "*Carrie?*"

The little girl was in her father's lap, her arms tight around his neck. She turned her head towards Arty but did not look at him.

"Can you do me a favor?" he asked. "Can you hop off your daddy for a minute so we can push him up against that wall over there?" He pointed to his left.

Carrie turned away from Arty and clung tighter to her father. Arty huffed in a deliberate manner, and stepped forward, grabbing Carrie under both arms and yanking her off her father. Carrie screamed and Patrick's face ballooned with rage.

"Honestly, Carrie," Arty said, still with the theatrics. "You really need to start pulling your weight around here."

The little girl flailed and screeched in Arty's arms as he handed her to Jim, who took hold of her in a tight embrace.

"Carrie?" Arty called again. "Carrie, please stop screaming."

Carrie continued to flail and holler. Arty sighed, then drove his fist into Patrick's face. Patrick grunted on impact, silencing Carrie like a switch. She stared at her father, and then at the man who had just hit him with a look of disbelief, as though Arty had just broken some kind of playground rule.

"How about that?" Arty said to Jim. "I think the kid gets it already." He turned back to Patrick. "Thank your daughter, bud. She just saved you a few more shots."

Arty gripped Patrick's chair, and with a solid jerk, spun him a quarter turn and pushed him all the way back against the wall.

He then glanced over at Caleb. The boy was curled into a ball on his mother's lap, his head tucked into her chest.

"How you doing over there, champ?" he asked.

The boy didn't budge.

Jim chuckled. "He looks like a fucking hedgehog doesn't he?"

Arty didn't respond to his brother. He was focused on Caleb. "*Hellooooo? Caaaaaaaleb?*"

The boy flinched upon hearing his name, but only burrowed harder into his mother's chest. Amy hollered until her eyes bulged. Her words were more decipherable through the gag now. Patrick's too. They had grown wet and thinner from the constant saliva and tears, and Amy's hateful words were gargled but clear. *"Leave hin aloe you huckin hastard!"*

Arty put a hand to his chest as though insulted. He looked over at Jim. "She thinks we mean to harm the lad." He returned to Amy and shook his head. "We're here to *entertain* the children, Amy. Not hurt. Never hurt."

Arty left the room. When he reappeared moments later he was carrying a green pillowcase filled with items that appeared heavy enough to stretch the material.

"Hey, Caleb," Arty said. "Look what *I've* got." Arty reached into the pillowcase and withdrew a flat rock the size of an egg. "What do you think? You think this is a good one? How many skips do you think I can get with this?"

Caleb's head popped up from his mother's chest and he looked at Arty with one eye. Arty stepped forward and held the rock in front of Caleb's face. Caleb jerked his head away as though the rock might bite him.

"He doesn't get it," Jim said from the corner.

Arty sighed. "I know. I guess *I'll* have to do the first one."

Arty tossed the rock gently into the air then caught it. He weighed it up and down in his palm, puckered his lips and frowned as if determining its value. "You know, I think this *is* a good one," he said.

Arty gripped the flat rock between his thumb and index finger, positioned his arm to the side. "Caleb, are you watching? Are you watching?" He smiled. "Because you're going next, champ."

Arty whipped the rock at Patrick, catching him square in the chest. There was a hollow thud on impact. Patrick's head dipped as he let out a strained gasp.

Jim laughed.

"How many skips did I get on that one, Jim?" Arty asked.

"I'd say about three good ones," he said. Jim looked down at Carrie and asked, "What do you think, sweetie? Is three about right?"

Carrie didn't respond. She wasn't ignoring him; she was in shock.

"What's *her* deal?" Arty asked.

Jim shrugged, still keeping a good grip on her. "Taking a personal moment I guess."

Arty nodded. "Fair enough. Her time will come." He spun. "*Caleb!*" The boy jumped. "Come on, buddy, I'm waiting on *you*."

Caleb began shaking, his whole body vibrating on his mother's torso. Amy's sobs of frustration changed to venomous snorts of spit and obscenities.

Arty walked calmly over to her and flicked her hard on the forehead. There was a *thock!* sound, and Amy winced from the blow. "Act like a lady," Arty said.

Patrick growled behind him and Jim laughed again.

Arty reached into the sack and grabbed a second rock. "I'm gonna do it without you, Caleb. Here I go…I'm going…I'm gonna do it without you…"

Caleb's reaction didn't change. Arty shook his head. He flung the second rock and cracked Patrick in the forehead this time, a flesh-colored egg appearing instantly. Caleb didn't see it, but screamed into his mother when he heard the smack of the rock on his father's skull.

Arty looked at the boy and shrugged innocently. "I thought you liked this shit, Caleb." He turned to Jim. "What gives?"

"They're just not getting it."

"No shit. I mean come on, little man, who would you rather have throwing these things, you or *me*?" Arty walked next to Patrick. "Because I can keep doing it if you want, but I think your old man might prefer less of an arm." Arty dug his thumb into the egg on Patrick's head. Amy cursed and hollered as Patrick groaned in pain.

Caleb stayed rooted to his mother. Arty threw up his hands. "He's never gonna get it."

"Maybe we need to change the rules a bit?" Jim asked.

"How's that?"

Jim threw Carrie into Arty. He caught her and felt her dead weight against him; there wasn't even the smallest attempt at a struggle.

It was now Jim's turn to leave the room. He returned with three knives—two in one hand, one in the other. Each knife was twelve inches long and sharp enough to shave with.

Jim handed the knives to Arty, and Arty handed Carrie back to Jim.

Arty held the knives up for all to see. "You want me to use *these*?" he asked.

"Sure beats a rock," Jim said.

Arty touched the point of the blade and pricked his index finger. A drop of blood grew on the tip. He watched the drop grow bigger until it dripped a red line down to his palm. He licked the red line up to the tip of his finger, sucked then smacked his lips on the wound and said, "Sure does."

51

The recent substitution to the game—the knives—caused a spastic uproar from Amy. Her garbled swearing increased despite her four-year-old son on her chest.

Patrick's reaction to the knives was different. It appeared a sort of heroic defiance, almost willing his captors to throw them; his chest was out and his head was upright.

Amy wanted to scold her husband's bravado. She understood his behavior (oh how she understood), but she feared it would only incite their antagonists. Or worse yet, make their sick game more enjoyable.

But she knew her husband. She knew he was a big teddy bear. But she also knew he had a breaking point. And that point had been broken a long fucking time ago. His rage was now bubbling beneath the lid, periodically hissing as it touched the burner beneath. She just prayed his wrath still clung to common sense. That dying with your boots on was not the goal now—salvation was.

"Alright," Arty said. "I'm gonna give this a try. Last chance, Caleb!"

No response.

"Fine."

Arty whistled the first knife towards Patrick. Amy watched right up until the last second before impact, shutting her eyes tight before the knife had a chance to find its home. She only opened them when she heard the knife pierce the drywall behind her husband.

He had missed.

"Shit," Arty said.

"It's alright, bro," Jim said. "You've got two more." Jim glanced at Amy, winked and said, "Don't worry; he's good at this. Could have been in the fucking circus."

Arty looked at the two knives in his hands, then at Caleb glued to Amy's chest. "I want the kid to watch this," he said.

Jim pushed Carrie into a corner and told her to sit. She did as she was told and fell into a catatonic slump, sucking her thumb and staring at nothing.

Jim then stepped forward and ripped Caleb from Amy's chest. Amy shrieked and fought so hard the chair fell over, her head and shoulder colliding hard with the wooden floor. The impact did not deter her tirade as she continued to scream and fight.

Both brothers laughed at the overturned chair as Jim hoisted Caleb up and into his arms. The boy was the opposite of Carrie's dead weight; he was a tightly wound ball trying to retreat into himself. Both he and his sister had shut down. It was as simple as that. Their young minds just couldn't process the horrific goings-on that were happening around them, and their only available coping mechanism was to switch off.

So when Jim felt the boy's rigid weight in his arms, turned and fixed on Carrie's blank stare in the corner, he fronted his brother and said, "These kids are going to be useless, man."

Arty was not so easily deterred. "Bullshit." He gripped knife number two in one hand, and peeled Caleb's head back from his brother's shoulder with the other, placing the blade directly in front of the boy's face. "You're going to *watch*, Caleb. You were too stupid to play, so now you're going to *watch*."

Arty spun and whipped knife number two at Patrick. The knife stuck deep within the drywall next to Patrick's head, missing again.

"Shit! I hit him *both fucking times* with the rocks!" Arty said.

"Relax," Jim said, hoisting Caleb up. "You're getting too wound up."

Amy was still turned over on her side, but she could see clearly. She knew that last knife would be thrown with serious intent, and she prayed with every drop of blood pulsating throughout her body that it too would miss. But what would follow after? The knives could easily be plucked from the wall for a second round, or...

Arty steadied his breathing, gripped the remaining knife's handle tight in his right hand, aimed it directly at Patrick's chest, threw it hard enough to rock his own balance.

And the knife buried itself deep into the drywall to Patrick's right.

Amy started to laugh. From her upturned, uncomfortable position, she laughed uncontrollably into her gag, and if her arms were free you can bet your sweet ass she would have pointed and mocked while doing so. Dying with one's boots on? Hadn't she been the one who silently hoped Patrick would abandon such bravado? So why was she laughing? Was she going crazy?

Both Jim and Arty exchanged looks. They looked truly dumbfounded for a moment. This wasn't right.

Jim set Caleb down, walked over to Amy, and yanked her chair upright.

Arty checked the television and saw their mother still asleep in the recliner. "Take her gag off," he said.

Jim shot his brother an uncertain glance. "Huh?"

"Do it."

Jim took off her gag and Amy instantly spat in his face.

"Yeah, that was a good idea," Jim said, wiping away the spit.

Arty went over to the green pillowcase and pulled something else from it. It was a bundle of thick lollipops fastened together with a rubber band.

"Looks like we're going to have to improvise again," he said. He pulled the rubber band off the bundle, unwrapped one of the lollipops, and jammed it into Amy's mouth. She gagged and tried to force it back out. Arty gripped her jaw and held her mouth shut, keeping the lollipop in.

Patrick grunted to the side of them but Jim just walked over and slapped him. "Shut up, stupid."

Arty unwrapped a second lollipop. "Grab her," he said, motioning towards Carrie with his chin.

Jim grabbed the girl and brought her over to Amy and Arty, her feet dragging across the floor as she was being pulled.

"Do you remember the candy, Carrie?" Arty asked, showing one of the lollipops to her. "Do you remember?"

Carrie turned away and down, looking at the floor.

"Do you remember when your mother told you that you weren't allowed to have any candy? Who ended up giving you some? Who was the nice guy who gave you the candy?"

Carrie's eyes were still on the floor. Jim gripped her face, squeezing her cheeks, bunching the soft flesh together. He guided her face up and towards Arty.

Arty gingerly placed the second lollipop into her little hand, squeezing it tight into a fist to imply that he insisted she keep hold of it.

"But look at Mommy now," Arty said. "*Mommy* is the one with the candy. Is that *fair?*"

Amy spat out the lollipop. It landed and stuck on the top of Arty's foot. She laughed again and said, "You didn't give her shit. You traded it for a *doll,* you faggot."

Patrick mumbled something behind them.

Arty closed his eyes and controlled his breathing. When he opened them he looked at Carrie. "Mommy's making this very difficult isn't she?"

Jim still had hold of Carrie's face; Arty still gripped the little fist that held the lollipop.

"Why don't we see if we can give your mommy *another* lollipop?" Arty asked. Despite his attempts at calm, his tone was becoming increasingly agitated. "How does that sound, Mommy? Does that sound fun to you?"

"Why don't you shove them up your ass instead?" Amy said.

Patrick grunted again. He was either asking his wife to stop antagonizing their tormentors, or cheering her on.

Arty closed his eyes again and breathed through his nose. He acted as though the comment had never been spoken. "It's a *game*, Carrie," he said. "A fun game where *everyone* wins. How does that sound?"

Carrie looked at Arty, her cheeks still bunched in Jim's grip. Arty gestured for his brother to release his grip. He did, and the little girl's face glowed red with the marks from Jim's fingers.

"Do it, Carrie," Arty said.

Carrie kept staring, her eyes unblinking, dazed. Amy went to speak, but Jim instantly slapped a hand over her mouth.

"Carrie...*do it*," Arty said.

Arty slowly let go of the little girl's fist, and Carrie dropped the lollipop to the floor.

Arty shook his head and immediately picked up the candy. He didn't bother to seize Carrie's hand again. Instead he jammed the lollipop into Amy's mouth himself.

Something snapped in Carrie and she started to cry again.

"Oh you want to try it now, do you?" Arty asked. "Too fucking late."

He unwrapped a third and jammed it in. Then a fourth. A fifth.

Amy gagged wildly, her cheeks bulging. Patrick threw an absolute fit behind them.

"Jesus!" Jim said. "Look at the *mouth* on her!" He turned to Patrick. "Hey, man, you wouldn't mind if I took your wife out of here for a little alone time, would you?"

Patrick's face was a deep purple in its fury, snot and spit spraying from his nose and mouth. He struggled so hard against his binds his chair bounced.

"Thanks, pal," Jim said. He patted Patrick on the head. "I promise I won't tear it up too bad."

Arty let out a long, wonderful breath. His faithful brother had revived the game.

Jim left the lollipops in Amy's mouth, but unfastened her from the chair. He re-tied her hands together in front, but left her legs as they were, wrapped in a tight bundle at the ankles. Amy's panic only made her gag harder on the candy still jutting from her mouth.

Jim reached forward, jerked her out of the chair by the hair, and hoisted her over his shoulder. Amy wriggled like mad, managing to spit two of the lollipops from her mouth. She hissed a wet, indecipherable curse and bucked harder, but Jim only held tighter; she was going nowhere.

Before leaving the bedroom Jim gave Amy a hard slap on the ass, looked over his shoulder at Patrick and said, "Don't wait up, stud."

52

The bedroom door across the hall was open a crack, so Jim Fannelli nudged it all the way open with the toe of his shoe, his hands preoccupied with the squirming Amy Lambert over his shoulder.

Once inside, Jim used the same foot—his heel this time—to shut the door behind him. He immediately threw Amy onto the only bed within the room's modest interior. The second she hit the mattress, Amy attempted to spring back up, but with both hands and feet bound she only managed to pitch herself *off* the bed and into a resounding face-plant on the carpet floor. The three remaining lollipops jabbed into the back of her throat on impact. She gagged hard, nearly vomiting.

"Whoops," Jim said.

Amy rolled onto her cheek and managed to spit out the remaining lollipops. She looked up in Jim's direction. "I'm gonna watch you die, you motherfucker. Do you hear me? I'm gonna watch you fucking die."

Jim made a sad face and began playing an imaginary violin. He then strolled over, snatched hold of her hair, and yanked Amy to her bound feet as though she was a piece of luggage.

Amy cried out in pain then instantly spat in Jim's face once upright. Jim closed his eyes and wiped the saliva off his cheek.

"That's twice you've done that now," he said. "I'm beginning to think you really don't want this—"

Amy spat on him again. Jim dropped his head, paused, then whacked Amy hard across the face, the impact of the blow shooting her backwards onto the bed in a dazed heap.

"You're making me feel like an abusive husband," he said. He made a stupid face, stuck his belly out, adjusted his groin, spoke in an ignorant drawl. "I dint wanna hafta do that shit to ya, darlin. But you done brought that shit on yaself."

"You're sick," Amy said.

Jim shrugged. "And?"

Arty heard the commotion from across the hall. Moments later, he heard Jim's palm cracking the side of Amy's face. When silence followed he looked at Patrick and said, "You think that shut her up?"

"Rough or gentle?" Jim asked.

Amy, fetal on the bed, said nothing.

"Is this gonna be rough or gentle?"

Still nothing.

"We can't wake my mother, Amy, so I'd appreciate an answer. Gentle and we can try the whole trust thing; rough and I have to gag you again."

Amy rolled onto her back, titled her chin in the air, and let loose an almighty scream. Jim pounced on her and slapped his hand over her mouth.

"I guess that means rough," he said.

Amy tried to buck him off but Jim clamped down harder onto her mouth, pushing her head deep into the mattress.

"And by rough I mean *painful,* Amy. I can get exceptionally creative when I want to." He took a deep breath to steady himself.

"So you have a choice: you can either lie back, shut your mouth, and enjoy it…or we can see how many of Arty's lollipops I can fit up your snatch."

"Well I guess that first whack *didn't* shut her up," Arty said. "She seems quiet now though. I wonder what they're up to."

Patrick's head was down and didn't move after Arty's comment.

"Are you fading on me, big man?" Arty asked.

Patrick gradually lifted his head and stared at Arty. His mask of rage was still evident, but there was a tint of fatigue to it now. If you coupled that with the abundance of wounds—the swollen eye, the egg on the forehead that had since turned purple, the cuts and bruises framing it all—then Patrick could have been a dead ringer for a prizefighter after twelve grueling rounds.

"You're looking a little weary." He got in Patrick's face and studied him. "Can't say I blame you though. It must be eating you up inside to think about your wife and my brother going at it in the other room."

Patrick mumbled something through his gag. Arty patted him on the head and said, "Good idea; I'll go check on them." He opened the bedroom door and stepped into the hallway, only to return a second later with a grin. "The door's shut. The door's shut and they're quiet. I guess she finally decided to play the game."

Patrick dropped his head again.

"At least *she* decided to join the game," Arty said, strolling to the far end of the room. "But your kids?" He huffed. "*Caleb? Carrie?* What do you have to say for yourselves?"

Arty looked down at the two children who were huddled together in a corner. Carrie's thumb was back in her mouth, and Caleb was curled into himself and no longer looking at his father. Both children were shells.

"Kids? Are you with me?" Arty asked. He turned back to Patrick. "I guess not. It's a shame too. We went through a lot of trouble planning this. I wanted to include *everybody*; not just you and Amy."

Arty headed back to the bedroom door and opened it for another look. The door across the hall was still closed.

"Don't be mad at Jim, Patrick," he said after shutting the bedroom door behind him. "He can't help who he is. I personally don't approve of his need to have most women we take. I feel it cheapens the game. But what are you gonna do? He's my brother and I love him." He then burst into a random cackle as though remembering a punch line to a recent joke. "He sure is a horny bugger though, isn't he? Like a rabbit on Viagra my brother is."

53

Amy had stopped fighting. She lay beneath Jim, his hand hovering over her mouth, ready to clamp back down in case she decided to scream again.

She had no such intentions. She now had a plan.

"I'm sorry," she whispered.

Jim appeared shocked. He even said, "What?"

"I'm sorry," Amy said again. "I'm very scared. I won't fight you anymore. Just please promise me you won't hurt my children or my husband."

Amy knew this attempt at bartering was futile given what she had seen from these men, but it helped support the idea that she was willing to be cooperative with her captor, let him think that her gumption had finally been stripped away, leaving nothing but a desperate naiveté. She needed to be careful though. If she appeared too desperate, too naïve, too willing…

"I promise," Jim said. He was wearing a smile that revealed his lie to such a degree it looked as if he wasn't even *trying* to humor her. She pushed her anger aside, remained focused.

"Can you sit up a bit please?" she asked. "I'm having trouble breathing with your full weight on me like this."

Jim didn't move. He studied her.

"*Please*," Amy said again. "I won't scream or run—just as long as you keep your promise."

Jim continued to study Amy. He squinted, cast her a sly, side-long glance. Then, with a quick burst, said, "Sure," and hopped off her, rolling onto his feet beside the bed.

"Thank you," she said. She sat up onto her knees and inched closer to Jim who had now relocated to the foot of the bed.

He watched her as she approached, a slight twitch to his manner as though perhaps she still had one good outburst left in her. But Amy was determined to portray the role of the passive hostage, willing to do whatever necessary to ensure the safety of her husband and children. She lowered her head and inched closer, the crown of her hair now touching Jim's chest. She stayed there for a few seconds, inhaled deep, the exhale choppy with fear, intentionally so. "Remember your promise."

She didn't look up, but could *feel* Jim's leer as he repeated his vow. She nodded into his chest and slowly lowered herself towards his navel.

With slow, calculated movements, Amy began working at the button on his jeans. Her wrists were still bound together, but this did little to impede her movements; she was managing fine, all things considered. She opened the button on his jeans. Paused. Performed the choppy breathing again before proceeding to the zipper. She made her hands tremor as she touched the metal. She prayed he was buying it. Prayed she looked like a terrified woman at her wits' end, resorting to sexual favors in order to save her family.

Not like a woman who was planning to bite her captor's dick off.

"What are you up to down there?" Jim asked.

Amy said nothing. She pinched the zipper's tip and started sliding it down.

"Ahhh..." Jim said. "Good girl."

With the zipper down, Amy attempted to grab both sides of Jim's jeans in order to pull them to his knees. The binds on her wrists prevented her from doing so.

"I think you might have to..." she said, her crown still in his chest, refusing to look at him.

"Help?" he said. "I'd be glad to help, lover."

Jim grabbed the edges of his jeans *and* cinched them downward. He wore no underwear and was already fully erect. The initial sight shocked Amy, despite her violent objective. Her choppy breathing was now equal parts act and real.

"You like?" he asked.

Amy said nothing. Her breathing was enough. Had she said yes it would have been too much. Too unbelievable for her to actually *like* what she saw. It would never sell. So she kept her head down, letting her calculated breaths become her words. He could have his pick. Were they breaths of desire, or breaths of fear? She knew his ego would choose desire. Scratch that. *Fear.* This man almost assuredly got off more to fear. And if Amy was to find even the tiniest morsel of joy in this situation, it would be that whatever fueled his sick desires was ultimately irrelevant. It would not stop her. Her objective was the same.

Let him think I'm afraid. Let him think I'm aroused. Let him think whatever the hell he wants. It doesn't matter. I'm biting that thing off and spitting it back in his fucking face.

She steadied herself, pulse hammering her chest. She lowered herself a few more inches. She was moving in for the kill. Her stomach churned, adrenaline teasing nerve-endings without remorse. Bile rose in her throat and she winced it down like cheap whiskey.

Here we go.

And then Jim spoke and she flinched, nearly crying out from being startled out of her zone.

"Wait," he said. "I want you to take your shirt off. I wanna see those titties you wouldn't show me in the supermarket."

Amy tried to swallow. Her dry throat refused. She coughed lightly to clear it. His penis was still hard, only a few inches from her mouth. Should she lunge for it? No. He would flinch at her sudden movement and pull away. She needed to ease into it. She needed to be the cat slinking along its belly towards its prey.

"I can't," she said, still looking at his penis, unable to look up. At this stage she feared her eyes would give away her intentions. "My hands are tied."

Jim stroked her hair, increasing the pressure with each glide of his hand. Before long he had removed the band on her ponytail, her hair falling around her face. He stroked some more, tucking it back behind her ears as if trying to give her profile to a camera in the room.

"We can manage, lover," he said. "Pull your shirt over your head and down your arms. You won't *need* your hands for what your about to do, will you?"

Amy sat up, trying to erase the doubts sprinting throughout her psyche. She needed to stay quiet and strike without warning. She needed to be the cat.

Still avoiding eye contact, Amy obeyed without thinking. Her shirt was off and resting along her forearms in one swift movement. Her breasts were out now, but still covered by a black bra.

"Nice," Jim said. "But you know the bra is gonna have to go too."

Amy made eye contact without intention. His question was preposterous. "What? I can't reach behind my back."

"Pull your straps down. Pull the whole thing down to your waist," he said.

Amy lowered her head again. She searched hard for the right response. "It'll look…*strange*," she said.

Jim reached out and pulled one of the straps down past her shoulder. "I don't think it will look strange, lover," he said. "And besides, I don't remember asking for your opinion." He tugged the second strap and let it snap back onto her skin.

Amy kept her head low and slowly removed the other strap with both hands. She paused there for a moment.

"Keep going," he said. "Pull it down to your waist."

She took a deep breath, her chest expanding, hating that the deep breath made her chest heave, assuredly exciting him further.

With both hands she gripped the center of her bra and inched it down to her stomach. She could not bring herself to look at her own breasts in this man's company. She closed her eyes and looked away.

Jim moaned lightly under his breath. "*Oh yeah…*" He briefly touched himself. "Nice and firm. I guess you never breastfed those two rug rats in there did you?" He aimed a thumb over his shoulder towards the bedroom door. "You know I read somewhere that if a mother doesn't breastfeed her kids, she loses that special bond between mother and child during those crucial developmental years. Is that true? Is there a bond lacking between you and Carrie? You and Caleb?"

Hearing her children's names made Amy's heart burn. She'd been desperately trying to put her family out of her mind during this most recent nightmare, and she would have bet anything that Jim knew this; that his speaking Carrie and Caleb's names as opposed to something like *your children* or *your kids* was intentional. It brought her anger back full-steam.

"I breastfed them," she said with an instantly regrettable defiance. She could feel the cold on her bare breasts and prayed her nipples were not hard for him. She did not look and see.

"Really?" Jim said. "Wow. I guess you've just got some winning genetics then, yeah?" He reached out with his index finger and circled the perimeter of her left nipple. Then her right.

Amy tried a swallow and her throat caught, forcing a cough. Her rage was the only thing keeping her from crying.

"Thanks," she whispered. It was barely audible.

Jim stopped his exploratory finger, brought his whole hand to her cheek, stroked it. "You're welcome," he said. His began caressing her hair again. Amy kept her profile to him. "Look at me," he said.

Amy didn't move.

"Turn and look at me."

Amy bit harder into her cheek and tasted the coppery hint of blood. She forced herself to turn and lock eyes with him.

He winked at her, leered, then established a quick, firm grip on the back of her scalp that made her gasp.

"Much better," he said. "Now...where were we?"

The pressure on her scalp was painful. She took her eyes off him immediately and attempted to lower her head back to his groin. He allowed her, but kept a strong hold on her hair.

Do I try and sell it again? Or are we past that? I need to say something. I need to hear my own voice...

"I think we were here," she said. Her voice was a weak, defeated offering—as she'd intended. She was inches from his penis for the second time.

He gripped her scalp harder. "Well then what the fuck are you waiting for?"

Amy swallowed dry again. She had no spit whatsoever. If she were with Patrick it would be difficult to do a decent job. But she didn't need to prolong this act. She didn't need to be concerned with performance. She would take him in her mouth for as long as necessary. Once the moment presented itself, she would chomp down with everything she had then jerk away violently like a wild animal. Hell, the dry mouth would even give her a better grip wouldn't it? Fuck yeah. Keep the damn thing from slipping out.

Amy knew the assault would not stop her attacker, but she was hoping (*praying*) the intense pain would buy her the precious seconds needed to hop off the bed, snatch the giant lamp on the dresser, and then bring it down onto Jim's skull, knocking the son of a bitch out. Maybe (*hopefully*) even killing him.

After that? After he was incapacitated? She had a plan. A damn good one.

Amy allowed the tip of his penis to touch her lips, her breathing coming in short, rapid bursts. She opened her mouth and allowed the first inch to enter. She didn't need to slide too far down onto his shaft. Biting the head off would do just fine.

She bit.

And her teeth clacked together, catching nothing. Jim had suddenly pulled out, his member unscathed. Still gripping her scalp, he ripped her face into his, their noses mashing. She saw lunacy in his eyes, smelled his sour breath as he started laughing.

"You think I'm fucking *stupid*?" he said. "You think I'm gonna let you bite my fucking dick off?" He gripped her hair harder, causing Amy to cry out. "You've got to be the most predictable bitch I've dealt with yet."

Amy's panic was electric. There was no plan B. Not even a sliver of one.

Jim stepped back and yanked Amy off the bed by her hair. She cried out again, moving with him willingly to relieve the pain on her scalp. Jim spun her around and pushed her up against the dresser, stomach impacting along the furniture's edge. With one hand still gripping her hair, he began to tear at her pants. Amy struggled but his strength overwhelmed her.

She was bent over now, her hands slamming down onto the dresser's counter, knocking over a small jewelry box and spilling its contents.

Jim's pants were still around his ankles, his manhood still erect and prepared to violate her.

Amy's pulse was off the charts, her chest and head pounding, each throb threatening a blackout. And then, as if handed to her by an invisible savior, her frantic hands fell upon a metal nail file that had spilled from the jewelry box.

She snatched it up and leaned forward, hoping her upper body would shield her find. She needed something else. She needed him to release the grip on her hair so she could spin around. She had no available target from where she was positioned. She needed to face him.

So she screamed. She screamed until her throat hurt. And it worked. Jim let go of her hair and slapped it over her mouth.

Amy didn't hesitate. She thrust her hips backward into his groin, doubling him over and knocking him back a step. She then spun, and with both hands gripping the metal file, drove all six inches of it deep into his scrotum.

The expression on Jim's face was that of a man who had jumped into a frigid pool. He froze, his breath gone. What followed was a pitiful groan of both excruciating pain and disbelief. Blood began to seep from the wound, and when Amy let go of her weapon, she saw that it remained stuck and standing to attention in a deliciously ironic similarity to his erection from only moments ago.

Jim backed up another step and looked down at his wounded groin. His hands shook as he went to touch the file. It looked as though he considered pulling it free, but fear of possibly making matters worse caused him to jerk his hands away.

Amy used both hands on the heavy lamp's neck, her adrenaline giving her the strength to lift it overhead with little effort. A forceful grunt that started in her abdomen matured into a ferocious battle cry as she brought the lamp down onto his skull, shattering the whole of its porcelain bulk on impact. Jim hit the floor hard—out cold.

Amy spit on him a fourth time.

The occupants in the bedroom across the hall heard Amy's scream. They heard Jim's low, guttural groan follow. Then another scream. The sound of something breaking.

It all made Arty smile. He thought his brother's groan was one of ecstasy. He thought Amy's screams were those of terror. He thought the sound of something breaking was Jim getting carried away like he usually did.

Moments later, when he heard his mother's cry for help coming from downstairs, and he took in the upsetting scene now being broadcast on the television, Arty realized he had it all wrong.

54

Amy was a whisper as she exited the bedroom, gently pulling the door shut behind her with the face of someone waiting for a balloon to pop; not a click or a clank could be afforded with Arty holding her family a mere few feet across the hall.

Her wrists and ankles still tied (there was nothing else in that jewelry box that could cut through her binds; and she certainly wasn't about to pull the nail file from Jim's bare balls, lest the pain wake him up), she shuffled softly past the closed door that held her family.

Upon reaching the stairs, Amy decided to do something she hadn't done since she was a child: she sat on that first step, then slid and thumped the rest of the way down on her butt. However, unlike a child, who would almost deliberately thump their butt as hard, and *loud*, as they could on each step, Amy's butt was fine china.

Arriving at the bottom, Amy hopped through the den and into the family room where Maria Fannelli lay in her recliner, asleep, the iPod's headphones still in her ears—still blocking out any and all noise.

Straight ahead, past the family room, was what Amy was hoping she'd find. It was the kitchen. And in that kitchen would be a knife. A knife she could use to cut her binds, and a knife she could use to make a life-threatening deal.

55

When Arty looked at the television and saw Amy holding a kitchen knife up to his mother's throat, his first thoughts were of his mother's safety.

Then of his brother Jim, and why he had allowed Amy to escape.

Then of a way to regain the upper hand.

56

Maria Fannelli's headphones were ripped from her ears, waking her instantly. She was seated in her recliner with someone standing behind her. Someone with one hand wrapped around her forehead and the other holding the blade of a kitchen knife against her neck.

To Maria's great surprise, the stranger was a woman. A woman had broken into her home and put a knife to her throat.

The stranger's demands were odd to Maria. The strange woman had first begun to yell at the ceiling for someone named Arthur to come downstairs. Now, the stranger insisted that *Maria* should be the one to yell—to yell for this Arthur to come and help.

"Call him," the stranger said as she pressed the blade hard against Maria's skin. "Call him and ask for help. Tell him you're scared and that you need his help."

Maria's voice caught. She coughed once, cleared it, and barely spoke above a whisper. "Help. I need help."

"Louder. Tell him you're scared."

Maria swallowed and her throat bounced against the blade. "Help! Help I'm scared!"

"*Louder!*" The stranger pressed the knife harder against Maria's soft skin.

"*Help! Help I'm scared! Please help!*"

Silence followed. The stranger was breathing heavy and seemed to be listening for sounds above them with great intent.

"*Arty, you fuck!*" the stranger yelled. "*I know you can see me! I'll cut her throat, I swear to God!*"

Maria wanted eye contact with the stranger behind her. Wanted to read her face, understand what was going on. She tried to turn her head. "Why—"

"Shut up," the stranger said, forcing Maria's head back around. "Shut up and I won't hurt you." The stranger paused and listened again. A brief shuffle of footsteps from above. "*ARTY, GODDAMNIT! GET THE FUCK DOWN HERE OR SHE'S DEAD!*"

And just as the stranger was about to repeat her threat, a man with dark hair and dark eyes appeared in the doorway, holding a gun to a little boy's head.

57

"Looks like we got ourselves a Mexican stand-off, yeah?" Arty said.

Amy did not expect this. She envisioned Arty sprinting down the stairs the second he looked at the television. She envisioned him helpless and begging for his mother's life. Instead it appeared as though he was able to keep his wits about him, present his own ace in the guise of her son.

"Let my family go and I won't kill her," Amy said.

Arty pressed the gun barrel of the six-shooter into Caleb's temple and cocked the trigger. "You kill her and I kill him."

Amy came close to dropping the knife. The sight of her son with a cocked and loaded gun to his head nearly caused her to lose her resolve. She wanted nothing more than to take Caleb into her arms and somehow whisk him far away from the nightmare.

"Mommy," Caleb said. His brown eyes were wide and glassy. Amy absorbed his fear and it all but drained her.

"Mommy's here, sweetie."

Arty's free hand released its grip on Caleb's shoulder. He patted the boy gently on the arm. "There, you see, Caleb? You've got nothing to worry about. Mommy's here. Now go on over to her." The little boy turned and looked up at Arty. "Go on," Arty insisted.

Caleb took a step toward his mother and Arty instantly snatched him back by the arm, causing the boy to stumble and fall at Arty's feet.

Arty laughed and pulled Caleb upright.

Caleb started to cry. Arty made an *awww* face at Amy, pretended to knuckle away a tear of his own.

Amy felt close to insanity. She wanted the man in front of her dead. No—she wanted him killed, and she wanted to be the one to do it. No apprehension, no struggle with morality. Dead. Killed. By her.

"You won't win," Amy said through clenched teeth. "I won't *let* you win. I swear on my very soul that my family will live through this and that you'll rot in hell."

Arty looked as if he hadn't heard her. "I saw what you did to Jim," he said. "It was upsetting. Upsetting, but I have to admit, a little exhilarating too. We've never had the game taken to this level before. I think it will be that much sweeter in the end, don't you?"

"It'll be sweet when you're dead."

Arty chuckled. "When I'm *dead*? What exactly were you planning to do? Kill everyone in the house? I thought you were just trying to make a deal here; trying to save your family."

Amy was flustered. It was her move, and she didn't know how to play it. She could only keep spitting threats and pray Arty would back down first. "Arty, I'm telling you one last time, and I am *not fucking kidding*, I will cut your mother's throat from ear to ear unless you let my family go."

Arty studied her. He did not appear concerned in the slightest. "Nah," he eventually said, waving a dismissive hand at her, "you won't do anything. It's not in you."

"I just stuck a nail file into your brother's ball sack. I think it's in me to cut an old lady's throat."

58

Patrick didn't know what was going on downstairs. What he *did* know was that Arty had left the room, taking Caleb with him, and that his brother Jim had not taken his place for a while now. That left him and Carrie alone.

"*Cawee,*" Patrick garbled through his gag. "*Cawee, helt Danny.*"

Carrie stayed curled into a ball in the corner of the room.

"*Cawee!*"

The little girl twitched and finally looked at her father. She blinked several times before focusing in on his face.

"*Cawee, helt Danny wit hi gag.*"

Carrie stood to her feet but remained in the corner.

"*Cawee, helt Danny wit hi gag!*" He prayed she understood him.

She walked towards her father and touched his knee. Patrick smiled with his eyes and said, "*Honey, helt Danny hake hi gag ott.*"

She reached up to his face and pulled at Patrick's gag. His daughter's hand on his cheek brought on an instant stream of tears. Less than an hour ago he was sure he would never experience her touch again.

"Good, honey, good," he said the second the gag was pulled down to his neck. "You need to do one more thing though, honey. Do you think you can do that? Can you do one more thing for Daddy?"

She nodded, her expression still projecting the glazed look of emptiness it previously held. This concerned Patrick, but wasn't something he could afford to ruminate over now. At least his daughter was *acting*, and at this point in time, her ability to take action, despite a lifeless demeanor, was most vital.

"Good, honey. Daddy's very proud of you so far." He then spoke slow and concise. "Now, what I want you to do next, is to take one of the knives out from the wall behind Daddy. Can you do that? Can you take one of the knives out of the wall?"

She nodded.

"Good girl. Do it now then, sweetie."

Carrie reached past her father's shoulder and clamped her little hand around the handle on one of the knives sticking out of the dry wall. She tugged once, twice, and then a third before the knife squeaked free causing her to stumble backwards, nearly falling over.

"That's my baby girl," Patrick said. He could feel his stomach swirling with adrenaline, his brow beginning to dampen; he expected Arty or Jim to appear at the door at any moment and pounce on his daughter. The thought terrified him and brought a quick and desperate tone to his voice. "Carrie, you need to cut Daddy free as quickly as possible. Do you see how Daddy's forearms are tied to the arms of the chair? All I need you to do is cut one of them free. I can do the rest once you cut one of them free. Can you do that? Can you cut one of Daddy's arms free?"

59

"So what are we gonna do here, Amy?" Arty asked. "Are you really prepared to commit *murder*? Here, in front of your son?"

"I'll do it."

"Oh I'm quite sure you could kill me or Jim..." He pointed at his mother. "But an innocent old woman like this?"

"If it hurts *you* I can."

"No you can't—you're trying to bluff. You had this all worked out in your head already, didn't you? You thought I'd see my mother with a knife to her throat and break down, give you whatever you wanted, right?" He pressed the gun barrel harder into Caleb's head, causing the boy to whimper louder. "But I'm not a fucking idiot, Amy. And I don't think the way you do. That's what makes me who I am. It's what has enabled me to survive as long as I have. That and the love of the woman you've got a knife pressed to.

"So, do you really think I'd let you bluff me into taking my freedom away while placing a knife to the throat of the most important person in my life? I won't let that happen, Amy. And I don't panic. Ever. That's why this little prick I'm holding here has a gun to his head. And it's also why I'm certain that I'd lose no sleep whatsoever after putting a bullet through his tiny skull."

Amy's chest hitched as she inhaled quickly, the image painted by Arty's words nearly crippling her.

"But you?" Arty continued. "Killing a sweet old lady? It's downright laughable. Someone like you would end up in therapy the rest of their life. Become an addict or a drunk. Maybe even off yourself once the grief sunk its claws in deep enough. How ironic would that last one be?" He grinned.

Amy's body shook, her eyes filmed with hot tears of rage and frustration. He was reading her inner dialogue near verbatim and filling her head with doubts. She tried desperately to shut them out, but the more he spoke the more his words dented the armor shielding her psyche. *Could* she kill an innocent woman? Maybe. *Would* it be something that affected the remainder of her life? Yes, of course it would. But then again, everything that's occurred these last couple of days would affect the rest of her life. Now was not the time for self-doubt. She had bluffed and it had failed. What lay in front of her now left no other options. Her baby's life was on the line. Her family's.

The self-doubt had to be crushed. Arty's words would need to be treated as fuel to her fire. She would, and *could*, go through with it if need be.

She repeated this mantra over and over in her head until it drowned out any negative thoughts that might cause her to balk. It was for her son. It was for her family. She would kill ten innocent women if it meant getting her family to safety. This innocent woman was an object. An obstacle. An obstacle that may have to be eliminated in order to save her son and family.

She repeated it again; she needed to objectify this woman's throat beneath her blade:

She is an obstacle. And I will eliminate that obstacle if it means saving my son and family.

And then again, tears of frustration drying up in the presence of her newfound defiance, her brow becoming furrowed with a purpose:

She is an obstacle. And I will eliminate that obstacle if it means saving my son and family.

"She's an obstacle," she said aloud. Her voice was solid. She didn't blink. "And I will eliminate that obstacle if it means saving my son and family."

Arty stared at her, his expression different now. Amy believed she had convinced him of her sincerity, of her will and inability to break. And just as he was about to retort with something Amy hoped was acquiescent, Maria Fannelli spoke:

"Young man, I'm not sure who you are, or what it is that you want, but if that little boy is this woman's child, then I urge you to put that gun away and release him to her before I call the police."

60

Every last bind had been cut and Patrick was now free. He stared intently at the scene unfolding on the television screen, then ripped one of the knives from the dry wall. His adrenaline was at a fever pitch. His legs and arms shook. He studied the big knife clenched tight in his fist. The rage he was feeling was unparalleled, and nothing short of ramming the knife deep into Arty's chest (repeatedly) would quench his thirst for vengeance.

"Carrie, you follow behind Daddy *quietly* okay? Be as quiet as you can but stay close to me. When we get downstairs I'll show you where to hide, but until we get down there I want you to *stay close* and be *quiet*. Can you do that?"

Carrie nodded.

"Good girl. Daddy's going to go get Mommy and Caleb and then we're going to go home."

"Are you going to hurt those bad men?"

Patrick glanced down warily at his daughter. She stared back up at him, the numb demeanor now gone, her eyes momentarily suppressing their innocence. Those eyes allowed Patrick to tell the truth.

"Yes."

Carrie's face became angry and righteous. "*Good,*" she said.

61

Arty looked at his mother in disbelief. "Mom, what's wrong?"

Maria Fannelli returned a bizarre look. "*Mom?* I don't have any children, young man. And I'll say it again: if that little boy is this woman's son, then—"

"Mom, stop it."

Maria frowned and snorted. "You can call me 'mom' all you like, but I can assure you; you're not my son, mister. I'm unable to *have* children."

Arty started breathing heavily. "Mom, you're having one of your spells. You're confused. It's me, Arthur. And I *am* your son. You have *two* sons actually. *James* and *Arthur.*"

"One of my spells?"

Arty felt his face grow hot. He looked at Amy, furious that she was witnessing this. His mother had gotten worse this past year, no question. But she had never forgotten Arty and Jim before. Never.

"Yes, Mom, you have spells; you forget things."

Maria shifted in her recliner, the knife still to her throat. "That's absurd. Where's Sam? I want to see my husband."

Arty looked at Amy again. Her expression was one of interest. She could have easily gloated at Arty's growing frustration over his mother's dementia, but instead she seemed more curious than anything. This angered him all the same. He did not want his mother's ailment to be the subject of her intrigue. He did not want her here at all. Arty could feel his uncanny ability to remain calm in the face of adversity waning.

"Sam—*my father*—is dead, Mom. He passed away a long time ago."

Maria went to sit up, but Amy pulled her back down and kept the knife tight to her throat. "Don't move," she said.

Maria tried to turn and make eye contact with Amy, but Amy would not allow it; she gripped the woman's shoulder and pressed it back into the recliner, pinning her.

"*What is happening?!*" Maria yelled. Her face came alive with panic. "*Where is my husband?! Who are you people?!*"

"Mom, stop it!"

"*I am not your mother! I don't have any children!*"

"Mom, you're confused! You're sick and you get confused!"

"*Where is Sam? I want my husband! SAM!!!*"

"Your husband is dead, Mom. He died over twenty years ago. You have a sickness that makes you forget thing—"

"*No!*"

"I'm your son. My name is Arthur, and I'm your son."

Maria Fannelli closed her eyes as if shutting out the world, refuting such wild claims.

"Mom, *please...*" Arty's voice finally cracked. His anchor had forgotten him.

"Tough break, Arthur," Amy said. "It sounds like she may need some medical attention..."

"*Mom...*"

"...and she's not going to get it like this. Now—you let my family go, and I'll let your mother go. After that, you can get her all the help she needs."

Arty hung his head. The gun arm fell to his side. His grip on Caleb's neck and shoulders, however, remained—a queer means of support perhaps.

His mother had forgotten him. In time her memory would likely return, but how soon until it happened again? And what if it *never* returned?

Amy had mocked him just now by calling him Arthur. She was enjoying this. She was reveling in his worst nightmare. This was not right. *He* was the one who gave the nightmares. He and Jim. Not her. Not anyone.

It was all coming apart. Jim was hurt badly, and his mother had forgotten him. His beloved anchor had told him she had no children. He couldn't bear it. His stomach burned. That bitch was mocking him, loving his nightmare. Something had to be done.

His mother would only get worse.

(*mocking him*)

She'll only get worse.

(*mocking his pain*)

Worse…

Arty lifted his head, his face stone. "She doesn't need medical attention," he said. "I'm going to take care of her just as I've always done." Arty raised the gun, pointed it at his mother's chest. "My mother will be with me until the day she dies."

He fired.

62

Patrick was on the very last step when he heard the gunshot. He flinched hard, and Carrie gripped his leg with the strength of a woman.

Patrick heard a second shot, and he flinched even harder.

"No," he whispered. "*Please, God, no.*"

63

The explosion echoed throughout the room. Caleb screamed. A mist of red popped from Maria's chest like a party favor.

Amy didn't realize she'd dropped the knife. She didn't even hear it clatter to the floor once it left her hands. The sound of the gun was so loud, and the scene before her so shocking, that her senses had been altered—time distortion giving everything a slow, dream-like quality. For a brief, comforting moment, she even embraced the notion that the scene in front of her *was* a dream, and that she was now close to waking, to shaking the mist of images until they were nothing but a stain on her memory, time her ally in removing the bulk of that stain.

She blinked; blinked again, and shook her head in tiny bursts. She wanted the images to disperse, for the mist to clear, for time to begin working on the stain. She wanted to wake next to Patrick in their bed back home. Wanted to tell Patrick about the horrible dream she'd had, and once that was done, she wanted to get out of bed and check on their children. Give each of them a silent kiss as they slept peacefully in their beds. She wanted to return to her room and slip back under the sheets and embrace her husband's warm body, maybe even make love in the middle of the night. She wanted it so badly. If only Arty's face would fade away. If only the strange house would dissolve to black, reappear as her giant ceiling fan in their bedroom back home, twirling and humming at a slow, hypnotic pace, its pleasant breeze caressing her face with security and comfort.

Time distortion had allowed Amy to entertain these thoughts in the span of seconds. But even time distortion could not ultimately blind her to certain truths.

Because Arty was not fading away.

The now-dead woman sitting in the recliner before her was not dissolving.

The house was not fading to black before reappearing as her ceiling fan with its comforting touch and reassuring hum.

The house was real; its contents and horrific goings-on therein real too, more so, if such a notion was possible.

Arty's voice was the final slap that brought her back, and the moment Amy returned, she knew her inevitable fate.

"I guess you lost your leverage," Arty said.

Amy took a step back from the recliner, held both hands up in front of her. "Wait, *wait*."

Arty shot Amy in the right side of her chest. She spun and dropped hard. Caleb screamed and cried out for his mother. Arty looked down at the boy, considered him, and finally said, "Aw hell, I'll do you a favor." He pointed the gun at Caleb's head.

64

The last thing Patrick could clearly remember was Arty pointing the gun at his son's head. Rage blurred what happened next.

Patrick dove at Arty with the impact of a train, Arty's body nearly folding in half as they were launched across the room, Patrick stuck to him in a savage embrace. The gun flew from Arty's grasp and slid to a halt beneath the family room's coffee table.

Patrick mounted Arty. A primal savagery took his tongue; obscenities were garbled sprays of spit and snot and fury as he rammed the blade into Arty's chest, piercing him just below the collarbone.

He brought the knife down a second and third time, each plunge more powerful than the last, each piercing Arty's chest plate, squeaking as the blade was wrenched from blood and bone.

Arty cried out, tried bucking Patrick off. It was futile. With wild eyes and a crazed delight, Patrick finally growled something coherent into Arty's face.

"You're going fucking nowhere."

Patrick stabbed again and again, short, frenzied hacks in the same spot. He changed rhythm and raised the knife overhead, ready to plunge it deep into Arty's neck, repeatedly if need be.

A sound stopped him.

It was a sound he knew well; the only sound in the world capable of penetrating the wrath that pounded the inner walls of his head. It was his wife's voice, and she was calling for help.

65

Amy was conscious. The pain along the right side of her chest was like a deep burn. It was excruciatingly acute at the bullet's entry, then radiated throughout the entire right side of her body. Her breathing was labored and her vision blurry, but she was still able to get to her feet using the back of the recliner as support. Once upright she spotted her son. He hadn't moved from where she'd last seen him. His eyes were impossibly wide and fixed on something to his right. Something else was different. Arty was no longer behind him. Where was Arty, and what was her son looking at?

Amy followed her son's gaze and she saw.

Patrick was free. He was free and mounted on top of Arty, driving a knife into their captor's chest repeatedly.

The sensation came back to her. The dreaming sensation. Was her husband really coming to her rescue?

She had to speak. It was the only way to break through her haze and establish some form of solidarity to the moment. If she called out, heard her own voice, and her husband responded, she would know it was real.

Her first attempt came out as a cough. Her second, a whisper. Her third was a weak shout that made Caleb turn but did nothing to penetrate Patrick's deaf rage. Her fourth shout was as loud as she could manage and it made her husband stop.

Patrick's head turned whip-quick in Amy's direction. His manner, the scene, Patrick appeared a ravenous animal startled from its meal. His good eye was huge and bulging. His mouth hung open in a deep pant like a wild dog's, chest heaving with each breath. His skin tone was pale, heightening the contrast of wet red that flecked his face and neck.

She had his full attention, but Amy called his name a fifth time in an attempt to bring her husband all the way back—she needed this savage to vanish, her lucid protector to emerge. She needed help. Amy could feel herself fading.

66

Patrick turned towards his wife. He knew she'd been shot, and he'd feared the worst. When he saw her upright and calling to him, his rage became something controlled by a switch—the animal was instantly gone, and he started sobbing with relief.

Patrick pushed off Arty's bloodied chest and jumped to his feet, Arty's limp body rocking beneath Patrick's weight before it settled motionless. Caleb was already attached to his mother's leg, weeping and refusing to let go. Carrie was still hiding.

"Oh God, baby," Patrick said, taking his wife into his arms. She cringed when he touched her and he instantly checked her wound. "How bad is it? Can you hold on?"

She nodded.

He smiled and coughed out another cry. He went to kiss her but stopped short. A frightening realization sunk deep into the pit of his belly. In his lust for vengeance, and now basking in the ecstasy of salvation, Patrick had overlooked a glaring truth.

Two.

One was dead, but there were two of them. Where was the other one? Where was Jim?

"The other one," he blurted. "Where's the other one?"

Amy looked as though she didn't understand.

"The other one, Amy! *Jim! Where's Jim?! Where's—*"

She gripped his arm tight. "It's okay, it's okay…" She moved her hand from his arm to his battered face, caressed it. "He's upstairs. He's hurt badly. Don't worry…it's okay."

Of course. Of *course* he was out of commission. How else would Amy have managed to come downstairs on her own?

Patrick wanted details. He wanted to know how she'd done it, and if Jim *was* truly incapacitated. But his wife's ragged breathing and crumpled posture buried those questions for a later date—

(*and there WILL be a later date, you motherfuckers,* he found himself thinking for a quick second, and with more than a little triumph)

—and forced him into action.

"Okay, good," he said. "Just hold on then, honey. I'm gonna get us to a hospital. Just hold on, okay?"

She nodded, hunched over, clutching her chest. Blood was seeping through her fingers. With her free hand, she rubbed Caleb's head at her waist then looked around the room.

"Where's Carrie?" she asked.

Patrick was bent over Arty's body, rifling through his pockets for car keys. He didn't look up when he answered his wife. "She's hiding. Carrie! It's safe now, honey! You can come out!"

Patrick resumed digging in Arty's pockets, but was coming up with nothing. "Shit! I can't find any keys."

Amy struggled for a breath and said, "Look around. They've got to be here somewhere."

Patrick gave up on Arty and stood. His head went in all directions around the family room, scanning tabletops and any other flat surface where one might throw their car keys. He saw nothing.

"I don't see anything," he said. "Jim. Maybe Jim has them."

Amy looked worried. "Don't leave me, Patrick."

"Honey, he might have the only set of keys. We need them to get out of here."

Amy shook her head. "Do you even know where *here* is? Do you even know where the nearest hospital is?"

She was right. In his haste, he had not thought things through clearly. He just wanted to distance his family from this place as quickly as possible. But his wife was right. Where the hell were they? And would they even know where to go once they left? They could not afford to drive around all night in Amy's condition.

"Call 911," Amy said. "They can trace the call for the address if need be."

She was right again. He cursed himself for not considering it sooner. Patrick rushed across the room and snatched up the cordless phone resting on a small oval table.

He started to punch the number nine and stopped. Carrie had appeared in the doorway of the family room. She was sobbing hysterically, but her tears meant nothing to Patrick—because his daughter's face was also wet with blood.

"*Carrie!*" he cried, dropping the phone to the floor, running to her. Patrick's was inches from his daughter when she was suddenly yanked out of view, disappearing from the doorway. A powerful arm took his daughter's place, and that arm drove a knife deep into Patrick's stomach.

Jim's entire body came into view. His face was the delirious mask of a clown—a man bent on brutal carnage without losing his comic zest for the atrocities.

Patrick thought he had been punched at first. When his stomach muscles started going into excruciating spasm, he realized something was very wrong. He looked down and saw the knife, buried up to the handle and sticking straight out of his lower abdomen.

"*Boo,*" Jim said. He ripped the knife out of Patrick's stomach and pulled back for a second stab. Except Patrick leapt forward into him, jamming Jim's movement before he could complete his thrust.

Jim struggled to push him away, but Patrick clung to him as if their clothes were sewn together, his eyes fixated on something protruding from Jim's face.

Patrick clamped his teeth down onto Jim's nose, jerked his head to one side, and bit the thing clean off.

Jim screamed, dropped the knife, and clutched his wounded face.

Patrick spat the nose on the floor, ducked down and scooped Jim up over his shoulder. Patrick spun, took a running start, then leapt into the air with his prey, the two landing on the family room floor with a brilliant boom.

Patrick immediately straddled Jim's chest and began hammering down punches. His wounded stomach cramped fiercely with the impact of each blow, but nothing short of a shotgun to the face was going to stop him.

Patrick continued hammering away like a piston, the sounds of knuckles cracking flesh and bone like a butcher pulverizing meat. Jim was close to unconsciousness and groping blindly at his assailant above him. And when Patrick finally stood, there was a brief second where an onlooker might have thought Patrick was showing mercy on his foe.

What he was doing, however, was trying to locate the coffee table, and the gun beneath it.

Patrick kicked over the coffee table, revealing the discarded six-shooter. Gritting his teeth from the pain in his gut, he bent and seized the gun, walked back over to Jim, dropped one knee onto his chest, rammed the gun barrel into his mouth, and pulled the trigger until the muffled explosions became empty clicks.

67

Patrick and Amy were admitted to The Western Pennsylvania Hospital in Pittsburgh, some twenty odd miles from Crescent Lake. The doctor had initially tried to separate them, but Patrick's glare changed his mind. They would be together, side by side as they healed, and never apart until they returned home.

Caleb and Carrie were already heading back to the Philadelphia area. Patrick's parents had received a call by one of the homicide detectives from the Allegheny County Police, and he explained the situation. The elder Lamberts were out the door the second the phone was put back on its receiver.

When the police had initially arrived at Maria Fannelli's house, Patrick was actually delighted to see his favorite sheriff walk through the front door. As the ambulance was busy attending to his family and the deceased, Patrick couldn't help slipping in a snide remark as the sheriff stood quietly in the corner while the Allegheny County detectives, who had been called in to assist a situation of this magnitude, surveyed the scene.

"You believe us now, asshole?" Patrick said.

Patrick was sure he saw one of the detectives smirk after his remark, and the sheriff just pulled his hat down over his brow, turned, and left without a word.

Both Patrick and Amy slept that first night in the hospital. They were heavily sedated after the doctor had attended to their wounds and neither one opened their eyes until well after noon the following day.

"Hi, baby," Patrick said. His head was turned on his pillow, looking at his wife lying in the bed to his left. She looked weary but even more beautiful than he ever thought possible. There she was, her hair matted, face pale, tired eyes circled in blue, and an large white dressing covering the wound on her chest—and Patrick was simply mesmerized by her beauty. His soul mate had almost been taken from him. But now they were safe. They were safe and they had triumphed. And Patrick's love for his wife became so suddenly intense it made his abdomen hurt. But in a good way. A good hurt.

Amy turned her head to the right. She smiled more with her eyes than she did her mouth. "Hi."

"How are you feeling?" he asked.

"Tired. You?"

"The same."

"You think the kids are okay?"

Patrick nodded. "My parents probably have them locked inside an impenetrable fortress right now, giving them whatever they want. You know how they are."

She said, "You think they'll *be* okay?"

Patrick shared his wife's worry and it showed on his face. "You mean in the long run…psychologically…"

Amy nodded against her pillow.

"Yeah. They're young. The memories will fade in time."

Amy looked at her husband in silence for a few seconds. Patrick wanted to think she was now experiencing the painful love and gratitude he was feeling. When she smiled with both her eyes and her mouth, he was sure of it.

"I love you so much, Patrick."

"I love you too, baby."

"You protected us just like you said you would."

Patrick shook his head against his own pillow. "It was all of us. We protected each other."

Amy rolled back to the center of the pillow and looked at the ceiling. After a brief pause she rolled back to her right and said, "Yeah, I guess we did. In a million years I never thought I'd be capable of sticking a nail file into a man's balls."

Patrick winced and hissed in a playful manner, cupping both hands over his groin. "Ouch," he said. "I gotta say that's pretty impressive, baby. As soon as we get home I'm getting rid of all the nail files in the house."

She giggled softly. "We can get rid of the files as long as you promise not to bite off my nose."

Now it was Patrick's turn to giggle. "Tasted like chicken."

Amy's eyes widened. "You didn't *swallow* it, did you?"

Patrick could not help a full-on laugh. The stitches on his stomach instantly complained and he put a hand on them. "No, no, I was just kidding—I didn't swallow the guy's nose."

"If Oscar was there you know *he* would have," she said.

They both laughed, both winced.

Patrick's smile faded. He said, "Poor little guy."

There was a long pause after that. Patrick looked at the ceiling, then to the wall to his right, then back to his left towards Amy. "Are we demonstrating some sort of defense mechanism right now you think?" he asked.

"What do you mean?"

"I mean, are we really laughing about the barbaric things we did?" The realization was there, but its impact seemed diluted. He didn't know why. "I killed two men."

Amy rolled back to the center of her pillow and looked at the ceiling again. She didn't roll back to face him when she replied, "Yeah, I guess we are…utilizing a defense mechanism. Maybe laughter after a traumatic episode like we experienced is normal. Part of the healing process."

"Yeah, maybe. Or maybe we just have sick senses of humor."

Amy broke her gaze from the white ceiling tiles and looked at her husband with one eye. "You're the one with the sick sense of humor."

"You love my sense of humor."

"You have your moments."

"That *had* to be an accident."

"What?"

"You really didn't just willingly give me the cue to sing Edwin McCain again did you?"

"I actually like that song," she said. "And you do realize that every time you sing it, you make it harder and harder to like, don't you?"

"It's too late now."

"You have no respect for the wounded."

"Here I go."

"Please don't."

Patrick started singing.

Amy bit down a smile and looked away. "Dork."

68

Amy felt eyes on her in the middle of the night. Jim was at the foot of her bed, naked and aroused and leering at her. She attempted a scream, tried to slink away from her sheets, but an invisible force held her down and stole her tongue.

She turned to her right, praying her husband was awake. He was dead. His eyes open and unblinking, the white sheet covering his body soaked through in red.

Jim laughed when she saw her husband's body. He laughed and then began to dance. His naked body hopped and twirled around the room, his skin giving off a pale glow in the dark room.

"*Help*," Amy attempted to say. "*Please help.*" The words were there, her desire impossibly strong, but her lips could not move.

She managed to raise a hand to her mouth where it flopped against her face as though belonging to someone else. She fumbled and tried to separate her lips, to pry her mouth open so her cries could escape. The dexterity of the foreign hand on her mouth was poor; for each finger that probed successfully there was another that hung limp and useless.

Jim's white body began to crawl up the bedroom wall directly in front of her, his arms and legs bent at odd angles and working in unison. He resembled a giant white crab scurrying up a dune in the moonlight.

Amy watched Jim's body scale the wall in front of her, then continue its trek to the ceiling where it hung overhead, a few feet from where she lay. Jim would stop every few inches and twist his head in impossible directions, never forgetting to lock eyes and grin at Amy before resuming his scuttle.

He was directly above her, the anatomy on his backside now strangely altered, taking on a smooth appearance, devoid of muscle tone and structure. Even the split in his ass had come together into a solid white. His body was that of a parasite's—the odd shape and deformities making this blatant to Amy within the bizarre truths of the dream world.

The parasite released its grip on the ceiling with its left hand and left foot, allowing the blood-red underside of its body to swing open like a door. From its neck down it was covered in an array of hungry erections, each one a thick pulsating blue, their heads small razor-toothed mouths dripping fluids as they opened and closed with desire, waiting to suck the essence from their host.

The parasite swung back towards the ceiling and re-attached itself, its backside to Amy once again. The head that still belonged to Jim rotated 180 degrees until it fixed on Amy. The wicked grin and glowing-yellow eyes encompassed the rest of his face, cartoon-like, an excessive caricature of the once-Jim Fannelli's features.

The mouth opened, still grinning, but spoke no words. It clicked and popped a foreign communiqué that Amy knew belonged to its race of parasite. She also knew that it was laughing at her as it got ready to drop from above and attach itself to her frozen body, the hungry erections ready to probe and fasten themselves to her skin while they fed.

Jim's head clicked a few more times, the body vibrating as it prepared to launch, and just as Amy found her voice, it dropped from the ceiling.

Amy's scream woke up Patrick and the medical staff who happened to be just outside the room's entrance. They rushed in and attended to her, wiping down her soaked brow.

Patrick was propped up in bed on both elbows as he looked helplessly to the medical staff assisting his wife.

"Just a bad dream," the nurse said, smiling at Patrick. "She'll be fine."

Patrick nodded and slowly lowered himself back down onto his bed. He listened to his wife's rapid breathing and the nurse's soothing words. His wife had weathered the first of many nightmares to come. Patrick closed his eyes, breathed in deep, and waited for his inevitable turn.

69

It was still dark outside when Patrick opened his eyes again. The steady hum of the hospital and all its gadgets therein provided a decent white noise that, in any other condition, would have sent him off to dreamland almost instantly. The stab wound on his stomach, however, was throbbing just enough to keep him awake.

He turned to his left and saw his wife rolled on her side, looking back at him.

"Hi, baby," he said. "Can't sleep either?"

"I've been in and out since that nightmare," she said.

"It was a bad one huh?"

She sighed. "Yeah. How 'bout you? You were moaning in your sleep just now."

"I was?"

"Yeah."

"My stomach hurts," he said. "Must've been that."

"I'll kiss it all better when we get home," she said.

He smiled. "It feels better already."

Amy rolled onto her back and looked at the ceiling. The sound of two nurses chatting started faint, grew loud, then went faint again as they walked past their door.

"You know what I don't get?" Patrick asked.

Amy turned her head back to her husband. "What?"

"Crescent Lake," he said.

"What about it?"

"That lake is square. It's not even remotely crescent-shaped."

Amy said, "You just realized that now?"

"Well, no, but…"

"Only my husband could have a menial epiphany like that at a time like this."

He smirked. "I guess we can figure out how the place got its name when we leave the hospital."

"Knock yourself out, honey. Me? I'm staying as far away from that fucking lake as possible." She rolled onto her back and closed her eyes. "Goodnight."

70

Patrick running through the woods. Someone is chasing him. He turns over his shoulder and sees a big man following close behind. The man is carrying a pitchfork in both hands and wearing a burlap sack with one eyehole over his head. A terror unlike anything Patrick has ever felt since childhood sweeps over him. He knows he cannot out-run his pursuer. He knows he will be caught. He knows that before he is killed the assailant will remove his hood and Patrick will see his face—the deformed face that haunted him throughout his childhood.

Patrick continues running anyway. In the distance, he sees an abandoned shed. He knows what's inside. Knows the victims of his pursuer are inside, mutilated and decomposing. He knows that no matter what he does, he will join them soon.

He enters the shed anyway. The shed is lit with random candles, casting a flickering glow on a scene littered with corpses. Some are freshly killed with wide, lifeless eyes staring back at him. Some are gray and rotted, riddled with bugs.

He slams the shed door shut and hoists two fresh kills up against it in an attempt at a barricade. He takes several steps back, waiting for his pursuer to try and enter. He scans the shed, looking for a weapon.

There is a bang at the door. The pursuer is trying to shove it open; the fresh kills are making it difficult, buying him precious time. Patrick spots a machete by one of the candles. It is next to the body of a man with no head. He knows it's a man by his clothes and the severed head inches from his torso. He was a fresh kill. The blood on the stump of the neck is wet. The eyes on the head are open and staring up at him. They start to blink when he grabs the machete. He cries out at the impossible absurdity of it, and they only blink faster.

Patrick turns to face the door. The banging has stopped. The man with the burlap sack and pitchfork is no longer at the door. He's somewhere though. He's close by— somewhere outside, looking for a way in. And he will get in. Patrick knows this. Knows it truer than anything.

His bowels are close to giving out; his bladder has already emptied. Patrick tightens his grip on the machete and takes another step back, away from the door. He steps on something. The tip of a boot. Someone is behind him.

Patrick spins and swings the machete. It slices into the man with the burlap sack's shoulder. The heavy blade becomes stuck in its new meaty home, Patrick losing his grip in a failed attempt to jerk it free. The solitary eye through the eyehole grows wide, a pained moan is heard. He's not dead. Because he can't die. And he's angry. Patrick's death will now be far, far worse.

The man with the burlap sack pulls the machete from his shoulder and drops it to the floor with a clatter. He is still holding the pitchfork.

It's time to die, Patrick thinks to himself. He is going kill me with that pitchfork and leave me here in this shed to rot. No one will ever find me.

But the man with the burlap sack doesn't kill Patrick. Instead, he removes his hood. Patrick sees his face and screams.

Now it was Amy's turn to look on with worry as the nurse rushed to her husband's side. His care was no different than what she'd received after her nightmare, but unlike Amy, Patrick's sheets needed changing.

Patrick stood and did not make eye contact with his wife as he walked to the bathroom. He closed the door behind him while the nurse stripped the bed. Amy was sure she heard her husband weeping behind the bathroom door. She started to cry too.

71

Homicide Detective Michael Henry waited a few days before talking to Amy and Patrick Lambert in detail. He'd taken brief statements from them the night they were brought to the hospital, however there were still things to discuss. He had questions, but most significantly, he had information.

"He's not dead?" Patrick asked.

Detective Henry shook his head. "Afraid not. He's currently being treated over in the east wing."

"He's in *this* hospital?" Amy blurted.

Henry nodded.

"Shouldn't he be in jail or something?" Amy asked.

"They've got to treat him first. Don't worry; we've got him under constant supervision. If he so much as sneezes, we're there to say 'God bless you.'"

Amy snorted. "Even God wouldn't waste His time on a psycho like that."

Detective Henry gave Amy a slight nod in agreement.

Patrick sat up in his bed. "What about the other one?"

"James Fannelli?" Henry asked.

"Yeah."

"Very dead."

"Good," Amy said. She reached behind her head and folded her pillow in half to prop her head higher. "What else?"

Henry pulled at his tie. He felt sweat on the back of his neck. "Your friends…"

"Lorraine and Norm?" Patrick said.

Henry lowered his head. Amy started to cry.

"Yeah, we kind of knew already," Patrick said. "Arty he…basically told us what they'd done."

"I'm sorry," Henry said. He let a moment of silence go by before continuing. "The mother is still alive," he said. "She's being treated here as well."

Patrick turned to his left, exchanged looks with his wife. She was wiping tears from both eyes. "What's her condition?" Patrick asked.

"She's stable, but she's been pretty out of it since she's been here. Came to for a short while, but just babbled a lot of nonsense. Her records show she suffers from dementia."

"Yeah, we know," Patrick said. "We got the whole inside scoop from the psychos themselves."

Henry gave a sympathetic smile. "Right; you mentioned it in your initial statement."

Patrick nodded with a slow blink.

Henry looked over his notes again. He flipped a page and ran his index finger down the paper, muttering to himself as he skimmed each line.

"What's going to happen to her?" Patrick asked.

Henry glanced up from his notes. He appeared startled out of thought. "Who?"

"The mother. What's going to happen to the mother?"

Henry lowered the notes to his side. "I imagine she'll be here a bit longer."

"We mean when she gets better," Amy said. "What will happen to hear when she heals?"

Detective Henry shrugged. "With her condition—and I'm talking about the dementia, not the gunshot wound—there's no way to be sure. You said in your statement that she had no recollection of being a mother, and she was calling for her deceased husband the night she was shot by her son."

"That's right," Amy said.

"Well then my guess would be that things for her will only get worse. Without her sons around to look in on her she won't be trusted to live on her own. She'll likely be committed to a rest home of sorts."

Patrick frowned and shook his head. "Poor ignorant woman. Maybe it's for the best she loses her memory after all. I mean, I'm sure the last thing she'd want to remember is giving birth to two fucking psychopaths that could shoot their own mother."

Henry fingered his notes again. He kept his head down as he read. "Her attending physician here was able to gain access to her medical history from a previous doctor in Philadelphia. According to those records…"

When Detective Henry had finished talking, Patrick and Amy asked him for a favor. At first he rejected their request, stating that it was unorthodox and unnecessary. The couple pleaded their case, running through the events of that final night in grizzly detail. Henry had looked away halfway through their plea. The Lamberts continued to talk, to outline the just cause of their favor; how it would bring closure to a nightmare that may never *have* closure.

When Henry turned back around and faced the couple, his face was red. Whether it was red with anger at the ordeal this poor family had endured, or red from frustration at the Lamberts' inability to take no for an answer, the couple hardly cared. The only thing they did care about was when detective Henry broke down and said, "Okay."

72

Amy and Patrick followed Detective Henry down the hospital's corridor towards the east wing. They held hands along the way, moving slowly, grimacing from time to time from the pain their wounds were causing them for moving around sooner than they should be. This was worth it though.

Henry glanced over his shoulder at the couple as they hobbled along, still in their hospital gowns, looking as if sleep had completely eluded them these past few days. "You sure you're up for this?" Henry asked, slowing his pace for them.

"Wouldn't miss it for the world," Patrick replied.

"Same here," Amy said.

Henry shrugged. "Okay—shouldn't be much further now."

The couple followed Henry around a corner as they approached the east wing. Ahead of them, a police officer sat outside one of the rooms, reading a magazine.

Henry nodded to the officer in the chair. The officer looked at Henry, then at the Lamberts, then back at Henry.

"It's okay," Henry said. "I'll take full responsibility."

The officer looked at the Lamberts one last time, smiled an obligatory smile, then lifted his magazine and resumed reading.

Henry placed his hand on the door's handle and looked over his shoulder. He made solid eye contact with both Amy and Patrick. "I'm trusting you on this. If you've got something else in mind…"

They both shook their heads at exactly the same time. "We gave you our word," Amy said.

Detective Henry gave one hard nod then turned back around and opened the door.

73

Arty Fannelli turned to the male officer sitting to the left of his hospital bed. "Are you *ever* going to be replaced by a female officer?" he asked.

The officer didn't look up from his *Sports Illustrated* when he replied, "Sorry, dickhead, you're stuck with me."

"Dickhead? Are you allowed to talk to me like that?"

The officer turned the page and continued reading. "Yup."

Arty pulled at his handcuff strapped to the bed's frame. "Are these really necessary? I've been here a few days now; I think you can trust me."

The officer frowned at something in the magazine, muttered, "*Overpaid prima donnas...*"

"Hello? Are you listening? I was stabbed eight hundred times for Christ's sake. Where the hell am I going to go?"

There was a knock at the door. The officer stood and threw the magazine onto his seat. Detective Henry walked into the room.

"Hey, you know he called me a dickhead?" Arty said to Henry.

"You are a dickhead," Henry said.

Arty laughed. "So what's up, Mikey? You stopping by to ask a few more questions?"

"Not exactly," Henry said. He walked over towards the officer on duty and stood by his side.

Arty said, "Well what is it then? You finally pulling Chuckles here off-duty? If so, can I put a request in for something with a bit more curves? No offense, Chuckles."

"Why would I do that?" Henry asked. "It's probably in your best interest to start getting used to men."

Arty smiled. "You *really* think I'm gonna serve any time, Mikey?"

Henry raised an eyebrow. "You don't?"

"Of course not. An anomaly like myself?"

Henry smirked. "*Anomaly?*"

"Oh I'm sorry, Mikey, am I talking over your head? I'll try and put it in layman's terms." Arty cleared his throat, loving it. "You see there are thousands of headshrinkers out there who will want to know why my brother and I did the things we did. They'll want to know why all their stupid little theories about evil and human be-havior were ultimately fed to them in one giant shit-burger.

"They'll keep me in cushy hospitals and kiss my ass in order to find out what makes me tick, and, more importantly..." He flashed a pornographic leer. "What *excites* me.

"Hell, there'll probably even be a fucking *waiting list* to come see me. Every budding shrink with a hard-on for stardom will be desperately trying to solve the riddle of the infamous Fannelli broth-ers so they can write the next bestseller.

"Was it nature? Was it nurture? *What?* It was *neither?* Holy shit! This truly *is* great! We can't send him to prison! We need to *study* him! Take CAT scans of his brain, find out how he's wired, ask him endless questions written by so-called experts who circle jerk to Freud. We need to find out what makes this guy so *unique*.

"I mean come on, fellas. I'm the kind of guy *movies* are written about, for Christ's sake. The kind of real-life boogeyman screenwrit-ers salivate over. How often do you come across someone composed of pure, unfiltered malevolence?"

Arty paused, a smile on the corner of his mouth. He remained fixed on the two officers, gauging the impact of his words. He never noticed the two visitors who had entered quietly to his right.

"And this will go on for as long as I want it to," Arty continued. "I'll give them a taste..." He held up his thumb and index finger as though pinching a bug. "A teensy- weensy taste. And then when the time is right, I'll give them a little more. And then a little more after that. I've got the tools and the smarts to keep the game going for a *very* long time. You see, Mikey and Chuckles, even when I'm confined I can orchestrate a game to amuse myself.

"So please, don't even—for one second—try some of your spooky cop talk in an attempt to scare me about the horrors of prison...because I'm not going there. Somebody of my stature belongs under a microscope; not behind bars. And we live in a sick enough society with a fucked-up-enough legal system to make it happen. And we both know that, don't we?"

Someone cleared their throat to Arty's right. He turned his head. Amy and Patrick were standing side by side, a big smile on both their faces.

"What the hell are *you two* smiling at?"

74

"Officer, would you mind giving us a minute here?" Henry said. "Go grab a soda or a coffee or something."

The officer shrugged, and then nodded to both Amy and Patrick on his way out.

Arty shifted in his bed and pulled at his cuffs again, metal on metal clinking. "What the fuck do you want?"

Patrick said, "Just wanted to touch base."

"*Touch base?*" He looked at Henry. "What the hell is this?"

Detective Henry said nothing. Arty turned back to the Lamberts. "I've got nothing to say to you two."

"No?" Amy said.

"*No.* You murdered my brother."

Patrick laughed. "Right...and it wasn't justified or anything."

"No, it wasn't. You two should have just known your role and accepted your fate. You're fucking *peasants* that were put here for *our* enjoyment. Period. Taking your life is akin to thinning a menial herd. You taking my brother's life is tantamount to blasphemy."

"That's the way you see it?" Amy asked.

"That's the way I *know* it, Amy," he said. "I'm surprised you even need to hear this again. I'm quite sure I made myself clear the first time around. What were you hoping for, a moment of regret now that my brother and mother are gone?"

Amy shook her head. "No, I knew better than to hope for something like that."

"Well good for you. Maybe you're not the stupid little cunt I thought you were."

Patrick took a step closer to the bed and Henry twitched. Patrick held up a hand and nodded an apology.

Arty laughed. "See? Even in here you're powerless, Patrick. I just tug those little strings of yours and you dance like the big predictable puppet you are."

"You call me powerless, yet here *you* are," Patrick said. "And your brother is likely room temperature right about now."

Arty snorted. "You keep thinking whatever you want to think, hotshot."

"I will, thank you."

Arty looked at Henry again. "Alright, are we done here? I still don't know what the hell this is—"

"Your mother's alive," Amy said.

Arty jerked his head towards Amy. He studied her hard, as if trying to read a bluff. "I call bullshit," he eventually said.

"Call whatever you want," Patrick said. "It's true."

Arty went back to Henry. "Is it?"

Henry closed his eyes and nodded once.

"I want to see her."

"What makes you think she'd want to see *you*?" Amy asked.

Arty ignored her. He kept his stare on Henry. "Detective Henry, I want to see her."

Patrick's turn now. "You *shot* her, asshole. You shot her with the intention of killing her. Why would she want to see you?"

Arty turned back to Patrick. "I was *freeing* her, you ignorant ass. I was ending her suffering. It's what she would have wanted."

"Nah," Patrick said. "You did it for yourself. It's what *you* wanted."

"You don't know shit."

"Oh I know some things," Patrick said with a smirk.

"Whatever." Arty looked back at Henry. "I want to see my mother."

"She's unconscious, Arty," Amy said. "Nobody knows when she'll come around."

"Shut up! Nobody's talking to you! Detective Henry! *I want to see my mother.* She'll want to see me. She'll want to see her only *living* son the second she wakes up." He shot a quick glare at the couple on the word *living*.

"What if she doesn't remember you again?" Amy asked.

"She will."

"Maybe," Patrick said. "Maybe not. She might tell you something you don't want to hear."

"I am her son; her flesh and blood. She'll remember me again."

"Then why did you shoot her?" Patrick asked with a chuckle. "If you're so sure she'll remember you again, then why did you shoot her? Why *free* her?"

"I don't have to justify anything to you. I was doing the right thing. You could never understand."

Amy inched closer to the foot of the bed. "You know, your mother said some things that night I found interesting."

"Good for you."

"She said she didn't know who you were."

"She was confused."

"She said she wanted to see her husband."

"She's *sick* and she was *confused*. She was talking nonsense."

"And she said that she was unable to have children."

Arty said nothing.

"Did you catch that bit?" Amy asked. "I'm pretty sure she only said it the one time, but she *did* say it."

"Like I said," Arty began, nostrils flared, "she is sick and—"

"The thing is, Arty, dementia can be strangely ironic," Amy interrupted. "You forget some things, and then you remember others—usually things from the past."

"*I know that.*"

"That's why your mother was calling to your father. She had regressed back to a time when she believed he was still alive."

"You said that already, bitch."

"She regressed back to a time when she and her husband had just found out that she was *unable to have children.*"

Arty laughed. "So what am I? A fucking mirage?"

Amy smiled and looked at Patrick. Patrick smiled back, turned to Arty and said, "No, you're very real. But you're also very adopted. You *and* Jim."

Arty laughed again. "You two reek of it."

Patrick smirked, looked over at Henry. "Detective?"

Henry nodded. "It's true, Fannelli. Your mother's attending physician was able to get hold of all her medical records dating back several years. A fibroid tumor was found in her uterus when she was twenty. Apparently the tumor was huge. Her uterus was removed as a result."

Amy took over. "Your mother, while not necessarily past her prime, was no spring chicken when she—" Amy held up both hands and mimed quotation marks "—*gave birth to you.* I mean, nowadays thirty-six doesn't seem too old to have your first child. But over thirty years ago? People were poppin' out two or three before they even *reached* thirty. Why would such loving, nurturing parents like yours wait so long to have children? Makes you wonder doesn't it?"

Arty shook his head. "This is bullshit. I would have known. My brother and I would have found out somehow."

"Different time, Fannelli," Henry said. "We're talking the 70's here. Adoption practices were a bit more lax back then. You *could* adopt at a young age and keep it a secret from anyone and everyone—including you and your brother."

Arty stuttered. "I would have...remembered."

Amy chuckled. "Doubtful."

Arty's breaths grew short and shallow. "I'm two years older than Jim. I would have at *least* been two."

Now it was Patrick's turn to chuckle. "Right. And we all remember so much at the ripe old age of two, don't we? Hell, I'll even give you four. Can you remember anything from when you were *four*, Arty?"

Arty pulled at his cuffs again, a clang instead of a clink this time. "I suppose now you're going to tell me Jim isn't my real brother either, right?"

"No, no," Henry said, "I'm fairly certain he is. There's a minuscule chance your parents adopted two American children from two separate families. I'd bet good money Jim is your biological brother."

"Do you know what all of this means, Arty?" Amy asked.

Arty didn't reply.

"It means that you and your brother aren't really the unique individuals you think you are. You *were* raised by loving parents...but you *weren't* born to them."

Arty said nothing. Patrick took over.

"Did you ever read *The Bad Seed*, Arty?" Patrick asked. "It was a fantastic book that came out in the mid-fifties. Written by a guy named William March. They made it into a play and a movie. The movie was damn good too, except for the fact that they changed the original ending. It wasn't really their fault though; their hands were kind of tied. You see at the time they had to comply with the Motion Picture Production Code, meaning the ending had to be morally acceptable; the bad guys weren't allowed to win, so to speak.

"Still, the movie was good enough to be nominated for an Academy Award. Patty McCormack was downright creepy as the little girl. You and your stupid brother *wish* you could be as creepy as that little girl."

Arty stayed quiet. He just glared at the couple—a mix of hate and confusion.

"I'm getting ahead of myself though. Let me give you the synopsis, okay? Basically the book is about this adorable, seemingly perfect eight-year-old girl who is actually downright evil. The little girl is a total sociopath who can flash her blue eyes and pearly whites one minute, and then kill a fellow classmate the next in order to get a penmanship medal she felt she deserved.

"The loving mother begins to suspect something is wrong with her child, and fears she may have inherited her nasty old grandmother's evil genes. You see, Arty, it turns out that grandma was quite the notorious serial killer in her day, and poor old loving mom fears that her innocent little daughter might have inherited those awful, awful genes." Patrick smiled. "Do you see where I'm heading with this, Arthur?"

Arty said, "Shut up."

"I'm surprised you didn't know about this classic, Arty, what with all your 'research' and all. I would have told you about it before, but I didn't have much of a chance." He turned to Amy. "Why is that you think, baby?"

Amy scratched her head, her eyebrows scrunched, lips pursed. Then everything popped, and her eyes were bright and wide, her mouth an O. "You were being gagged and tortured at the time, honey. You couldn't have!"

Patrick slapped his forehead. "That's right. Why didn't *you* tell him about it then, honey?"

Amy gave her husband a silly look and sang, "*Honey*...I was being gagged and tortured too."

Patrick slapped his forehead again. "Duh!"

Arty yelled, "*Shut up!*"

"You remember your little spiel about *Serial Killer Stanley?*" Patrick said. "That's what you called him, right? *Stanley?*" He looked to Amy again.

"Yeah, I think that was it," Amy said. "Although I kind of liked *The Three Stooges* reference better. Found it more amusing."

"Yeah, I did too. I like the Stooges. Again, I would have told you and your brother that, but..." Patrick wrapped an imaginary gag around his mouth and head, made his lips disappear, then splayed his hands with a helpless shrug.

Amy laughed.

"Henry, I want these fucks out of here now. I have rights; this is beyond fucking absurd."

Detective Henry pretended to look out the window. Patrick was sure he saw him smirking.

"Let's not get off track," Patrick continued. "It's contagious, this lecturing stuff. I can see why you and Jim felt the need to bore us for so long with how cool you thought you were."

"Henry!"

Patrick continued. "Sorry, sorry…let's get back to our buddy Stanley. So! Arty…you said Serial Killer Stanley was a serial killer because he came from a long line of serial killers, yes? Those were your words, if I'm not mistaken." Patrick's haughty delivery was the equal of a prosecutor to an ignorant defendant.

"Shut the fuck up!"

"Did you know *The Bad Seed* was based on a true story? That there really was a serial killer grandma that had an eight-year-old, serial killer granddaughter?"

This was a lie, but Patrick hardly cared. He was having too much fun. "I guess the point I'm trying to make here, Arthur, is that in this case—in *your* case—it looks like *heredity* was the winner. Hey, you know what I just thought? What if your *real* father's name was actually Stanley? How fucking funny would that be?"

Amy laughed again.

"So you know what I'm thinking here, Arty?" Patrick said. "I think—no—I *bet*. I bet my newly saved life that your biological parents, the *real* people responsible for bringing you into this world, were just as sick and fucked up as you and your brother are." Patrick quickly corrected himself, "Oh, sorry…as *you* are. Guess I'd have to say *were* if I'm talking about Jim, yeah?"

Arty finally spoke in a tone below a shout, though it clearly held no guarantees it would remain as such; his face was near purple with rage, veins bulged his neck and forehead, looking as if they might split the skin. "You don't know that. You don't know that for sure."

Amy shrugged. "You're right. Nobody does—including you. We might be able to find out though. Do some digging maybe? If we *really* tried I'm sure we could come up with something." She looked at Detective Henry. He raised both eyebrows and nodded in agreement. Amy continued.

"But I don't think you want us to do that, do you, Arty? In fact, I don't think *we* would want to do it either. I think it's best if we just let it fester inside that rotted head of yours. Because deep down I think you know the truth. We *all* know the truth. And if you'll forgive the pun…that *seed* we just planted? That *seed* that's gonna keep on growing and growing…? That's enough for us. That seed will put a smile on the face of my husband and I for the rest of our very long lives."

Patrick took another step closer towards the bed. He wanted to hammer the point home. "So enjoy your time in prison, Arty. I wouldn't hold my breath on waiting for any budding shrinks to come look you up. Especially not after my wife and I make certain that everyone knows the *true* origins of the 'infamous' Fannelli brothers."

Patrick began guiding Amy towards the door. Before exiting he looked at Arty, smirked and added, "Maybe Amy and I will send you a card on Mother's Day."

Detective Henry barked a laugh, instantly covered his mouth and said, "Ah shit. Come on." He ushered the Lamberts out of the room.

75

The silver Highlander headed east on the Pennsylvania Turnpike towards Valley Forge. The sunglasses Patrick wore shielded both the sun and the bruising that was still evident around his eyes.

Amy was next to him in the passenger seat, her hand on his knee throughout the entire trip. She gave it a little squeeze.

Patrick glanced at her and smiled. "What?"

She smiled back, took a deep breath. "It's just nice to know you're there."

He took her hand off his knee, brought it to his mouth and kissed it. "You'll never get rid of me, baby."

"I hope not." She shifted her torso slightly and winced.

"You alright?"

She gingerly patted the right side of her chest. "Still sore."

He kissed her hand again. "That's to be expected. Doctor said it would take awhile."

"How about you?" she asked.

He let go of her hand and touched his stomach. "Still sore. Who would have ever thought two suburbanites like us would be shot *and* stabbed?"

She chuckled softly. "Not me."

"At least we'll have cool scars."

"I don't want a cool scar, thank you. A big pink hole over my right boob—I'll be quite the stunner in a bikini."

"Thank God he didn't shoot you *in* the boob."

Amy shook her head. "My husband: a man of priorities."

He smiled and winked at her. She put her hand back on his knee and gave it another little squeeze.

"Well hey, how do you think Oscar feels?" he asked. "Poor little guy got his tail sliced off. How you doin' back there pal?" Patrick reached behind him and stuck his fingers through the metal grate of the pet carrier in the back seat.

Oscar instantly licked his fingers and wagged his stump.

"He should have been a cat," Amy said. "Nine lives and all."

"I'll tell you what I don't get," Patrick said. "Those sickos had no trouble taking the lives of all those people, yet when it came to a dog..."

Amy shrugged. "Not part of their stupid little game I guess. I won't even pretend to understand."

Patrick grunted.

Amy reached back and let Oscar have a lick of her fingers as well. "I still can't believe they found the bugger. I can't wait to see the look on Carrie's face when we get him home. I'm praying it helps speed up the healing process."

Patrick sighed. "Yeah."

The symbol of a gasoline handle was lit on the Highlander's dashboard. Patrick paused before exiting the car and turned to his wife. "You want anything?"

"Something to drink please."

"Coke?"

"Fine."

Patrick exited the SUV and began pumping his gas. When he finished he went inside the mini-mart to pay. As he exited with a bottle of Coke in hand, he noticed a man filling his black Volkswagen behind the Highlander. The pump was running hands-free, and the man was leaning against the hood of his Volkswagen, both arms folded, staring at the rear of Patrick's car.

"You go to Penn State?" the man asked when Patrick arrived. He was a young man who looked to be in his mid-twenties. He was dressed in faded blue jeans and a white sweatshirt. He was smiling pleasantly when he asked the question.

Patrick said nothing. He walked around his SUV, opened the passenger door, and gave Amy her Coke. She pulled the door shut, and Patrick pressed on it afterwards to ensure it was shut properly. He then calmly walked over to the smiling man and launched him clear across the hood of his Volkswagen with a thunderous right hook.

Patrick got back into the driver's seat of the Highlander and looked at his now wide-eyed wife. He shrugged. "Better safe than sorry."

76

After a few months, the Lamberts were finally ready to entertain. Nothing big—just a few friends over for dinner and drinks.

The "subject" was carefully avoided at first, almost to an awkward degree, making conversation hollow and generic. But as the drinks continued, and the mood lightened, it was all but impossible for someone not to take that first plunge.

Long-time friends, Jamie and Alexis Brown, were those first two.

"So how are you two coping?" Jamie asked. "I mean really."

The remaining couple, Tom and Jane Jenkins, shared an uncertain glance.

"I think we've crossed the last big hurdle," Patrick said after he and Amy shared their own uncertain glance.

With the exception of police and close family, the couple had not shared any details about their ordeal at Crescent Lake to anyone, yet knew it would ultimately surface one day and need to be addressed. They had even rehearsed what should and should *not* be divulged. The gist of the tragedy had already been learned (how could it not after the media coverage it had received), but it was the *details* that were shaky ground. A vague synopsis of the goings-on could be discussed, but gruesome particulars (Patrick biting off a nose; Amy jamming a nail file into a man's balls; et al) were better left locked away in a vault that even the Lamberts struggled to open.

"How so?" Alexis prodded.

Taking a healthy pull from her chardonnay, Amy said, "Patrick and I have been seeing a therapist who has helped us a great deal. He helps us try to place the incident in the same category as a bad dream. It will surely haunt us, likely forever, but time will hopefully be our ally. The more we can distance ourselves from everything and remove all traces of the affair, the less impact it will have over time. At least that's what we're being fed." Amy ended with an awkward laugh. The table's placating laugh that followed was even more awkward.

"What about the trial?" Jamie asked.

"Of course we'll eventually have to revisit some unpleasant memories at the trial, but we're not even thinking about that right now. Right now is all about healing immediate wounds." She took another decent swallow from her glass. "Like I said; lessen the impact..."

"Speaking of wounds, how are...?" Tom motioned his hand over his own torso, hinting at the physical wounds Amy and Patrick had endured.

Patrick touched the scar on his stomach; the wounds on his face had long been healed. "Well, they're a reminder of course." He looked at Amy who rubbed the spot above her right breast. "Something that has unfortunately *tattooed* us with the memory of everything, but...as Amy said, we're hoping time will be our ally."

"Any pain?" Jane asked.

"Not too bad anymore," Amy said, rubbing her chest again. "It was pretty bad at first. God bless Codeine and wine."

Another placating laugh from the table, though less awkward than before.

The six adults sat in silence for a beat. Some took sips from their drinks, others poked at the remains on their plates. It was only a matter of time before the next question was carefully measured and delivered.

"How about the kids?" Jamie asked. "How are they holding up?"

Patrick said, "The psychologists we've worked with said they have youth on their side. Said that at their age, their resiliency can prove surprisingly strong."

Alexis said, "You seem as if you don't agree."

Patrick gave a partial shrug. "I'd have to agree as far as Caleb is concerned, but Carrie…" He glanced at Amy. His look asked his wife if she felt comfortable with continuing, and it asked if this was indeed one of those details that was better left alone. She answered him by answering the table.

"Carrie's been struggling ever since we got home," she said. "She was sleeping with us up until a couple of weeks ago. She still wakes up screaming and crying from nightmares."

Alexis put a hand to her chest. "Oh, the poor thing."

Tom wrinkled his brow. "Wait…so Caleb's okay?"

"We don't know," Patrick said. "He *seems* okay. In fact, he seems a little *too* okay. And to be honest, that has us a bit worried. We asked the doctor about it; we were worried that he was in shock, or so traumatized by everything that he had somehow suppressed it. But one of the doctors told us that if he hasn't exhibited any distressing behavior thus far, then he *should* be fine. I'm not sure I agree with all that, but hey, what the hell do I know?"

"I'm not sure I agree either," Tom said. "How could it *not* affect him?"

"The doctor said it most assuredly did, but that because of Caleb's age, he likely couldn't comprehend what the hell was going on. Again, it goes back to the whole resiliency thing with kids—the younger they are, the more resilient, I guess. Perhaps he's already done what Amy and I are hoping to do, and chalked the whole thing up to a bad dream."

Tom's frowned remained. "Strange that he hasn't even shown the slightest signs of post-traumatic stress."

Amy shrugged. "Both kids slept with us when we got home. We insisted on it. But after a few days Caleb wanted to go back to his own bed. He's been fine ever since; he putters around here as though nothing happened."

"Which is fine by us," Patrick said. "Carrie's been struggling so much, it helps us devote a little more attention towards soothing her without having to worry if Caleb is receiving equal care."

"As odd as it may sound," Amy began, "I suppose their reactions mimic their personalities. Carrie has always been the high-strung, extroverted one. Caleb could be sitting next to you on the sofa and sometimes you'll forget he's even there."

"He's a tough little bugger—just like his old man," Jamie said with a smile.

Patrick returned the gesture, but it was labored.

Jamie played with something on his plate, his attention obviously elsewhere. Patrick sensed something coming he wouldn't like.

"How did you do it, Patrick?" Jamie asked. He then looked at Amy. "How did you both do it?"

Patrick ate a mouthful of food as a means to buy time. After swallowing, he feigned ignorance. "Do what?"

"How did you manage...to do what it was that you did...to come out alive?"

"*Jamie,*" Alexis said.

Patrick and Amy shared what seemed like their one-hundredth glance before Patrick fixed on Jamie. "Like I said, Jamie—we're trying to forget it."

Jamie held up a hand. "Okay, I'm sorry. I was just...no, I'm sorry."

Patrick smiled genuinely. These were his friends; they had been drinking; they were curious. Likely, he'd be the same way. "It's okay, man. Maybe some day."

A whine emerged from beneath the table. All six adults leaned to one side and looked below them. Oscar stood by Patrick's feet, wagging the stump that used to be his tail.

"Now here's someone we could all take a lesson from," Patrick said. "The poor thing had his tail sliced off, and all he cares about is getting some leftovers."

The table laughed—a good laugh this time; no placating; nothing awkward.

"I guess if you can find *one* good thing to come from all of this..." Alexis said.

Amy snorted. "Speak for yourself. He eats more than all four of us combined. I don't know where he puts it in that little body of his. That mangy mutt is going to eat us out of house and home."

Another good laugh from the table.

When it faded, Tom asked, "You don't think he's a reminder? The dog?"

It was a good question, one that Patrick had never really considered. He looked at Amy for help. She looked mildly annoyed at the query.

"He makes Carrie happy. We're not about to take that away from her," was all she said.

Tom smiled and nodded fast, seemingly realizing that he too had just joined Jamie Brown on the Inappropriate Dinner Conversation Team. "Good, good, I'm glad," he said.

Dessert and coffee were done, and a brief silence returned once again. Clinks and tinks from glasses, plates, and silverware played a broken tune.

Carrie's sudden scream from upstairs broke the silence.

Both Patrick and Amy leapt from the table, the squeak of their chairs on the wooden floor like sneakers on a basketball court.

The couple bounded upstairs, the dinner guests leaving their seats and forming a group at the base of the stairs.

Carrie was upright in bed, sobbing, her sheets soaked with sweat. Amy wiped her daughter's matted hair from her eyes and flashed on Carrie's insistence to have her bangs cut when they first arrived at Crescent Lake. She began to cry with her daughter as she held her tight. Patrick sat at the foot of the bed, rubbing his daughter's shaking legs. He lowered his head and fought back his own tears.

Patrick returned to the group at the base of the stairs alone. He explained that Carrie had a nightmare and that Amy was consoling her. He did not have to ask everyone to leave. They took the cue.

Hugging his final guest before shutting the door behind them, Patrick returned upstairs to Carrie's room where she had managed to fall back to sleep in Amy's arms.

"Are you going to stay in here with her tonight?" he whispered.

She shook her head, then slowly slid her way out from beneath her daughter, gently lowering her head back down to the pillow.

They checked Caleb's room next. He was fast asleep; Carrie's screams hadn't woken him.

"He could sleep through an earthquake," Patrick whispered as he shut his son's door.

The two walked into their bedroom where Amy sat on the bed and put her face in both hands.

"You okay?" Patrick asked.

She looked up, sighed. "Yeah. I just want it all to be over. I want the bad dream to end."

He sat beside her. "I do too, baby." She leaned in and rested her head on his chest. He kissed the top of her head and started running his fingers over her back. "Tell you what, why don't you go get ready for bed. I'll go downstairs and clean up."

"No, it's okay. I'll come down and help."

He pulled her in, squeezed, and kissed the top of her head again. "I insist."

She took her head off his chest and kissed him. "I love you."

Patrick had cleared the dining room table, and was now elbow deep in suds at the kitchen sink. He thought about Jamie's question:

"How did you do it? How did you manage to...do what it was that you did...to come out alive?"

He set the plate he'd been holding back into the sink and shut the water off. How *had* they done it? How had *he* done it? That man who did those things. That man who shot, stabbed, and mauled like a savage beast. Was that him? Standing here now, safe in his suburban kitchen, knowing Jim was dead and that Arty was locked away, he felt as though he *hadn't* done those things—that someone else had. He felt a vague connection to it as though it were a scene in a film he had seen more than once. Now, in retrospect, he felt removed from the blood lust that had surged through his veins during that horrific moment.

A tingle began at the base of his spine, and then tickled ice cold all the way to the top of his head...because he *had* done those things. My God. He *had*.

And to answer your question, Jamie, I have no fucking idea how we managed to do it. No fucking idea at all. I guess when it comes to family...

Patrick thought of the nose he'd bitten off Jim Fannelli's face and immediately filled a glass of water. He gargled with it then spat. He repeated the process, and then set the empty glass to one side. He placed both hands on the sink's ledge to steady himself, his head down.

"This is going to take awhile, isn't it?" he said quietly to the sink full of dishes and water and soap. "A hell of a lot longer than Amy and I think it—"

A second scream that night cut him off. It was not Carrie's this time, it was Amy's: a short, painful cry.

Again Patrick found himself sprinting up the stairs. In his bedroom he found Amy sitting on the floor, clutching her right foot with both hands. Her left foot was covered in a bedroom slipper; her right was bloodied and dotted with silver thumbtacks.

"*What the hell?*" Patrick said.

Amy continued clutching her foot with both hands, rocking back and forth in pain.

Patrick dropped to his knees and began examining her foot. "What the hell happened?"

Amy kept a tight grip on her ankle with her left, and began slowly plucking the tacks free with her right, wincing after each withdrawal. "My slipper," she said.

Patrick spun on both knees and spotted the solitary slipper. He picked it up and turned it over. A dozen silver thumbtacks spilled out. "*What the fuck?* Who did this?"

Amy continued working on her foot. "How the hell should I know?"

Patrick hopped to his feet and immediately went to Carrie's room. She was in the same position they had left her earlier, fast asleep. He closed the door and went to Caleb's room. His son was turned on his side away from him, lying still. Patrick called his name. Caleb didn't answer. His tiny torso beneath the blankets rose and fell with each breath. He was asleep.

A wave of panic swept through Patrick's head. Had one of their friends done it? No. *No way.* Even the hardest of practical jokers would have found such a gag awful even under normal circumstances.

Jim was dead. He was sure of it. He was dead. Dead. He saw it. Dead.

Arty was locked away. Locked *far* away from them. Had he gotten out? Tracked them down? No. Impossible. It was absolutely impossible. But Patrick did know one thing: he would call right now. He would call and check. Call right fucking now and check to make sure that bastard was still locked up tight.

Patrick thought of serial killer Ted Bundy; he remembered reading how Bundy had managed to escape the police *twice* after capture.

My God, what if he escaped, Patrick? That means he was here. God Almighty he was HERE.

"No," he said. Insisted. Pleaded. "*No, no, no.*"

Patrick locked Caleb's door and pulled it tight, then did the same for Carrie's. He sprinted back to his bedroom, his eyes wide and wild. He began going through their closets, pushing and shoving clothes out of the way, ripping them off their hangers and tossing them over his shoulder, checking every conceivable hiding spot.

Amy was still on the floor attending to her foot. Her own eyes grew wild from her husband's frenzy. "What? *What?*"

Patrick ignored her; he just continued with his frantic search. The bathroom next.

"*Patrick!*"

He emerged from the bathroom a minute later. Satisfied their entire bedroom was empty save for him and his wife, Patrick turned to Amy, his eyes still lidless. "Stay here and keep this door locked."

He flipped the lock, pulled the door tight, and checked the handle to ensure it didn't budge. He heard Amy call after him one last time as he bolted downstairs to make the call.

Curled over on one side, his back to the bedroom door, four-year-old Caleb was desperately holding in a giggle, wishing he could have seen the look on his Mommy's face after playing his funny joke on her.

Turn the page for a special excerpt of
Jeff Menapace's pulse-pounding sequel...

VENGEFUL GAMES

Available now!

1

Although the interior of the house was black with night, Monica could have slinked her way upstairs and into their bedrooms eyes closed. She had been in their home—alone—several times already. Her job demanded this kind of tactile homework. She had to be perfect. Always. But it was never a burden. She loved her job. It was why she was so good.

Monica never cared to know the reasons behind her assignments unless they were critical to the job. Reasons meant little to her. It could be a terrorist hiding in suburbia, or a school teacher having an affair. She didn't care. It was the work itself she prized. Her first solo assignment at nineteen was carried out with the exactness of a veteran—her hand never shook, her movements never second-guessed.

At the top of the landing, Monica made an immediate right into the boy's bedroom. He was a freshman in high school. Five-foot nine. Scruffy brown hair. Skinny. She'd studied him on his way home from soccer practice. Every day after school until five. He walked home.

Monica now stood over his sleeping body and withdrew a pistol from her leather bag. Teenagers were always so easy. They slept like the dead. The boy snored deeply, his mouth ajar. She smirked at the opportunity and placed the suppressor of her Glock into his mouth. The boy never opened his eyes, even when the two quiet thumps bounced his head and turned the back of his pillow red.

Mom and dad were down the hall. She didn't have to hurry with this one, and that was just fine by her. Quite often a job would require a quick in and out with little time to savor and enjoy. But with this one, she could (and would) secure the situation, and then take her time.

She glided into the master bedroom, hung at the foot of the bed, watched their sleeping silhouettes. She felt the familiar tingle flutter its way down her spine until it made a pit-stop in her belly, swirling hot and bad, waiting for the chance to continue its exquisite journey south.

Monica had once read that Adolph Hitler would often ejaculate while delivering passionate speeches to his minions. A crazy notion to most, but she understood the moment she'd read it. She desired sex as often (she assumed) as most women did, but achieving orgasm was near impossible no matter how earnest the man's efforts may have been. But when an assignment like tonight's allowed her to take her time? She was able to explode with ecstasy—multiple times.

One poor fellow unknowingly volunteered to be her first successful effort at sexual gratification when Monica was only twenty-two. The young man was not an assignment, just another random penis stepping up to the plate in hopes of hitting it out of the park. Unfortunately, the man, despite his efforts, could not even manage a bunt, and in a desperate attempt for fulfillment, Monica—she on top; he still inside her—reached for one of her instruments (always hidden close by), and slashed his throat.

Staring down at disbelieving eyes, a mouth gurgling red, and frantic clawing at a throat that no longer worked, she came instantly.

Future sexual encounters of the same nature occurred, but they were infrequent. More sport than anything else. The job satiated her appetite with far greater satisfaction.

And so now, just as the female subject (40; dirty-blonde hair; five-foot two; Pilates at twelve on Tuesdays and Thursdays) lifted her head off the pillow to likely obey the blind suspicion subjects sometimes had—the suspicion they were being watched—she did not receive two quick bullets like her son had. Instead she got a lightning-quick injection to the side of the neck that put her back into a deep sleep. The husband (42; brown hair; five-foot ten; work hours eight to six; happy hour with colleagues on Wednesdays and Fridays from six to eight) barely stirred, even when he received an injection of his own.

Monica left the sedated couple, entered their bathroom and hit the light. Her reflection in the stretch of mirror above the dual sinks was exceptionally kind: dark, seductive eyes, full lips, healthy dark hair that usually bounced at the shoulder (now pulled back tight for job efficiency), and a body that defied the majority by being slim and tight in the usual trouble spots; full and firm in the oft-desired.

These physical gifts were accentuated—and coveted by every female eye she passed—by a powerful and sophisticated aura, product of conditioning from years in the most elite of boarding schools. If she were wearing a power suit instead of the unassuming but apt attire needed for her current assignment, she could easily pass for a seven-figure knockout parading down Wall Street.

Monica placed her leather bag on the sink, glanced into the bedroom at the couple, and felt the familiar tingle begin its feathery dance down her body. Now she would take her time.

Monica sat on the edge of the bed and lit a cigarette. Inhaling deep, she glanced over her shoulder, searching for the remote. It was on the nightstand next to the wife's corpse.

She stood, strolled past the chair that held the husband's bound and mangled body, flicked an ash on his scalp, picked up the remote from the nightstand, and returned to her spot at the foot of the bed.

Crossing her legs, she took a second drag, leaned back on her elbows, and blew a long stream into the air. She tweaked the toes of the dead woman next to her, then clicked on the television.

The news was replaying a top story from a few days ago. The incident had caught her attention the night it aired, and she had given it a brief glance. Multiple murders in the sticks of western Pennsylvania. A place called Crescent Lake. Torture. Sick games. Something out of a movie, they had said.

Now they apparently had the whole story.

She turned up the volume and looked on with the casual eye of an athlete watching their own sport. She hoped this local station had the balls to air recordings of the aftermath. The breaking report she had witnessed days ago on assignment in New York had given her nothing but a woman with a bad dye-job, blabbering in front of a cabin in Bumblefuck, Pennsylvania.

For the moment this one looked to be no different. Same bullshit drama in front of a cabin. A man reported this time, one with a bad toupee and capped teeth. He carried on as though auditioning for a Hollywood role.

Four murdered…two men responsible…brothers…one of the brothers eventually killed in an act of self-defense…the other brother critically wounded and in custody.

Her casual interest was waning.

The reporter disappeared, and Monica was finally rewarded with a brief shot of a large black body bag being carried out of a cabin and into an ambulance.

She rolled her eyes. Painfully unfulfilling. She took another drag of her cigarette and blew perfect smoke rings.

Toupee returned for a brief moment to provide new details about the naughty brothers. And then, for the first time, their pictures—side by side headshots that took up the whole screen.

Monica sprang upright, the remote falling from her hand, the battery casing breaking open as it hit the rug. She leaned forward and gawked at the screen. The brother on the left—the one they'd declared dead. He looked exactly like her.

The finished cigarette burned her fingers and she cursed and dropped it. She quickly stubbed it out with her toe, pocketed the butt, pushed off the bed and rushed close to the screen. A lock of her thick, dark hair came free from her ponytail and fell over one eye. She slapped it away from her face as though it were a bug.

The other brother, the one that was still alive and in custody, there was a resemblance there as well. And then she heard the word and her open mouth gaped wider.

Adopted.

Both brothers had been adopted. The pictures disappeared and she snatched at the screen as though she might be able to bring them back.

Toupee stood in front of a lake now. More cabins rimmed the corners of the screen. If he had been auditioning for a Hollywood role before, he was now trying to take home the Oscar with his dramatic recap:

"Once again, an idyllic autumn getaway becomes a nightmare for an innocent family, as two psychotic brothers subjected these unfortunate people to unspeakable horrors for their own sick amusement..."

A photo of the family's cabin, and then of an isolated house where apparently further atrocities took place.

"...the family survived the brothers' wrath, even fighting back and taking the life of one of the sadistic brothers in a heroic display of self-defense..."

A solitary picture of the deceased brother now—the one that looked like her. Monica touched the screen, caressed his face.

"The same cannot be said for the four victims here at Crescent Lake, whose lives were brutally snuffed out for unknowingly playing the role of obstacles in the sick games the brothers were orchestrating..."

A repeat shot of the same black body bag being taken out of a cabin and into an ambulance. Her fingers fell from the screen, dropped to her side.

"Ironically, it would later be known that one of the survivors of that night of horror was actually the adoptive mother of the two sadistic brothers. A widow, this elder woman, whose name is being withheld, was tragically unaware of the evil she was raising until it

was too late. She too proved to be an obstacle, and is now in critical condition..."

Toupee on his own again, in front of the lake, pouring it on.

"What compels men to do such things? How does one develop the urge and ability to torture an innocent family for their own enjoyment? To slaughter four people without pity? Attempt to take the life of their own adoptive mother who, along with her now deceased husband, lovingly took these boys into their lives out of the pure goodness of their hearts...?"

The side-by-side headshots leapt forward again as the commentary continued. Monica caressed the screen with both hands this time, one for each.

She knew. All those questions they were asking. The whys? The hows? She knew why. She knew how. *God* how she knew.

Monica rushed towards her leather bag, fished out her cell, dialed.

A male voice picked up on the first ring. "Code in."

"Neco. 8122765," she said.

"Waiting for voice authentication...clear. Everything okay?"

"Fine. You can send the cleaner in an hour. I want you to check something for me first."

Monica "Neco" Kemp hung up after ten minutes then dialed a second number. It rang twice.

"What's up, baby girl?" A male voice, deep and powerful.

"I found them."

ABOUT THE AUTHOR

A native of the Philadelphia area, Jeff Menapace has published multiple works in both fiction and non-fiction. In 2011 he was the recipient of the Red Adept Reviews Indie Award for Horror.

Jeff's terrifying debut novel *Bad Games* became a #1 Kindle bestseller that spawned three acclaimed sequels, and now the first three books in the series have been optioned for feature film and translated for foreign audiences.

His other novels, along with his award-winning short works, have also received international acclaim and are eagerly waiting to give you plenty of sleepless nights.

Free time for Jeff is spent watching horror movies, The Three Stooges, and mixed martial arts. He loves steak and more steak, thinks the original 1974 *Texas Chainsaw Massacre* is the greatest movie ever, wants to pet a lion someday, and hates spiders.

He currently lives in Pennsylvania with his wife Kelly and their cats Sammy and Bear.

Jeff loves to hear from his readers. Please feel free to contact at http://www.jeffmenapace.com/contact.html to discuss anything and everything, and be sure to sign up for his FREE newsletter (no spam, not ever) where you will receive updates and sneak peeks on all future works along with the occasional free goodie!

CONNECT WITH JEFF ON
SOCIAL MEDIA:

http://www.facebook.com/JeffMenapace.writer

http://twitter.com/JeffMenapace

https://www.linkedin.com/in/JeffMenapace

https://www.goodreads.com/JeffMenapace

https://www.instagram.com/JeffMenapace

OTHER WORKS BY
JEFF MENAPACE

Please visit Jeff's Amazon Author Page or his website for a complete list of all available works!

http://author.to/Jeffsauthorpage

www.jeffmenapace.com

AUTHOR'S NOTE

Thank you so much for taking the time to read *Bad Games*, my friends. And remember, the games are far from over! You've still got *Vengeful Games (Book 2)*, *Bad Games: Hellbent (Book 3)*, and *Bad Games: Malevolent (Book 4)* to sink your teeth into!

Please know that every single reader is important to me. Whenever I'm asked what my writing goals are, my number one answer, without pause, is to entertain. I want you to have fun reading what I write. I want to make your heart race. I want you to get paper cuts (or Kindle thumb?) from turning the pages so fast. Again—I want to entertain you.

If I succeeded in doing that, I would be very grateful if you took a few minutes to write a review on Amazon for *Bad Games*. Reviews can be very helpful, and I absolutely love to read the various insights from satisfied readers.

Thank you so very much.

Until Amy is able to look at a nail file the same way again...

Jeff